MR FOX

Helen Oyeyemi

WINDSOR
PARAGON

First published 2011
by Picador
This Large Print edition published 2011
by AudioGO Ltd
by arrangement with
Pan Macmillan Ltd

Hardcover ISBN: 978 1 445 85882 1
Softcover ISBN: 978 1 445 85883 8

British Library Cataloguing in Publication Data available

Printed and bound in Great Britain by
MPG Books Group Limited

For my Mr Fox

(whoever you are.)

In the darkness they wondered if they could do it, and knew they had to try to do it.

MARY OLIVER

Mary Foxe came by the other day—the last person on earth I was expecting to see. I'd have tidied up if I'd known she was coming. I'd have combed my hair, I'd have shaved. At least I was wearing a suit; I strive for a sense of professionalism. I was sitting in my study, writing badly, just making words on the page, waiting for something good to come through, some sentence I could keep. It was taking longer that day than it usually did, but I didn't mind. The windows were open. I was sort of listening to something by Glazunov; there's a symphony of his you can't listen to with the windows closed, you just can't. Well I guess you could, but you'd get agitated and run at the walls. Maybe that's just me.

My wife was upstairs. Looking at magazines or painting or something, who knows what Daphne does. Hobbies. The symphony in my study was as loud as it could be, but that was nothing new, and she's never complained about all the noise. She doesn't complain about anything I do; she is physically unable to. That's because I fixed her early. I told her in heartfelt tones that one of the reasons I love her is because she never complains. So now of course she doesn't dare complain.

Anyway, I'd left the study door open and Mary slipped in. Without looking up, I smiled gently and murmured: 'Hello, honey . . .' I thought she was Daphne. I hadn't seen her in a while, and Daphne was the only other person in the house, as far as I was aware. When she didn't answer, I looked up.

Mary Foxe approached my desk with her hand stuck out. She wanted to shake hands. Shake hands! My long-absent muse saunters in for a handshake—I threw my telephone at her. I snatched it off the desk and the socket spat out the wire that connected it to the wall and I hurled the thing. She dodged it neatly. The phone landed on the floor beside my wastepaper can and jangled for a few seconds. I guess it was a half-hearted throw.

'Your temper,' Mary said.

'What's it been—six, seven years?' I asked.

She drew up a chair from a corner of the room, picked up my globe and sat opposite me, spinning oceans around and around on her lap. I watched her and I couldn't think straight. It's the way she moves, the way she looks at you. I guess her English accent helps too.

'Seven years,' she agreed. Then she asked me how I'd been. Real casual, like she already knew how I'd answer.

'Same as always—in love with you, Mary,' I told her. I wished to hell I wouldn't keep telling her that. I don't think it's even true. But whenever she's around I feel as if I should give it a try. I mean, it would be interesting if she believed me.

'Really?' she asked.

'Really. You're the only girl for me.'

'The only girl for you,' she said, and laughed at the ceiling.

'Go ahead and laugh—hurt my feelings . . . what do you care,' I said mournfully, enjoying myself.

'Oh, your *feelings* . . . well. Let's go further in, Mr Fox. Would you love me if I were your husband and you were my wife?'

'This is dumb.'

'Would you, though?'

'Well, yes, I could see that working out.'

'Would you love me if . . . we were both men?'
'Uh . . . I guess so.'
'If we were both women?'
'Sure.'
'If I were a witch?'
'You're enchanting enough as it is.'
'If you were my mother?'
'No more,' I said. 'I'm crazy about you, okay?'
'Oh, you don't love me,' Mary said. She undid the collar of her dress and bared her neck. 'You love that,' she said. She unbuttoned further and cupped her breasts. She pushed her skirt up past the knees, past the thighs, higher, and we both looked at her smoothness, her softness, her lace frills. 'You love that,' she said.

I nodded.

'This is all you love,' she said, pulling her own hair, slapping her own face. If it wasn't for the serenity in her eyes I would've thought she'd lost her mind. I stood up, to stop her, but the second I did, she stopped of her own accord.

'I don't want you like this. You have to change,' she said.

The symphony ended, and I went to the Victrola and started it up again.

'I have to change? You mean you want to hear me say I love you for your . . .' I allowed myself to smirk, 'soul?'

'It's nothing to do with that. You simply have to change. You're a villain.'

I waited a moment, to see if she was serious, and whether she had anything to add. She was, and she didn't. She stared at me—really came on with the frost, like she hated me. I whistled.

'A villain, you say. Is that so? I'm at church

nearly every Sunday, Mary. I slip beggars change. I pay my taxes. And every Christmas I send a check to my mother's favorite charity. Where's the villainy in that? Nowhere, that's where.'

My study door was still open, and I began listening out for my wife. Mary rearranged her clothes so that she looked respectable. There was a brief but heavy silence, which Mary broke by saying: 'You kill women. You're a serial killer. Can you grasp that?'

Of all the—

I hadn't seen that one coming.

She walked up to my desk and picked up one of my notepads, read a few lines to herself. 'Can you tell me why it's necessary for Roberta to saw off a hand and a foot and bleed to death at the church altar?' She flipped through a couple more pages. 'Especially given that this other story ends with Louise falling to the ground riddled with bullets, the mountain rebels having mistaken her for her traitorous brother. And *must* Mrs McGuire hang herself from a door handle because she's so afraid of what Mr McGuire will do when he gets home and finds out that she's burnt dinner? From a door handle? Really, Mr Fox?'

I found myself grinning—the complete opposite of what I wanted my face to do. Scornful and stern, I told my face. Scornful and stern. Not sheepish . . .

'You have no sense of humor, Mary,' I said.

'You're right,' she said. 'I don't.'

I tried again: 'It's ridiculous to be so sensitive about the content of fiction. It's not real. I mean, come on. It's all just a lot of games.'

Mary twirled a strand of hair around her finger.

'Oh . . . how does it go . . . we dream, it is good we are dreaming. It would hurt us, were we awake. But since it is playing, kill us. And—we are playing—shriek . . .'

'Couldn't have said it better myself.'

'What would you do for me?' she asked.

I studied her and she seemed perfectly serious. She was making an offer.

'Slay a dragon. Ten dragons. Anything,' I said.

She smiled. 'I'm glad you're playing along. It's a good sign.'

'It is? Okay. By the way, what exactly is it we're talking about?'

'Just be flexible,' she said. I seemed to have accepted some challenge. Only I had no idea what it was.

'I'll keep that in mind. When do we start this thing?'

She drew closer. 'Presently. Scared?'

'Me? No.'

The crazy thing is, I actually did have the jitters, just a little. Suddenly her hand was on my neck. The gesture was tender, which, coming from her, worried me even more. My hand covered hers—I was trying, I think, to get free.

'Ready?' she said. 'Now—'

dr lustucru

Doctor Lustucru's wife was not particularly talkative. But he beheaded her anyway, thinking to himself that he could replace her head when he wished for her to speak.

How long had the Doc been crazy? I don't know. Quite some time, I guess. Don't worry. He was only a general practitioner.

The beheading was done as cleanly as possible, and briskly tidied up. Afterwards Lustucru set both head and body aside in a bare room that the couple had hoped to use as a nursery. Then he went about his daily business as usual.

The Doc's wife had been a good woman, so her body remained intact and she did not give off a smell of decay.

After a week or so old Lustucru got around to thinking that he missed his wife. No one to warm his slippers, etc. In the nursery he replaced his wife's head, but of course it wouldn't stay on just like that. He reached for a suture kit. No need. The body put its hands up and held the head on at the neck. The wife's eyes blinked and the wife's mouth spoke: 'Do you think there will be another war? After the widespread damage of the Great War it is very unlikely. Do you think there will be another war? After the widespread damage of the Great War it is very unlikely. Do you think . . .' And so on.

Disturbed by this, the doctor tried to remove his wife's head again. But the body was having none of it and hung on pretty grimly. What a mess. He was forced to leave her there, locked in the nursery, asking and answering the same question over and over again.

The next night she broke a window and escaped.

Lustucru then understood that he'd been bad to the woman. He lay awake long nights, dreading her return. What got him the most was the idea that her vengeance would be fast, that he would be suddenly dead without a moment in which to understand. With that in mind, he prepared no verbal defences of his behaviour. Eventually his dread reached a peak he could live on. In fact it came to sustain him and it cured him of his craziness, a problem that he had not even known he had. After several months there was no sign of his horror beyond a heartbeat that was slightly faster than normal. His whole life, old Lustucru readied himself to hear from his wife again, to answer to her. But he never did.

* * *

'Hey . . . what's going on here?' I asked. We'd changed positions. I was in a chair, sprawled across it, as if I'd fallen. I assumed we were still in my study—I couldn't say for sure because Mary's hands were pressed firmly over my eyelids.

'Mary?'

She didn't answer.

'What's going on?' I asked again.

'I'd rather you didn't look at me just now,' she said.

'Are you all right?'

'What do you think? After what you did, you—you great *oaf*.'

‘Are you saying that that was us? Actually us? Me and you? The doctor and his lady wife?’

She was curt. ‘Yes, yes. I just need a couple of minutes, if that isn’t too much trouble.’

I whistled ‘I Can’t Get Started’ until what she was saying sank in. That’s my go-to tune, my haven during many a mindless hour. I experimented with the length of the notes, drawing a couple of bars out here, rushing over a couple of bars there, fast, slow, fast, fast, slow, slow, slow. The tremor in Mary’s hands told me she was laughing silently. That was reassuring. I broke off halfway through the third rendition to ask if I could look at her yet.

‘No, better not—’

She didn’t need to tell me it was bad. Put it this way—she was close, right in front of me, but her voice was coming from another direction entirely, from my far left.

‘Listen—how did we get—I mean, how did that happen? How did we do that? How is that even possible? For us to do that together?’

‘It’s all very technical,’ she said, haughtily. ‘You couldn’t possibly understand.’

‘Try me.’

‘This isn’t a good time, I’m afraid.’

I missed her hands when she took them away. ‘Don’t look—I mean it,’ she warned. A moment passed, I heard a clicking sound, and she gave a ragged gasp. I kept my eyes closed.

‘Mary—that’s just the way the story went. I didn’t know that was us. Maybe if you’d explained beforehand—’

‘Oh, you knew. Of course you did.’ Her voice was thin. ‘But never mind. Serves me right for letting you go first. The next move is mine, and I assure you, you're not going to like it.'

be bold, be bold, but not too bold

February 17th, 1936

St John Fox
c/o Astor Press
490 West 58th Street
New York City

Dear Mr Fox,

I read Dr Lustucru with great interest. It really wasn't bad. In fact I congratulate you on it. Whilst not expecting a reply I feel compelled to ask why none of your books contain a photograph of their author. Are you particularly ugly, particularly shy, or is it simply that you transcend physical existence?

Best regards,
Mary Foxe
85 East 65th Street, Apartment 11
New York City

June 2nd, 1936

Mary Foxe
85 East 65th Street, Apartment 11
New York City

Dear Mary (you will forgive my familiarity, as it is potentially less presumptuous than calling you 'Miss' when you may be a 'Mrs', or 'Mrs' when you may be a 'Miss'),

Thanks for your letter—such courtesies mean a lot to me.

I'm replying to confirm that I'm astoundingly ugly. I have been the sorrowful owner of several dogs, each of whom I named Nestor, each of whom has found my features exhausting and run away from home.

I have a hunch that you, however, are the complete opposite. True? I invite you to enclose a photograph of yourself by return.

Cordially,
S.J. Fox
c/o Astor Press
490 West 58th Street
New York City

July 2nd, 1936

St John Fox
c/o Astor Press
490 West 58th Street
New York City

Mr Fox,

Having reread my initial letter to you, I don't believe it merited such an insulting reply. If you are so sensitive about your looks perhaps you ought to refrain from responding to enquiries about them. And if the short piece in January 4th's New York Times is correct and you have indeed recently obtained your third divorce, isn't it extremely unlikely that dogs would be repelled by you yet women continually attracted? They say sarcasm is the lowest form of humour and I agree.

M.F.
85 East 65th Street, Apartment 11
New York City

July 6th, 1936

Mary Foxe
85 East 65th Street, Apartment 11
New York City

M.F.,

How delightfully easily insulted you are, how unnervingly well-informed. You also appear to be British ('humour').

As you can see, I have rushed a reply out to you, so great is my anxiety that your opinion of me has been lowered. Has it? Say it ain't so.

St John
c/o Astor Press
490 West 58th Street
New York City

PS—your failure to include a photograph with your last letter has been noted.

July 11th, 1936

St John Fox
c/o Astor Press
490 West 58th Street
New York City

You seem bitter, Mr Fox. Are you having trouble with the next book?

M. Foxe
85 East 65th Street, Apartment 11
New York City

July 16th, 1936

'Mary Foxe'
85 East 65th Street, Apartment 11
New York City

Dear 'Mary Foxe',

Is this your true name? Have we met someplace; are we acquainted? Have I wronged you in some way?

Be direct. Allow me to make amends,
St John Fox
c/o Astor Press
490 West 58th Street
New York City

July 22nd, 1936

St John Fox
c/o Astor Press
490 West 58th Street
New York City

Dear Mr Fox,

I found your questions asinine.

Yours sincerely,
Mary Foxe
85 East 65th Street, Apartment 11
New York City

July 28th, 1936

Mary Foxe
85 East 65th Street, Apartment 11
New York City

My dear Miss Foxe,

That's quite some vocabulary you've got there. But this is not the day and age to waste paper, ink and stamps. What is it that you want from me?

S.J.F.
177 West 77th Street, Apartment 25
New York City

August 2nd, 1936

St John Fox
177 West 77th Street, Apartment 25
New York City

I've written a few stories, and I'd like you to read them.

M.F.
85 East 65th Street, Apartment 11
New York City

August 6th, 1936

Mary Foxe
85 East 65th Street, Apartment 11
New York City

Why me?

S.J.F.
177 West 77th Street, Apartment 25
New York City

September 1st, 1936

St John Fox
177 West 77th Street, Apartment 25
New York City

Mr Fox,
I apologise for the brevity of my previous note, which was due to a combination of factors: I was surprised by the frankness of your letter and the fact that you had included what appears to be your actual home address. Also I had been having a difficult week but wanted to reply promptly, so was forced to do so without niceties. Why you? My answer is unoriginal: I-have-long-been-an-admirer-of-your-work-and-have-found-it-a-great-encouragement-whilst-in-the-midst-of-my-amateur-scribbling-to-imagine-you-reading-what-I-have-written. There, that's over with. In short, I ask for nothing but your honest opinion of my stories. I'm aware that even asking this is an imposition, one that I would certainly resent if our situations were reversed, therefore I'll take no offence at your ending this correspondence by dint of silence and shall remain,

Your interested reader,
Mary Foxe
85 East 65th Street, Apartment 11
New York City

September 10th, 1936

Mary Foxe
85 East 65th Street, Apartment 11
New York City

Little Miss Foxe,

If you'd really been doing your homework you'd know that I am the last person in the world to consult with about your writing. It surprises me that you're able to make reference to the January New York Times piece about my third divorce without also recalling the February piece that described me as 'a suffocating presence across the breakfast table . . . harsh destroyer of the feminine creative impulse'. Why don't you write to the author of that piece? I'm sure she has some handy hints for you.

Sincerely,
S.J. Fox
177 West 77th Street, Apartment 25
New York City

September 13th, 1936

St John Fox
177 West 77th Street, Apartment 25
New York City

Mr Fox,

You are suspicious of me. Don't be. You feel exposed by recent scrutiny of your private life and you sense that I am mocking you or preparing the way for some kind of punchline, that I will send you some satirical pages about a writer with thirty seven ex-wives, all of whom hate him and blame him for their own failures. I find it disappointing that you so transparently view your every interaction as a narrative. It is cliché, if you'll forgive my saying so.

I had a birthday in June and became twenty one years old. No I am not pretty. Not at all pretty, I'm afraid. Yes I am a Brit, in fact directly related to the author of Foxe's Book of Martyrs (I am very proud—I consider Foxe's Martyrs to be the sixteenth century's best book). I grew up in a rectory, my father is a vicar, as a child I suspected him of having written the Bible. I am sole occupant of one medium sized bedroom in a penthouse apartment not so very far from you; the place is full of Objects I am afraid I shall accidentally break. For almost a year now I have been tutor and general companion—there is not really a name for my job—to a fourteen year old girl who was asked not to return to school because the majority of her fellow pupils were frightened of her. On weekends the family usually leave town, and that is when I take the opportunity to type what I have written in my notebook. I am not sure what I mean by writing this to you, or how much, if at all, my listing these things will strike you as reassuring, or even interesting. I'm not what you think I am, that's all.

M. Foxe
85 East 65th Street, Apartment 11
New York City

October 17th, 1936

Mary Foxe
85 East 65th Street, Apartment 11
New York City

Dear M.,

Your letters have interested me more than any I've been sent in a long while, and if you'd still like me to read your pages I'd be glad to. You must give them to me in person, though—I only read the work of people I am personally acquainted with. And before you make a smart remark, yes, I knew Shakespeare. I really am that old.

I almost always pass an hour or two at the bar of the Mercier hotel of a Sunday—not even eavesdropping—everybody tries too hard to be shocking nowadays—just drinking. It would be my pleasure if you could join me there next Sunday. 7pm. No need to write back this time, just show up, and let's see if we can pick each other out. If you have your pages in full view I'll consider you a spoilsport.

Warm regards,
S.J.
177 West 77th Street, Apartment 25
New York City

* * *

I received that letter on Wednesday morning and opened it at the breakfast table while Mitzi Cole licked grapefruit segments and Katherine Cole sat with her eyes closed, repeating 'split the lark split the lark split the lark split the lark' in what she thought was an English accent. After a few minutes, Mitzi joined in: 'split the lark split the lark split the lark split the lark' but gabbled, her words hastily jammed into the pauses Katherine took to breathe.

Katherine opened her ice-blue eyes to intone: 'And you'll find the music.'

Mitzi poked my wrist with her spoon. 'Anything of note?' she asked.

I shook my head. 'Just a letter from my father.' I hadn't exactly lied—beside my plate there was an envelope addressed in my father's handwriting, but unopened.

The Coles have a musical clock hung on a bracket in their living room; it is lantern-shaped with a circular opening for the clock face. It chimes the hour every hour from seven in the morning to ten at night, and it also plays a snatch of 'Für Elise'. It makes me laugh now to think that 'Für Elise' ever used to send a chill down my spine. Katherine has said several times that the clock offends her sensibilities, but Mr Cole likes it, so it stays. When the family interviewed me in London, the second or third thing Mr Cole told me after shaking my hand was that he had no culture, none at all. Mitzi, tiny, white-blonde and warmly rounded, like a soft diamond, had immediately interjected: 'God bless our Papa Bear; he doesn't need any culture.'

The clock chimed nine just as Katherine turned to her mother and said: 'You know, your elocution is really terrible.'

Mitzi smoothed Katherine's hair and said, 'Why, thank you, my sweet.'

Katherine replied: 'You had grapefruit juice on your hands and now it's in my hair.' Shc lcft thc table immediately—with purpose more than petulance. Mitzi and I heard the bathroom taps go on and we looked at each other.

'I find it slightly ridiculous that Katy is my child,' Mitzi remarked, and resumed with her grapefruit. She was simultaneously reading the dictionary—(I saw she had just begun the letter 'K') and looking through a Bergdorf Goodman catalogue, choosing clothes for Katherine.

Katherine returned to the table damp-haired. Mitzi tapped a page of the catalogue with her pen and asked, 'Honey, what do you think of this little skirt suit here?'

'It's great, I'll take it,' Katherine said, without looking. Katherine is Mitzi miniaturised, brunette, and wiped entirely clean of conscience. I have the strong feeling that unless Katherine is closely watched she will one day do something terrible to another person, or perhaps even to a large group of people. The key is not to aggravate her, I think.

Mitzi placed a large tick on the catalogue page.

Let's see if we can pick each other out . . .

I looked at the walls as I ate my toast—everything was butter and marmalade. The blondest wood that Mitzi had been able to find, yellow countertops, yellow tablecloth, linoleum of the same colour but in such a shocking hue that I can never quite believe in it and constantly find myself walking or sitting with only my toes on the ground, never my full weight.

Katherine's white silk blouse was wet from her washing, possibly ruined. I would take it to the dry-cleaner's before our morning walk. Her pine green skirt was cut so simply that I knew it cost the equivalent of at least three months of my wages.

'Better change your blouse, Katherine,' I said. If she heard me, she gave no sign. I took Mr Fox's letter (*If you'd still like me to read your pages I'd be glad to* . . . glad to, he'd be glad to . . .) and the letter from home, took them to my bedroom and tucked them in alongside the others, between the covers of my copy of Foxe's *Martyrs*, a book to which Katherine had shown an aversion, so I knew they'd be safe from her eyes.

Mitzi had switched on the wireless set; a band was swinging Gershwin, trombones loudest. I returned to the kitchen to clear the plates and cups.

'I've been reading some of your poems,' Katherine told her mother. Mitzi went wide-eyed with alarm and said: 'And?'

'They don't make any sense,' Katherine said. 'You know that? I have some questions.' She pulled a square of paper out of her skirt pocket and unfolded it. Mitzi looked to all four corners of the room for help. I turned quickly and ran water over the dishes.

'Oh it's blank,' Mitzi whispered, hoarse with relief. 'Honey, it's blank. What a dirty trick to play on your old ma.'

'April Fool's,' Katherine explained.

'It's October,' Mitzi told her.

Katherine didn't say anything for some time; she

seemed to be brooding. No one else said anything either. The band on the radio heaved into another song and I began drying the dishes. I would give Mr Fox just three stories—I already knew which ones. The previous weekend I'd looked at the stories I'd typed, reading them over and over. If Mr Fox doesn't think you're any good, I asked myself, what will you do?

The dishcloth was yellow, too—as I dried each cup I checked my hands for jaundice. Katherine appeared at my side. She had changed into a grey dress. 'Come on, Mary,' she said, handing me my coat. 'Let's go for our walk.'

It had rained overnight, and in the trees it was still raining. Every branch along 65th Street shed leaves on us. The leaves were dark and their moisture made noise. There was a sense that at any time they might bite—they were like bats. The Mercier Hotel was down the block on our way to Central Park. Pigeons stumbled across the white portico that jutted over the doors, and I could distantly hear the bustle, see people moving behind the smoky glass.

We stopped at the dry-cleaner's with Katherine's blouse and a couple of Mr Cole's suits, then I told Katherine about the literature assignment I was setting her: read *The Woman in White* and *The Count of Monte Cristo*, then answer the question 'What is a villain?' I had two copies of each book in my satchel for when she settled down to read at the park. I meant to read along with her, to see if it was possible to catch her thinking. It wasn't the reading itself that would throw Katherine—she read everything. The problem was eliciting a response from her afterwards. If asked for a review she impersonally rehashed every detail of the story. 'Oh, everyone's got a view, haven't they . . . everyone's got something to say,' she'd tell me, when all I wanted to know was whether she'd liked the book or not.

As I'd expected, Katherine wasn't listening to what I was telling her. She picked leaves off her black beret. 'Say, do you think Ma'll let me bob my hair like yours?'

We crossed at the light, hand in hand.

'Your hair suits you as it is.'

'But I want a bob. Ma says it's quaint because it's so out of style.'

I blushed hard. No point asking whether Mitzi had really said that.

Katherine looked sideways at me. 'Why *do* you bob your hair? Waiting on a flapper revival?'

'I bob my hair because I don't care about trends, only about what suits me, thank you very much for asking,' I said, severely.

Really I bob my hair because I've given up on it. It's so palely coloured that if I pull it back from my face I look bald. My mother used to kiss my cheeks and run her fingers through my hair. She'd hold locks of it up to the light and say: 'Look at that colour, spun gold. You'll be such a beautiful woman . . .'

I always understood that it was a story, like all her other ones, the fairy tales she told. I've taken no harm from its not coming true. I don't expect it to come true.

* * *

I spent Sunday morning typing fresh copies of the

three stories I meant to give Mr Fox. Usually I make plenty of mistakes, and I waste quite a lot of paper that way. But this time mistakes were minimal—adrenalin lent me precision. I played 'Mama Loves Papa' over and over on Katherine's gramophone, which she'd placed in my room before leaving for Long Island with her parents. All three had left wearing starched tennis whites; they planned to take turns playing doubles on their tennis court, to help Mr Cole forget the hassle of his working week. I haven't been to the Long Island house, but I've seen photographs, and I hope the Coles never think to ask me along. Beside the tennis court they have a swimming pool and a topiary maze. Also a cook. What would I do in such a place? Die, I expect. Some Depression the Coles are having.

Mitzi occasionally asks me how I spend my weekends, and I tell her I volunteer at a soup kitchen on Times Square.

When I'd finished typing, I slid the pages into a black folder and put the folder in my satchel. My stomach sprang up my throat and I tried to be sick in the bathroom, but had no such luck. I lay on my bed with *The Count of Monte Cristo*, rereading his astounding escape from the Château d'If. Good for you, Count of Monte Cristo. Your escape is one in the eye for jailers everywhere. I've given up trying to position my bed in such a way that the sky can be seen from the bedroom window—there just isn't any sky in this part of Manhattan. On sunny days clouds are reflected in the plate glass halfway up the tallest buildings, but that's the best this place can do.

It's odd the way I keep to my bedroom even

when the apartment is empty, more so when it is empty, actually. I can't explain it—it's not an attachment to the room itself, not anything to do with a sense of security or ownership. Not timidity, not disorientation. Maybe the Coles chose me for this very reason, they looked at me and thought, this girl is no threat to our home, to our cut crystal and heirloom silver, our framed landscapes and lace, oh, our lace. She's English but she's not hoity-toity. She knows her place, she sure does know her place. There's something ghostlike about this girl . . . she will appear at certain times and in certain places and at other times she will recede into a disinterested dark. Mary 'Ghost' Foxe.

*   *   *

I would be at the bar before he arrived, I decided. To spy him before he spied me. I would sit close to the door with a glass of wine, drinking it slowly with my eyes half-closed. Then, at 7 p.m., I would look up and examine all those gathered around me. It would be like the ending of an Agatha Christie mystery, all possible culprits together in a locked room.

At 7:03 I would stride over to the man whose appearance was the least remarkable and say: 'Mind if I join you, Mr Fox,' without a question mark. We would talk for one hour, I would hand over the stories and be back by 8:10, 8:30 at the latest. The Coles would be home at 9.

I chose to make my entrance at 6:30. His inviting me for 7 made it unlikely he would arrive before 6:30 himself. Unless 7 represented the latter half of the 'hour or two' he passed at the bar, in which case he would be already seated, ice cubes melting into his whisky. None of the characters in any of his stories drink whisky, they drink everything under the sun but that, I've noticed, so whisky is probably a drink Mr Fox reserves for himself. He'd wait until ice and alcohol had merged completely before taking his first sip. Whilst waiting he'd . . . what? Did he really go to the bar of the Mercier hotel alone 'most Sundays', or did he have a drinking buddy named something like Sal, flat-headed sleepy-blinking Sal, a sports journalist whose lethargy concealed an encyclopaedic knowledge of every professional boxing statistic since the sport began? Good old Sal, uncomplicated company. Or perhaps Mr Fox liked to drink with admirers of his books, young newspapermen with rolled-up shirtsleeves, smartly dressed girls who typed rejection letters on behalf of various publishers and literary agencies. He probably liked actresses. He hadn't yet been married to or linked to an actress, only writers, but maybe a Broadway starlet was on the cards, an antidote to his run of bad luck. If I found Mr Fox sitting at the bar with a simpering actress, I wouldn't bother speaking to him, I'd leave immediately.

At ten minutes to six I walked into Katherine's room and opened her wardrobe, which was so tidy it looked empty. I took her green skirt off a hanger and put it on; it fitted well. Next I went into Mitzi's room. The clock chimed six and hammered out 'Für Elise'. I sat at the dressing table in Katherine's skirt and my own black brassiere (twenty minutes left—it would take me ten minutes to walk down to the Mercier) and used everything in sight. I powdered my face, rouged my cheeks, painted my eyelashes, combed my eyebrows. When I had finished, I washed my face clean, because the results were exactly as I had expected and I looked ghastly. With three minutes remaining I buttoned up Katherine's silk blouse, turned the gramophone off and left.

The lift attendant asked if I was going on a date. I ignored him. It's quite an experience, ignoring the speech of someone you're sharing a lift with. I suppose it should only be done when one has absolutely nothing to say. He tugged his cap and said: 'Well la-di-da and good evening to you too,' when I got out at the ground floor.

Inside, the Mercier was all brass and mahogany and polished rosewood. Red velvet, too, and perfume soaked so deep in tar that it smelt dirty; a nice sort of dirty. I took a cramped corner table that a couple had just vacated. They looked happy together, walked out with their coat collars turned up and their fingertips just touching. I put my wine glass down between their empty glasses and asked the waitress not to clear them away. From the bar's vast marble crest to the bank of tables and chairs that surrounded it, hardly anyone sat alone. There were a few more couples, but mainly mixed groups of five, six, seven, the women sipping at cocktails with prettily wrinkled noses, the men using their cigars and whisky tumblers to emphasise the points they were making.

At 6:40 someone said: 'Hi there.'

I looked up at a man with a beer glass in his hand. His hair was slicked across his head with each strand distinct, like the markings on a leaf. He grinned.

'All on your lonesome?'
'Are you Mr Fox?'
He winked and drew out the chair opposite me. 'Sure, I'm him. I've been looking at you, and—'
I dropped my satchel onto the chair before he could sit down. 'I'm waiting for someone.'
The man moved on without argument, took a seat at the bar, swivelled his stool to face my table and smiled at me whenever I looked his way. I couldn't help looking every now and again, for comparison's sake. I began to feel certain that the man at the bar was Mr Fox after all. His eyes were quite beady, there was too much white to them and they sat too close together, but his smile was pleasant, soothing despite them.
At 7:10 a waitress came over with another glass of wine for me. 'Gentleman at the bar's taken a shine to you. Sends this with his compliments. Says his name's Jack.'
I nodded and let her put the glass down before me. I didn't drink from it. It sat there, buying me time to wait here alone in this place. I looked into the wine and felt myself drowning in it. Mr Fox didn't come, he didn't come, he didn't.
It was 8:30 when I left the bar. The night was very stark, alternate streams of town cars and chequered taxi-cabs, blaring horns busily staking claims—here is the road and here is the sidewalk. But the road looked so much livelier, what if I tried the road?
I often think it would be such luxury to go mad, and not have to worry about anything. Others would have to worry for me, about me. There would be some sort of doctor there to tell me, *Don't worry, Mary, it's just that you are mad. Now be*

quiet, and take this pill. And I would think, So that's all it is, and I would be so glad. But aloud I would say: 'What? I'm perfectly sane! *You're* mad . . .' Only mildly, though; just for show, really.

* * *

November 1st, 1936

St John Fox
177 West 77th Street, Apartment 25
New York City

Abominable Mr Fox,
Contemptible Mr Fox,
Nefarious Mr Fox,
Vile Mr Fox,
Loathsome Mr Fox,
Putrid Mr Fox,

I closed my thesaurus and pulled the letter out of the typewriter with such haste that it tore; half of it was left in the scroll above the type bar. When I touched the two halves together they didn't even fit any more.

Katherine was on my bed, reading a book I hadn't set her. She looked up when I crushed the letter to Mr Fox in my hand—that's Katherine for you, she'd hardly blinked while I was pounding the typewriter keys, but the moment I quietly made something smaller between my fingers, she was all interest.

I asked her what she was reading.

She shrugged. 'Some book.'

'So you've already finished reading the books I set you, have you?'

She turned a page. 'Not yet, I'm getting to it.'

'I shall tell your mother that you're not applying yourself.'

Katherine seemed intrigued. I had never threatened her before.

'You probably should. After all, it's my education that's at stake. Maybe I need a new teacher or something. You missing London?'

I laughed at her indifference, the way she'd spoken without even bothering to inject a nasty insinuating tone into her words.

'Katherine, I could die horribly here in this chair, and my blood could spray all over the room and cover the pages of that fascinating book you're reading, and I believe, I really do believe, that you'd just wipe the worst away and keep going.'

Katherine stretched her legs. 'That's a pretty gruesome thing to say, Mary.' She shook her head. 'Pretty gruesome.'

She left the room, and I picked up the book she'd been reading. On the cover was an illustration of a steamboat. I glanced at the back. Vampires in the Deep South.

Katherine returned with *The Woman in White* and settled in the chair before my typewriter. 'Happy now?' she asked. I said I was happy. I had gone from standing by my bed to lying on it. I had been quite tired the past few days; sleeping longer than usual, feeling the shock of waking throughout my body, as if I had been flung against a wall. Katherine started typing. I didn't open my eyes (when had I closed them?) but I said: 'Hands off my typewriter, Katherine.'

She didn't stop. I hadn't really expected her to. I like to hear the marching of typewriter keys, the shudder of the spacebar, the metallic 'ding' as the paper is scrolled up. Those sounds are encouraging, sounds made by someone who is interested in you and in what you're saying, someone who understands exactly what you're getting at. 'Hmm,' the typewriter says. And 'Mmmm. I-see-I-see-I-see.' And sometimes it chuckles . . .

When I woke up my bedroom door was closed.

'Katherine,' I called.

'What?' she called back. So she had not absconded. I relaxed somewhat. She would not have to be collected from a police station at a quarter to midnight, as she had on the Coles' London trip. Katherine had given Hester, her previous companion, the slip in Covent Garden in order to engage in a vigorous bout of shoplifting. Having deemed Hester unable to cope with Katherine, the Coles had sacked her, then advertised for an immediate replacement. They hadn't employed an English companion before and wanted someone well-spoken and unapproachable, as if these traits could cow their daughter.

I looked inside my typewriter. There's a city in there. Black and grey columns and no inhabitants.

'I've done all my algebra. And I'm on page two hundred and goddamn five of this book you're making me read,' Katherine announced.

'Don't say "goddamn",' I replied. 'Walkies now!'

She barked quite realistically.

*   *   *

One evening I encountered Mr Cole alone in the kitchen, bending over the toaster, using it to light his cigar. 'Couldn't find my matches,' he said, when he straightened up. I said, 'Ah,' and began going away again. My cup of tea could wait. But he reached out—not very far—he is built quite powerfully and I'm like a doll beside him—and grabbed my hand. He twirled me around the room, propped me up with my back against the counter, then took a puff on his cigar (he had not troubled himself to put it out the entire time). He leant so close to me that I could very clearly see the roots of hairs that had escaped his razor. I looked at his mouth because I thought he was going to kiss me and I hoped that if I paid attention he would not kiss me. That would have been my first kiss and it would have tasted of ash.

He didn't kiss me, but he put his hand on my breast. He continued to smoke whilst squeezing my breast through my brassiere and dress. I know I should have felt angry or violated, and I did try to, but his expression was distracted, as if he was doodling on a pad whilst mulling over another thing. Mainly I felt very confused. He had been looking at my forehead, but as he squeezed for the third time, he looked into my eyes. And let go immediately. 'Places to go, people to see, Mary.' He walked backwards to the door, removing his cigar from his mouth for long enough to place a finger over his lips and wink. I wish there was someone I could have written to after that, someone I could have written to to explain how awful it was to have someone touch you, then look at you properly and change their mind.

Mr Cole was at home when Katherine and I returned from our walk, sitting in an armchair with Mitzi on his lap. Mitzi opened her arms to Katherine, inviting her to join the tableau. Katherine regarded her parents with frozen eyes and swerved around them, opting for the dining room, where a coloured maid in a white cap stood beside a stacked trolley, covering the table with trays full of vol-au-vents that no one would eat.

'How much time do I have to get away before the ladies descend?' Mr Cole asked. He seemed genuinely worried. Mitzi squeezed his neck and cooed that he was a grumpy bear, wasn't he, wasn't he.

Mitzi only hosted her women's club once a month, so it was tolerable. The wives of her husband's colleagues would gather at the Coles' apartment and fill it with cigarette smoke. Nothing was consumed but cocktails and crudités; everyone was trying to reduce. They'd go around in a circle, these women, each telling the others what she'd been reading, what she'd seen at the theatre or at the pictures, which art exhibition was most divine. Katherine and I would barricade ourselves into my room or hers, with a chair against the door in case Mitzi had too much to drink and was suddenly possessed with a desire to display her offspring. We sprawled in a nest of our own laps and legs, reading and crunching animal crackers. Katherine swore she wouldn't have anything to do with any goddamn women's club when she grew up. My only reply was: '*Don't* say "goddamn".' Sooncr or later Katherine will be expected to contribute to her mother's gatherings, and having endured it once, the next time will be easier, and so on until this brief moment when Katherine and I are in perfect agreement is lost, and it'll be strange to both of us to remember that we ever understood each other. Katherine is completely different from me, and it's more than just the fact that her father's money will erode her until she is no longer abrasive to the rest of her social set, until she is able to mingle and marry amongst them quite contentedly. It's also that she's already very pretty. A little long in the nose, but on the whole, very pretty. After a while it will seem odd that she has these looks and makes no attempt to use them. Why doesn't she smile and bat her eyelashes, the way her mother must have practically from birth? I wanted to tell her. Don't look at people so strongly, Katherine Cole. Let your gaze swoon a little. Don't speak so firmly; falter. Lisp, even. Your failure to do these things made me mistake you for someone like me.

'Katherine is improving in English literature,' I told her parents, because I felt I should say something. Then I hurried to my room. Katherine joined me when the clock struck seven. And there we stayed, safe from the clinking of glasses and the lilting sound of civilised conversation. Katherine had been teaching herself how to read Tarot, and she told my fortune, laying down card after card, telling me what each one was supposed to predict. They were all bad cards. A heart spiked with sword blades, a lightning-struck tower, a demon holding a man and a woman on the same chain, a hooded figure walking away from cups that lay empty on the ground. She was taken aback; she reshuffled the cards. 'Let's start again,' she said.

'Let's not,' I said. 'That's cheating.' We put on shoes and coats and slid past the lounge and out of the front door. In the garden at the side of the building, we knelt by the pond and fed the koi carp. There had been more rain earlier in the evening, so we turned up plenty of their favourite food without much effort. The fish surged to the surface of the water and ate the earthworms live from our fingers. Lamps lit the rosebushes as bright as day and sirens sounded and resounded, their screams strangely pure, choral. I had been all over this city on my own, looked down from its heights, looked up from its swarming pavements—I'd spoken to no one, everyone passed me by at a clip. It occurred to me that I was unhappy. And it didn't feel so very terrible. No urgency, nothing. I could slip out of my life on a slow wave like this—it didn't matter. I don't have to be happy. All I have to do is hold on to something and wait.

* * *

Once Katherine was asleep I read and marked her illustrated history project on the Church of England. I had to give her a C because she spoilt an otherwise thoughtful piece by suddenly concluding that the Church of England was Anne Boleyn's 'fault'. A Church is not the 'fault' of anybody. Next, I set about preparing a lesson on stars, galaxies and planets, poring over fat books I had withdrawn from the public library on Katherine's ticket. There was so much information. I had to select things that would interest her, place them strategically alongside the things that were bound to bore her, the figures and units of measurement, in such a way as to disarm her objections to the important facts. I didn't finish until 1 a.m., and by then it was too late to reach for my typewriter and add to the other pages I had been accumulating. So I sat beside the typewriter in the dark, and I pretended that I was working at it, then I pretended that all the work was finished and I touched the keys that would make the page say

THEENDTHEENDTHEEND

* * *

November 9th, 1936

Mary Foxe
85 East 65th Street, Apartment 11
New York City

Mary,

Many thanks for your letter of November 1st. Here is what I propose: to have my secretary wait for you this Saturday at 1pm, in order to collect the pages you want me to look at, and to buy you a consolatory lunch if you're hungry. Salmagundi, on Lexington and 61st, is a personal favorite of mine—if you object to the time, place, date, or all three, then please say so by return. Otherwise, save your stationery.

Yours most chastened,
The abominable, contemptible, vile, *execrable*, etc.,
Mr Fox
177 West 77th Street, Apartment 25
New York City

*   *   *

I telephoned Katherine at the Long Island house. Mitzi answered, and I told her that this was an impromptu French oral examination, to keep Katherine's skills elastic.

'Bonjour,' Katherine said, when she came to the phone. She was slightly out of breath—all that tennis. 'Comment ça va?'

'Got a letter from Mr Fox,' I said.

She laughed, and I heard her clap her hands. 'What did he say? Did he sock it to you?'

She stopped laughing as she soaked up the realisation that I couldn't speak. I was in too much of a state.

Once I'd recovered I asked: 'Why did you send it, Katherine?'

'I just thought it would be fun.' As she spoke I pictured her standing before me, eyeing me with all the defiance of Lucifer. In a smaller, meeker, voice she said: 'Stop hating me . . . who is he, anyway?'

'Just a man,' I said. In my mind I was already reorganising the contents of the black folder. I'd kept working on the stories, and they were stronger now, and better; I was sure of it. It was just as well he hadn't met me at the Mercier.

* * *

On Saturday afternoon I stood paralysed on the pavement outside the restaurant, which had these smart black-and-silver revolving doors; every time someone stepped into them I knew I was meant to take the next empty space and push myself into the lobby. But when I finally did I found that I couldn't stop pushing at the door until I had spun back out into the street again. I tried to be firm with myself, but with each glimpse of the restaurant full of marble and women genteelly eating salad, I lost my nerve to join them and ran inside the doors like a rodent in a glass maze. On the corner a man in a suit was standing beside an apple cart. 'Apples,' he said. 'Getcha apples!' No one was buying, so he began juggling them. 'Look what I've sunk to,' he sang. 'God I hate these apples, I'd rather starve to death than eat these apples, tra la la.' He was a tenor. Finally he started telling the people passing that he had kids at home. Someone suggested he feed the apples to his kids. He caught my eye. 'You're my witness. When you're out of work people think they can talk to you anyhow!' I nodded and went back in for another bout with the revolving doors. By now people trying to enter the restaurant from the street were asking me if I was crazy or what; the fifth time I saw the maître d' frowning menacingly, and the sixth time a woman came to meet me out on the street. She seized my arm as if I was a naughty child about to scamper off somewhere. 'That's enough of that,' she said. 'You'll tire yourself out.'

I coughed out an 'Ouch, do you mind?' and hoped the apple-seller wasn't looking. The woman's grip was surprisingly strong. She wore a brown skirt-suit and a tiny brown hat tipped coquettishly over one eye.

'Let go of me,' I said.

When she didn't, I pleaded: 'I'm meeting someone.'

'Who?' she asked.

'I don't see how that's any of your business—'

She shook me a little. 'Mr Fox's secretary,' I said. 'I'm meeting Mr Fox's secretary.'

'Then it's just as well, isn't it, that I'm her.'

She released me at last, and we stood nose to nose. I glared, and she just looked back, with an air of melancholy.

'You'd better prove it,' I said. For some reason, I'd thought the secretary would be a man.

'You're . . . Mary Foxe?' she said, looking me over.

'I'm Mary Foxe,' I said.

The woman produced an envelope from her handbag, pulled my letter out of it and showed me.

Abominable Mr Fox,

I read, then winced, and returned it to her, apologising. She said: 'Don't apologise, I think it's funny.' But she didn't laugh, or even smile.

'What's your name?' I asked.

'Doesn't matter,' she said.

I handed her the black folder full of stories and I asked her what Mr Fox was like.

The secretary blinked slowly, thinking. 'He's kind of quiet,' she said.

She wandered away with the folder sticking out of her handbag, leaving me alone on the sidewalk. I watched her, thinking she might suddenly remember something and turn around. Once I was sure that she'd gone I hailed a cab.

* * *

A week went by; he didn't write to me. He had my folder and he didn't write to me. Then three more silent weeks, six, eight. My fingernails crept down into their beds, my eyes grew glassy, I brushed my hair with my back to the mirror. I had no interest in looking at myself; it was the sensation of teeth against my scalp that subdued me.

It was all I could do not to write to him again.

'You should go get your stories back,' Katherine said, when I briefly explained the situation to her. 'He's probably going to steal them or something.'

'How would you know they're good enough for him to want to steal them?'

'Oh, I know,' Katherine said, sagely. 'I read 'em. All of them. I especially like the one about the disappearing zoo. That's the best one.'

I grabbed her before she could escape and, unexpectedly, found myself hugging her. I liked the fluffy weight of her head against my chest. She was just as surprised as I was. I neutralised it by calling her a bloody nosey parker.

'Maybe that goddamn secretary stole the stories,' Katherine suggested.

'I told you not to say that word.'

'Which? Secretary? Stories? Maybe . . . ?'

Maybe, maybe, maybe.

One morning Mitzi said I ought to take a break. That was alarming. I stopped buttering my toast and said: 'Why? I'm fine. Thanks all the same, Mrs Cole, but the weekends are enough for me.' I made a swift analysis of my behaviour of the past two weeks or so. I had not said or done anything particularly strange; I had behaved more or less as I always did.

Mitzi rose from her seat and cupped my face in her flower-scented hands. I was so nervous I could have bitten her. 'Honey, no one's saying you're not doing a good job. You're doing a wonderful job. Isn't she, Katy?'

Katherine said yes and stuck her tongue out at me.

'It's just that you can't give your weekends to a soup kitchen and your weekdays to this little fiend of mine and just go on and on without stopping. What if you burned out or something? Honey—I'm telling you, I'd never forgive myself.' She had a new bracelet on, stacked with emeralds brighter than her eyes. I hate rich people.

'Your face is all pinched,' Katherine told me helpfully.

So that morning, instead of taking Katherine to the Metropolitan Museum of Art, I went to get my stories back.

177 West 77th Street was easy to find. It was a posh apartment block, much like the Coles', but smaller. More exclusive, I suppose. I entered the building behind a grocery delivery boy who pulled a small township of brown-paper bags along on a trolley behind him. The building directory indicated that Mr Fox, at number 25, was on the fourth floor. As I waited by the lift I caught sight of myself in the polished steel doors. I was grinning. On the fourth floor I approached number 25 casually, as if I might not stop, as if I might well walk past it and continue on down the red-carpeted corridor. But I did stop at 25. And I rang the doorbell, and I knocked, hard.

The secretary answered the door. She wasn't wearing any lipstick or powder, and she'd yanked her hair up into a knot on the top of her head. She had a pencil behind each ear and one in her hand. She looked very, very young.

'What can I do for you?' she asked. She didn't appear to recognise me.

'My name's Mary Foxe,' I said.

'Mary Foxe,' she said, as if repeating the name would help jog her memory.

'I corresponded with Mr Fox about some stories of mine—he said he'd read them, but I suppose he's too busy—I've come to take them off his hands.'

She hesitated. Oh God. She'd thrown my stories away. Or there was a mountain of manuscripts somewhere behind her, and she'd never find mine.

'I met you outside Salmagundi on 61st and Lexington a couple of months ago,' I said. 'There was a bit of a fuss with some revolving doors.'

Her eyes lit up at last. 'Oh, right,' she said. 'Right.'

She looked over her shoulder, though no one had spoken. 'Be right back.'

She closed the door before I could peer into the flat. It seemed strange to me that Mr Fox's secretary should be at his flat—I mean, secretaries belong in offices.

Ten minutes later she opened the door again and handed me my folder. I looked through it quickly—all the stories appeared to be there. The pages were well thumbed, and some parts were underlined.

'He—er—he read them?'

Suddenly I felt as if I could knock this woman down and charge into his study, pull up a chair, and settle down to talk. As if she knew what I was thinking, she took a firmer stance in the doorway. She twirled her pencil between her slim fingers. 'Yes. He did.'

I didn't like the look in her eyes. My throat went dry. 'And?'

She shook her head. 'You don't really want to write . . . what you want is love. Go find yourself a beau. You're so young, Miss Foxe. Go have a little fun.'

'Did Mr Fox say that? Or is this coming from you?'

She looked down.

'It's coming from me,' she told the floor.

'I want to talk to Mr Fox,' I said.

I stepped towards the secretary and she held her pencil out at eye level, in an unmistakably threatening gesture. The point was very sharp.

'What did Mr Fox say?' I said. 'Just tell me that, and I'll go.'

She didn't answer, and I said: 'Are you Mr Fox?'

She laughed. 'No.'

'You are, aren't you? You're Mr Fox –' I caught sight of a bare passageway, a telephone on a stand, the receiver off the hook—I heard no dial tone—'you're him.'

She frowned. 'I'm not.'

'What did he say, then?'

'Wait.'

The door closed again. When it opened, the secretary was holding a lit taper. The flame cast her eyes into shadow.

'He said . . .' She paused, and sighed. 'He said I should do this.'

She touched the taper to the black folder, and it caught fire. She blew the taper out before the flame struck her fingers. But I didn't let the folder go. The leather cover burned with a harsh sound like someone trying to hold back a cry between their teeth. Still I held the folder. I felt the skin on my fingers shrink. I watched words turn amber and float away.

I liked these stories. Katherine liked them. I'd worked hard on them.

There was so much smoke in my eyes.

But I held on.

Mary Foxe had known that it was more than a matter of snapping her fingers and having Mr Fox change his ways—she'd known it would be difficult, but this was beyond all her expectations. She'd been asleep for days, in a four-poster bed in a dark blue room. There wasn't a part of her body that didn't ache. Her brain ached most of all. She'd felt terrible burning his stories, which she'd actually thought were rather good. She couldn't have let Mr Fox get away with beheading her, though. That was exactly the kind of behaviour she had set out to discourage. She was aware of a large clock ticking outside the bedroom door, but it didn't wake her up. Mary was busy having a very long dream.

In her dream, she was a spinster. Fastidious, polite, and thirty-eight years old. Her features were plain and unremarkable—they had always been plain and unremarkable. She had been a dutiful daughter when her parents were alive, and now Dream-Mary lived in the attic of the house her parents had left her. The remainder of the house she had hoped to let to a family—but no family liked the idea of living there with her up in the attic like that. So Mary let the house below to a solicitor named Pizarsky. He was out all day—that was good. He was punctual with his rent—also good. In the evenings, however, he hosted parties that were exclusively attended by attractive young ladies who giggled for hours on end. That was tiresome.

Mary and Mr Pizarsky kept their exchanges as brief as possible:

'Morning, Miss F.'

'Good morning, Mr Pizarsky.'

'Here's the rent, Miss F.'

'Thank you, Mr Pizarsky.'

'Off home for Christmas now, Miss F.'

'Merry Christmas, Mr Pizarsky.'

On Valentine's Day, Dream-Mary bought herself a single red rose, then immediately ran back into the shop, confused and embarrassed, to return it.

Most days Dream-Mary stayed at her desk until sunset, working in the special quiet of the otherwise empty house, the settling of floorboards and the ticking of clocks. She wrote romance novels under the pen name Wendy Darling. Hers were gloriously improbable tales, stuffed with happy coincidences, eternal devotion and the unwavering recognition of inner beauty. They were in great demand, Mary's novels. They were read-them-once-and-throw-them-away sort of books, really. And Mary had seen people doing just that, throwing her novels away, or very deliberately leaving them behind on park benches and bus seats once they had finished. She tried not to let it get her down. She didn't like to brood. She kept a framed photograph of her parents on her desk, to remind herself of their story, which amazed her. They had fallen in love and kept it up far into old age; that was all. Her father was the hero in every story she wrote, and her mother was the heroine. They had been gone five years, but she brought them together again and again, thirty-five lines of cream-coloured foolscap folio at a time. And they never tired of finding each other, even when she was reduced, in the final chapters, to typing with just one finger, her little finger, jabbing out words until her hand curled up and could do no more. She completed a novel every other month and took August and December off.

It was Dream-Mary's custom to read the local newspaper as she ate her evening meal in the dining corner of her attic. She read it thoroughly, without omitting a single paragraph or page. It was much more difficult to be alarmed by the events of a day that was almost over. After that she would go for a walk, to keep fit. And upon her return to her attic she would say a few phrases aloud, experimenting with a friendly tone of voice. She didn't often socialise, but it was important to keep her hand in. She rehearsed small talk about the weather, and about children and the cost of living. From Mr Pizarsky's party below, a gramophone puffed jazz up at her like smoke rings until she stopped trying. She put on her nightgown, did her stretching exercises, applied cold cream to her face and went to bed. Her days were pleasant and her mood was even.

One evening Mary went for her after-dinner walk as usual. She went through town, passing the tidy shop fronts, their signs beautifully lettered in glossy paint and print, striding over the mushy bank of sawdust outside the butcher's. The entire neighbourhood was at home; wireless sets buzzed gently at her as she passed. Each house stood in its own square of garden, each garden with its own picket fence and its own garden gate. Not a curtain twitched. Mary climbed Murder Hill. It was a funny old hill. It started off as easily as walking on flat ground, and continued to seem flat, even after she had begun to feel short of breath. She looked down at all the chimney tops and picked lavender.

When she returned from her walk she found the house suspiciously quiet.

There was no rustling or giggling, no chiming of glassware to be heard anywhere in the house, she noticed. No party this evening. Mr Pizarsky appeared, carrying a cake; it prickled with lit candles, at first glance there appeared to be hundreds of them. 'Happy birthday, Miss Foxe,' he said, smiling warily.

He was right. It was her birthday. Dream-Mary thought she might be sick. 'Mr Pizarsky,' she said. 'You shouldn't have.' It was meant to sound light-hearted, but it didn't.

He looked crestfallen. 'You don't like cake.'

'No, I do. How did you know it was my birthday?'

In the kitchen, Mr Pizarsky carefully dropped his burden onto the table. He stared at the candle flames. They both did. It seemed rude to look at each other just then.

'I gave my room a good spring cleaning last week,' he said. 'I found a birthday card. Dated.'

So he slept in her old room. She hadn't known that, hadn't checked to see whether or not he'd been keeping the lower half of the house in order, whether he had changed any aspect of the furnishing. The hallway and main stairs were tidy enough, and as long as the house didn't fall down she didn't care. In the last few weeks of her mother's illness they'd spent whole afternoons in that room. Afterwards she'd moved out of that part of the house in a hurry. And she hadn't gone back for anything since, had waited in the parlour while prospective tenants looked the property over. She must have left a great many things in there.

'I've taken a liberty, haven't I?' Mr Pizarsky gestured towards the birthday cake. 'Even as I bought it, I wasn't sure. You like to have secret birthdays? You English . . . I am forever offending you.'

'No, no—' Mary searched for her manners and caught hold of them again. 'It's a lovely surprise.'

She pretended to make a wish and blew out the candles—only thirty of them, she counted. Such flattery. She found two small plates and put a slice of the cake on each, then remained standing, holding her slice away from her. He stood too—he couldn't very well sit down and eat while she stood there, not eating. As they exchanged remarks she was aware of treating him shabbily.

'I hope you didn't cancel a gathering on my account, Mr Pizarsky.'

'No, I've been abandoned tonight.'

Mr Pizarsky was unkempt for a man of the law—his hair wanted combing, and the elbows of his jacket could have done with a thorough darning.

'I'm sure they'll come back,' Mary soothed.

'I hope she will. That is to say—to tell you the truth, Miss Foxe, there is only one of them I particularly care for. The others are just her friends.'

She hadn't taken a proper look at any of the girls that crowded the downstairs rooms most evenings; they all looked exactly the same to her.

'Well—best of luck, Mr Pizarsky. Is your name Russian?'

'I'm a Pole, Miss F . . . though I have met Russians who bear the name. Have you ever been to my country?'

'Poland? No—no. I haven't been anywhere. Brighton. The Lake District and the Cotswolds, a few times. London sometimes.'

'A pity. Mine is a lovely country, in parts—simple and honest and strong. The landscapes, the buildings, the mead.'

'Oh—I must go there one day.'

He smiled sadly, with his mouth closed.

'One day. Not now. The rioting. And more to come.'

'Really . . . ?'

Her question was feeble, but he considered it with a quizzical twist of his mouth.

'Why, yes, of course! "Really", you say. You don't think riots are so bad. Are you thinking of them as you do the weather here? A nuisance, but it's not so difficult to get on with things despite them?' He described the three riots he had witnessed first-hand, in three different cities. He made the anger of the poor and put upon sound like a storm on the ground; it scorched buildings when it woke, its first touch killed. 'That is why I am here,' he finished. 'Otherwise, pork pies and jellied eels be damned; give me my country.'

Mary suspected her father would have especially liked this man.

'Are you—forgive me, I know nothing about

solicitors—but is it quite usual to find solicitors like you, Mr Pizarsky?'

She had delighted him. 'Let me see . . . perhaps not. I was a poet.'

'Oh a poet . . . but what's that?' Wishy-washy, that was how she found most poetry—it just missed the point over and over again.

'What's that,' he agreed, laughing. 'What's that . . .'

He took her plate from her hand. 'And now I will release you, even though you are unfair and have told me nothing in exchange.'

She assured him that there was nothing to tell.

'Perhaps you could sing a song, then,' he suggested. 'Or turn a cartwheel—or—you could laugh, yes, laugh wonderfully, just as you are doing at the moment.'

She left him with the cake and went up to her attic. She put on her nightgown, did her stretching exercises, applied cold cream to her face and arranged herself on her bed with a stack of pillows supporting her head and neck. She looked up through her attic windows, up into the cloudy night. So Mr Pizarsky had been a poet? That was how he'd said it: 'I was a poet.' As if the poet had died. He was in hiding, perhaps. He might have written something that someone powerful hadn't liked . . .

. . . there she lay, casting him as a character in one of her own romances. He didn't cut anything like a dashing figure. And he'd need to be four inches taller before he could even make an appearance in her prose. *No more nonsense. At the count of three I shall go straight to sleep*, she informed herself. *One. Two. Thr –*

Mary Foxe woke up, feeling refreshed. And a little regretful. What if she were to abandon the task at hand? Mr Fox was a hard nut to crack. It was good that he didn't know how Mary tried to take care of him, alphabetising his reference books and checking and correcting his spelling and grammar while he lay asleep with his wife in his arms. If he knew how Mary loved him he would turn it against her somehow; he would play with it. Because that was what Mr Fox did—he played. And there was something appealing about this Mr Pizarsky . . . perhaps she could find him, or someone like him, out in the world. She imagined their courtship—quiet, restrained, but full of tenderness. She would learn more about Poland and he would learn more about England and they would clear up many funny little misunderstandings. They would pore over maps together—*I was born here, I went to school here* . . . They'd go to the seaside, and sit on the pier under umbrellas, in the rain. He would take her to the pictures and bring her violet creams. He would declare himself without words, bring her a daisy and retire with haste. And just thinking of how much he desired her but dared not presume, she would swoon over the tiny flower, dragging its petals across her lips and the backs of her hands, then shyly, languorously, along her inner thighs . . . and in time, and by being a good woman, and a patient woman, she would have won a good and patient man.

Mary turned onto her side. The pillow she was lying on was covered in spidery words; tiny, but legible. She rubbed her nose against one of the words and smudged it. The words were carefully spaced so that the pale green of the pillowcase haloed them. 'What . . .' Whole paragraphs. And they were numbered. 7, 8, 9. She turned again. Her head was surrounded with more writing. There was yet more under her hands, long lines of words meandered all along the duvet, some running horizontal, some diagonal, some fitting into each other like puzzles. And numbered, all numbered. Laughing in an appalled sort of way, Mary Foxe pulled the pillow out from under her head and read:

1. *I may not be here when you wake up. If I am not here, read on.*
2. *Mary Mary, quite contrary. I'm the easy option. You won't want me.*
3. *I have bought you more pillowcases and another duvet cover, in case you cannot stand what I have done to these ones. I took them off the bed before I wrote on them, so there's no need to worry about the ink bleeding into the pillows, etc.*
4. *My English is probably better than yours. I deliberately muddle my grammar when I speak. It puts people at ease. They become friendly when I get things wrong—they speak slowly, use shorter words, to help me. I hate it, but it's the best way to get on. You have never done this with me. Thank you.*
5. *I often sing Christmas carols in June, and I don't think it's bad luck. Do you?*
6. *It was on April 2nd last year that I discovered you had a dimple in your right cheek. You smiled at me for some reason (why? I had done nothing to deserve it. Please explain, if you remember April 2nd.) On the calendar in my*

office I made a note: 'M.F. revealed dimple today.' What do you think of sentimental men? I'm sure you hate them. And you'd be right to.

Mary sat bolt upright. Was Mr Pizarsky a dream, or not? She studied her surroundings. She had no idea where she was. There was a vaseful of foxgloves on her bedside table, their petals the pale, shocking blue of the veins in a wrist. She moved on to the next pillow.

7. *I learnt English when I went to war. People think I'm lying when I say that, but that's how it was. We were in Galicia, Poles in Russian uniforms, trying to court independence; we only managed to occupy a slice of the place while the Germans and the Austrians made off with the rest. We were fighting so very hard and achieving so very little aside from staying alive. BUT THAT'S EVERYTHING, my father wrote to me, when I told him that in a letter. I studied to take my mind off things. At dead of night in the mess hut—Pride and Prejudice, an English to Polish dictionary, and a candle. I could have burnt the place down. But I had to do it. I needed words, lots of words to think about while I was going about the rest of the day. And I didn't want anything affected. I wanted nothing to do with those Romance languages. I wanted clipped words, full of common sense. Thoughts to wear beneath my thoughts. Allow, express, oath, vow, dismay, matter, splash, mollify. I liked those words. I liked saying them. I still do.*
8. *I helped to load cannons. People are not good at war. Can I really say that, when all I know is that I and those around me were not good at*

war? Don't say our hearts weren't in it—they were. But we got sick, some of us unto death. Spanish flu and the rot of trench foot, and there were such smells, they made us sick to our stomachs. A few of our men dropped cannonballs and broke their legs. That sort of thing. And then there was my cousin Karol. The first time he successfully shot a man, he didn't see a way to stop shooting; he knew he had to do more, and with greater speed than the first kill. He couldn't aim steadily at anyone else so he turned his rifle on himself—and missed, and missed, each time he did it was as if he was playing some sort of horrible trick on himself, the worst kind of bluff. He told me all about it. 'Calm down, Karol,' I told him. 'You must keep your head.'

9. *Wake up, Mary.*
10. *I had a great uncle; he was rich and we shared a Christian name. He liked me. I made him laugh, without even trying. I said naive things that I really believed in. Things about life, and money. He almost killed himself laughing at me. He liked to slap me on the back and tell me I looked like a peasant. When he died he left me a lot of money. I liked him then. Before that, I must say I had often daydreamed about punching him in the throat. His neck was very fat. He owned factories, and I used to think that people like him were the source of all that was evil in the land.*
11. *Wake up, wake up . . .*
12. *When I was in Galicia I tried not to think of my fiancée. I didn't write to her much, and in her own way she reproached me for that. She had*

every right to, so I won't dwell on the maddening, indirect ways in which she reproached me. Anyhow I lost her. When I came back she looked through me and seemed displeased—I might have been the ghost of Banquo for all the pleasure she took in my company. She's happy now—she married my cousin, a good boy, who is tender with her (yes, Karol—I believe I mentioned him in point 8).

Round and round. Blissfully, Mary rolled in the words, propped her head up on some and her heels on others. She liked this man.

13. *When I saw you for the first time, I thought you had a secret life. You had your hair up out of the way and you were wearing your reading spectacles and your dress was buttoned up all the way to your chin. Still, I noticed—if you will excuse my noticing—the fullness of your lips, and the way they parted every now and then as if responding to changes in the breeze. And fleetingly, so fleetingly that it's possible you weren't aware you were doing it, you moved your hand from your cheek to your neck to the centre of your chest; you held your own waist and smoothed your skirt over your hips. Yes, you looked as if you had a secret, or you were a secret in yourself. I had seen better lodgings further out—better lodgings for a bachelor, that is. A set of rooms I would have had all to myself, and I could have cycled to work and back. But I rented this house because of the lady who lived in the attic. To see if I could catch her out.*
14. *I took a lot of my inheritance money and I told everyone that I would be a lawyer. And I came*

here to study. When I got here I was restless and nothing interested me. At the end of every evening I got very drunk and vowed to give up my studies, and every morning I was back at the books. I am just trying to show you that my nature is not a consistent one. Sometimes I do what I say I'm going to do, but more often I don't. It's a failing. The least of my failings, and the only one I feel up to admitting at the moment. The rest will emerge if you choose to see it. I don't know if I'm the kind of man that is acceptable to you; I have heard that your father was a priest.

15. *Shall I tell you how many times I came up these steps while you were typing? Vowing that today would be the day that I asked you to the pictures. And I'd buy you a pound of violet creams, two pounds of them, whatever you wanted. But then I'd hear you at your typewriter, and I'd go away again. I decided that since I could not approach you, I would make you jealous. I asked my sister Elizaveta if it would work, and she said no. She also said you sounded too old for me. My mother and sisters are all very concerned about who I will marry. I am an only son.*
16. *This Mr Fox. Is he better looking than me?*

Cold blew onto Mary Foxe's blood, as if she had no skin at all.

17. *My hand is getting tired. That must be why I slipped up just now.*
18. *You're slipping yourself, Mary. Good thing you woke up before our little picnic on Murder Hill. A blue-eyed poet with some stories, a good line in wry humility and some English as a second*

language bullshit . . . is that all it takes to turn you fickle these days? Never mind . . . we'll pretend it didn't happen. A hundred years hence (or a hundred washes, whichever comes first) these words will be gone . . .

The game was still on.

fitcher's bird

Miss Foxe referred to herself as a florist, but really she was a florist's assistant. She swept plant debris off the shop floor, and she wrapped flowers for the customers and did everything else that the shop owner, Mrs Nash, didn't feel like doing. Miss Foxe wasn't allowed to cut and arrange the flowers used in the window display; nor was she allowed to advise people on the perfect floral gift. Miss Foxe knew much more about flowers than Mrs Nash, but all she could do was listen while Mrs Nash told the anxious relatives of spring-time invalids to send pink azaleas. Evidently Mrs Nash was not aware that in the language of flowers azaleas meant 'take care of yourself for me'. A touching thought, but by giving a sick person a bunch of azaleas you were telling them that they were on their own. Mrs Nash's agenda was simply to shift stock. In summer Mrs Nash prescribed marigolds left, right and centre—for birthdays, apologies, and romantic overtures—even though those flowers were better as especial comfort to the heartsick. But Miss Foxe kept all that to herself, for fear of losing her job. As it was, Mrs Nash snapped at her and called her slow and asked her if she was an idiot nineteen times a day. Miss Foxe liked to be near the flowers, especially in winter, when it was easy to forget that there had ever been such a thing as a flower.

Flowers, and thoughts of flowers, were Miss Foxe's main occupation. She didn't especially care for motion pictures; she found them too noisy. She would have liked to have had friends to lend books to, and borrow pie dishes from. But it was difficult for Miss Foxe to reach that stage with anyone. She spoke so quietly that people couldn't understand what she was saying and quickly lost patience. When she paid for things in shops, the change was invariably placed on the counter instead of in her hand. Miss Foxe occasionally wondered whether she had spent her life approaching invisibility, and had finally arrived at it. She encouraged herself to see her very small presence in the world as a good thing, a power, something that a hero might possess.

Miss Foxe's other passion was fairy tales. She loved the transformations in them. Everybody was in disguise, or on their way to becoming something else. And all was overcome by order in the end. Love could not prevail if the order of the tale didn't wish it, and neither could hatred, nor grief, nor cunning. If you were the first of three siblings, then you were going to make a big mistake, and that was that. If you were the third sibling, you couldn't fail. *Here is the truth about everything*, Miss Foxe would think, after a night with Madame D'Aulnoy, or Madame de Villeneuve.

Flowers and fairy tales were all very well, but they began to take their toll on her. Independently and in unison they made insinuations, the flowers and the fairy tales. When Mrs Nash was being especially nasty, Miss Foxe imagined herself surrounded by leafy branches that changed as her tears dripped onto them—glossy green tips shrank and smoothed into skin, the branches gripped her firmly, like arms . . .

One morning Miss Foxe gave in. It was high time she found herself a companion. But how, and where? She knew what kind of man she wanted; someone passionate, someone who would understand her. But she didn't meet people. Every man who came into the flower shop was invariably attached, or had someone else in mind.

Miss Foxe went to bars, and was overlooked with a thoroughness that chilled her marrow. She had chosen seedy bars on purpose, bars where (she had heard Mrs Nash say) the men were voracious and anything went. And it was true. Even cross-eyed girls who laughed like hyenas were bought drinks. Anything went but Miss Foxe. She wasn't bad-looking—it was just that it took a great deal of effort to be able to actually see her, especially in noisy, crowded places.

Miss Foxe tried libraries, but talking wasn't allowed.

Miss Foxe tried bookshops, but was frightened off every time she saw the titles of the books the interesting-looking men happened to be holding. Such weighty and joyless words: *Fear and Trembling*, *Anatomy of Melancholy*, *The Nicomachean Ethics* and the like.

One afternoon Mrs Nash barked at her. 'You've been late back from lunch five days running now. Explain yourself. And don't fob me off with any more lies, or you'll be out of work.'

Miss Foxe explained that she had been trying different things.

'What does that mean? Spit it out.'

'I've been looking in the bookshops for a gentleman friend,' poor Miss Foxe stammered.

Mrs Nash threw her head back and laughed for ten minutes without stopping. Then she said: 'You'd better advertise.'

And that is what Miss Foxe did. In a national newspaper, no less.

Fairytale princess seeks fairytale prince. Sarcastic and or/ironic replies will be ignored; I am in earnest, and you had better be too.

If the advertisement sounded as if Miss Foxe was fed up, that's because she was.

As a result of her advertisement, Miss Foxe received seventeen moderately interesting propositions, fifteen pages of lunatic verse (from fifteen different lunatics), twelve sarcastic and/or ironic replies (six of each) and a single foxglove wrapped in clear cellophane. The foxglove was accompanied by a card that read: *Fitcher*. The name was printed above an address not too far from where Miss Foxe lived.

Miss Foxe held the flower and walked all around her bedroom in quick circles. Her steps sped up so that she was almost running. She felt her heart beating in her fingertips. She knew the foxglove's meaning in the language of flowers—beauty and danger, poison and antidote. The digitalis made the heart contract. If your heart was too slow, then it worked to make you well. If your heart was sound, the digitalis killed. This Fitcher, whoever he was, understood the beautiful risk of the fairy tale. She wrote to Fitcher at once, and three days later he met her at a coffee shop after work.

Fitcher bemused Miss Foxe. He looked at her. He looked at her eyes, her ears, her teeth, her neck, her breasts. And he was a quiet man, but not in the way that she was quiet. His quiet was of the measured kind, entered into to conceal his thoughts. He stepped noiselessly upon the floor. She dreaded that at first.

'Is Fitcher your only name?' she asked him.

He answered: 'I have no other.'

They spoke of fairy tales, and found their tastes were exactly matched. Encouraged, she met him again, and again. At their fourth meeting, as they walked between glass cases at the British Museum, Fitcher threaded Miss Foxe's fingers through his own. She froze. She did not find it easy to be touched by Fitcher; she found that her hand was warming his, and that though his hand was strong, it moved gently with hers.

At their sixth meeting, Fitcher brought Miss Foxe a nightingale in a gold-painted cage. He set the cage down on the shop counter and draped a black cloth over it. And the bird sang out its hope, the silly little romantic calling out for a mate, not caring if this nightfall was a trick.

Mrs Nash approved of Fitcher. 'A proper Romeo, that one,' she said.

'He doesn't talk much, though,' Miss Foxe confided. 'It worries me.'

'It's better that way,' Mrs Nash returned. 'Pay attention to what he does, not what he says—that's the rule.'

And to this she added various other adages, such as 'It's in his kiss', etc.

By their seventh meeting, Miss Foxe had grown

so sure of Fitcher that she felt ready for the next step. She invited him to her flat, where she cooked him dinner and they drank wine by candlelight. Fitcher seemed appreciative, but as usual, said little. At last they were sitting on the sofa, together. She fed him bites of lemon tart. Fitcher looked as if he was enjoying both the food and the attention. Once that was over with, Miss Foxe reached behind the sofa and produced an antique sword that had been in her family for many years. It was half her height, and heavy, but shiny and sharp, as she had recently had it oiled and sharpened. She laid the sword across their laps.

'Take this sword,' Miss Foxe said, solemnly, 'and cut off my head!'

Fitcher and Miss Foxe both fell to thinking of their favourite fairy tale, The White Cat, and the enchanted princess, pleading with her love to strike the blow that would release her from her animal form.

'Are you sure?' Fitcher asked. From Miss Foxe's bedroom, the nightingale sang in its cage.

Miss Foxe sighed. 'Don't you believe . . . ?'

'Oh I do,' said Fitcher. 'I do.' And without further argument he unsheathed the sword and cleaved Miss Foxe's head from her neck. He knew what was supposed to happen. He knew that this awkward, whispering creature before him should now transform into a princess—dazzlingly beautiful, free, and made wise by her hardship.

That is not what happened.

I walked into my study—I don't know where from. Where *had* I just come from? What had I been doing? My step, at least, was sprightly—maybe I'd just come from a book launch, or an award ceremony, or a meeting with an effusive film executive. I searched my pockets for clues, but my pockets were empty. Well. Wherever I had been, Mary Foxe had been there too. Was I certain about that, or was I guessing? I whipped open the study door and regarded the hallway with a measure of suspicion. Everything was in order. I turned back to my study and registered the condition it was in—books and crumpled paper and broken records were scattered around me as if they had rained from the sky. The windows stood wide open, and a cold wind flowed in and made the torn pages of my books whisper. One of my shelves had fallen, or been pushed, down, and I had to walk across the back of it to get to my desk, which was soaked in ink. Thorough. The rampage had been thorough. I whistled, and then I closed the windows. The sound must have alerted Daphne, because she came and knocked on the door. Which wasn't closed, so why knock . . .

'Come in,' I said. I picked up half of a coffee mug and half of a phonograph record and idly held them together. A domestic chimera. Daphne came in with her arms full of books, and her eyes blazing like two poisoned moons. 'How'd you like the mess, St John?' It would've been better if she'd screamed. The question was in monotone, and was accompanied by a hardback German edition of my first book, *Stinging the Bees*. More followed—

books and flat statements, all aimed at my head—I was stunned and defended myself as best I could with my arms, but there was nowhere to hide. Daphne said she hadn't finished yet. She said she ought to burn the house down, and she just might do it, while I was sleeping. She said I was a dead man walking. She said she was going to Reno. She said she should never, never have married a tarnished individual like me. Finally, at the top of her voice she said: 'WHO IS SHE? THIS WOMAN YOU'RE HUMILIATING ME WITH.'

She ran out of books and stood there, crying, her hands fluttering over her face. I'd fallen into a crouch to weather the storm, and I waited a second before I straightened up. My ear was bleeding a little, and when she saw that, she sobbed even harder. We looked at the crack she'd made in one of the windows—the Japanese edition of *The Butcher's Boots* is no slim tome.

'Who is she?'

'Who is who?'

Daphne turned on her heel and made for the door.

'Where are you going?'

'To Reno. You'd better not contest the papers, either.'

I crossed the room and caught her hand, which seemed like the coldest and most fragile little thing in the world just then. I held her hand, patted it. She looked away and just let me hold it, as if it was of no use to her any more. My wife was pretty, I noticed. Sort of elfin, but vulnerable-looking with it. All these wispy curls surrounding a heart-shaped face.

'Don't go to Reno,' I said. She looked at me out

of the corner of her eye.

'That's it? That's your best shot at making me stay? "Don't go to Reno"?'

'I hadn't finished, D. I also wanted to tell you that you're paranoid. I don't even know what you're talking about. All I've been doing is trying to win us some bread.' I raised her hand and kissed her wrist—she likes that. 'Give me a week or two and then we'll go someplace nice, just you and me.'

She was melting; she made a face. 'Of course just you and me . . . who else would go with us, dummy?'

Quite clearly she had no solid evidence. It was interesting to know that I'd married someone who could cause this much destruction on a hunch. It made me like her more.

'D . . .' I pulled her into my arms. She buried her face in my sweater and reached up with her handkerchief, pressing it against my ear. 'Greta says I shouldn't listen to a word you say. You're a liar.'

I took custody of the handkerchief; it was awkward, her holding it, and she was applying more pressure than was necessary. 'Greta lies more than me.'

'How would you know that?'

'I don't, but I've got to defend myself.'

'You're the liar. If you hadn't been up to anything you'd be furious that I wrecked your study. You'd have thrown a hot iron at my head or something.'

'Is there a hot iron to hand?'

She sniffled. 'Yes. I was pressing my divorce dress.'

Daphne had bought a divorce dress with my

money. Even more interesting. I'd had her down as a starry-eyed idealist who didn't notice my flaws. I'd have to keep an eye on her.

'Your heart is—*jerking*,' she mumbled.

'Oh, so you can hear that?' I said into her hair. 'It's saying: Da—phne, Da—phne. How embarrassing. Don't tell anyone you heard.'

'She keeps calling,' Daphne said. 'And hanging up. While you've been God knows where—'

'Who keeps calling and hanging up?'

'That girl you've got on the side. Don't deny it, St John, I just know.'

'You just know.'

'Yes.' She looked up at me, so piercingly that my first instinct was to look away—but that would have been a mistake. 'But I don't want to leave you. Not really. So just drop her, and we'll forget about it.'

'Daphne. There is no girl on the side.'

'Say whatever you want, just drop her. Please.'

'I can't,' I said. 'She's in my head.'

I saw her expression and I talked fast. 'What I mean is, she's not real, honey. She's only an idea. I made her up.'

'What?'

'I know this sounds unlikely, but you've got to believe me. If you don't, I've got nothing else to tell you.'

'Keep talking, St John.'

'Not a lot to tell. Her name's Mary. You'd like her, I think. She's kind of direct. No-nonsense. I made her up during the war. She started off as nothing but a stern British accent saying things like, "Chin up, Fox," and, "Where's your pluck?" Just a precaution for the times I came dangerously close to feeling sorry for myself. Don't look like that, D, I don't need a doctor. Anyhow—you see now, don't you, that she couldn't possibly call the house? That's just people getting wrong numbers, or one of your brothers phoning you up to ask for money and then losing his nerve.'

'Less of the stuff about my brothers. Back to Miss A Hundred Per Cent Imaginary, Miss Only An Idea. Do you take her out to the movies?'

I couldn't tell if she was kidding. 'Absolutely not,' I said, vehemently.

'Do you tell her secrets?'

'It isn't like that.'

'Is she pretty?'

'Uh . . .'

Daphne gave me a knowing look.

'Prettier than me?'

'D . . .'

'You say "it isn't like that", so tell me what it's like. I'm just trying to figure out whether you're crazy or not.'

'I'm not crazy. At all times I remain fully aware of her status as an idea.'

'So she's kind of like a character in one of your stories?'

'Kind of.' I resisted the urge to pat her on the head and tell her not to worry about it.

'So nothing I should worry about?'

'No, ma'am. Absolutely not.'

Daphne kissed my cheek and backed away. 'Okay, honey. Sorry about the mess.'

I nodded and waved a hand, as if it was nothing. I was proud of myself. In the old days I would have lost my cool. But other things were happening now; I needed to focus on those and I didn't seem to have anything left over for rage. There's also the fact that all the men in her family, and a few of the women, are basically thugs.

'I think I'll go see a movie with Greta now.'

'Have fun.'

She closed the door very quietly behind her. Pinching my ear through Daphne's handkerchief, I crossed the fallen bookshelf again and sat down at my desk, watching ink drip onto the carpet. Mary Foxe was trying to ruin my life. By rights I should be on the edge of some sort of nervous breakdown. But I was happy.

'Impressive conflict management,' Mary remarked, from beneath my desk. Her arms were tucked around her knees, and her chin was resting on them.

'Well, hello there.' I held out a hand to her and she came out from under the desk. She settled on my lap with her arms around my neck. Nice. Carefully, I span the chair around, for a garden view, and we watched the rain falling on the old cedar tree.

'Would you mind terribly if you die next time?' she asked.

'Yes, I'd mind. To be honest, I don't like the sound of that at all. Why do you ask?'

'I just want to see . . .'

'No.'

'No?'

'*No*.'

'But, Mr Fox,' she said. 'It's all just a lot of games . . .'

like this

. . . they will say: 'The one
you love,
is not a woman for you,
Why do you love her? I think
you could find one more beautiful,
more serious, more deep,
more other . . .'

Neruda

There was a Yoruba woman and there was an Englishman, and . . .

That might sound like the beginning of a joke, but those two were seriously in love.

They tried their best with each other, but it just wasn't any good. I don't know if you know what a Yoruba woman can be like sometimes. Any house they lived in together burnt down. They fought; their weapons were cakes of soap, suitcases, fists and hardback encyclopaedias. There were injuries.

The man liked to make things. He took a chisel to stone with kindness and enquiry, as if finding out what else the stone would like to be. But his woman kept him from working—that's why they were poor. They wondered why things were like that between them when other people loved each other less and had peace. There were days when she'd open her eyes and be him for six hours in a row; she knew all his secrets and nothing he had done seemed wrong to her, she knew how it was, how things had been, she was there. There were days when he touched the tip of her nose and it was enough, a miracle of plenty.

But who finds happiness interesting?

One day the woman stamped her foot and wished her man dead. So he died. (And now you know what a Yoruba woman can be like sometimes.)

She had a devil of a time getting him back after that one. Books and candles and all the tears she could cry, and yet more—she had to borrow some from friends, and some from trees at dawn. Finally she had to give up all the children she might ever have had. In the dead of night they were scraped under the knife of a witch with a steady hand and a smile . . .

It was the most expensive thing she had ever done. Once the woman was barren, her man returned. He wasn't grateful. He was tired; it hadn't been easy coming back. He said, Let's have no more of this. She nodded slowly, saying, I don't dare go on. She was still weak, and though he was only a little stronger he carried her to the car and sat beside her in there; he spread a map across their knees and told her to choose a place where he could leave her. She would not choose. Paris, then, he said. He remembered a visit he had made there long before he met her. He remembered how the river had charmed him, how it had seemed to talk to the sun and to the city it flowed through, bringing news from the sea rolling in under the bridges. He remembered lion heads carved above great, heavy doors, and how in their old age the heads had yawned instead of roaring. He thought that she would like it there, and that she would not be lonely.

He showed her the route that they would take,

and they agreed that at any point before Paris she could say 'stop' and leave him then. She hadn't packed any of her belongings. She wore a brown dress, flat brown shoes and a shabby coat of the same colour. The coat belonged to the man, and he had put a little money in an inside pocket. The woman's hands spent the entire journey folded on her lap, safe and still. Sometimes she looked out of the car window at the things that passed them by. Sometimes she looked at him. They didn't really talk. At one point he coughed and said, 'Excuse me.'

When they got to Dunkirk she didn't feel able to say stop, nor could she say it at Lille, or Amiens. She wasn't particularly worried about where she would go or what she would do. Those things didn't seem important. Silently, he changed his mind again and again, but at every turn he remembered how she had told him to die.

At Paris, on a tiny street that ran alongside a vast, busy one, he let her out of the car, and she was like a moth in her drab dress as she leaned in and told him that she had never meant him harm.

He mumbled that he hoped she would be well.

He drove away and the buildings around her drew closer together. With her eyes she climbed their sepia stonework, the curls and flourishes. There was a ring on her finger; he had given it to her in exchange for their thousandth kiss, and she turned it around and around, trying to find a way out of her skin. I have loved a fool who counted kisses, she thought. The sky passed above like glass. She sat down on the pavement and watched people walking around. There was a cafe directly opposite her. Couples went in holding hands and the dust on the windows hid what they did next, where they sat, what they had to drink. A woman came out of the cafe alone. She was dressed entirely in navy blue. In one perfectly manicured hand she held twelve fountain pens. In the other she held a white cup. She took a seat on the pavement, too.

'Drink this,' said the woman in blue.

'What is it?' asked the woman in brown.

Blue became brisk: 'It'll buck you up. Hurry.'

Listlessly, obediently, Brown drained the little white cup in one gulp. Bitter espresso, that's all it was.

'Now. Take these.' Blue handed Brown the fountain pens. 'You have to go soon. You've got a lot to catch up on.'

Brown did not feel particularly bucked up. If anything, she felt duller. 'Go where? Catch up on what?'

'Writing,' Blue replied. 'You write things. I was never any good at it, but you will be. That's where you'll live and work.' And she pointed at the front door of a house a few steps away. The door was painted bright blue, so you couldn't miss it.

'Er . . . what?'

Blue laughed; her laughter was delightful. 'Oh . . . you'll see.'

'Who are you?'

'That man who just dropped you off and drove away . . . I'm the one who was meant for him,' Blue said, calmly. 'There was a terrible mistake a few decades ago; there are many cases like ours, and they're only just being sorted out. From now on, I'm in charge. I'll take care of everything. All you have to do is go through that door and into your proper place in life. And you will forget him. You will forget today, you will forget everything.'

Brown was astonished, and said nothing.

'Doesn't that please you?' Blue asked.

'No it doesn't,' said Brown. 'I don't want to forget about him. I don't want my proper place in life. I don't want to go in at that door. I don't want—'

'Your heart is broken, poor little fool,' Blue interrupted. 'You have no idea what you want.'

'It isn't broken,' Brown said, stubbornly.

Blue spread her hands: 'Well . . . what do you propose doing instead?'

All around them people were speaking a language Brown didn't understand; it was like silence with sharp edges in it. Sound broke against her eardrums. It didn't hurt, but it wasn't pleasant. Brown looked at Blue carefully. Their skin was more or less the same shade of brown, but after that there were only differences. Blue was much better-looking than Brown was; smaller and tidier-looking, too. There was a sweetness to the corners of Blue's mouth, and her manner was warm. She would be good to him. Speaking as quickly as she could, Brown told Blue about the man she was meant for; just small details off the top of her head, the things that years boil down to. Blue produced a small book and pencil, nodded, listened, and made notes.

Then Brown went through her new front door with her hands full of fountain pens.

She didn't look back, so she didn't see Blue throw the notebook away. She didn't see the car, returning to the spot where it had left her, inching along as her lover stuck his head out of the window, looking for her. Blue walked over to him, and as the man spoke, Blue tilted her head and listened with an expression of great sympathy . . .

*   *   *

Brown walked into her home under a row of crystal chandeliers, their octopus arms outstretched, their hearts layered with old gold. The high ceiling was painted with a map that looked both old and new—it was faded, the paint cracked, but the fade was bright. The map showed that the world had edges you could fall off, into blank white. *Here . . . be . . . dragons*.

Upstairs, on a desk by a window, there lay a fountain pen that looked identical to the ones she held. Brown picked up the fountain pen and shook it. The cartridge sounded empty. She wished she'd bought new cartridges instead of new pens; it would have been far more economical. Beside the desk was a wastepaper basket full of crumpled paper. There were more fountain pens in there, too. She didn't really want to sit down at this desk, it seemed to be a place of nerves and wretchedness. But there was a fresh pad of paper open, and the chair was drawn out, so she sat down. She laid the new pens down one by one. She looked at them, twiddled her thumbs, picked a pen up, put it down, examined the notepad. She was clearly supposed to write something, but not a single idea made itself available to her. Was it meant to be a letter? Or a report? The fact that it was to be handwritten suggested a personal aspect. Her writing was to be addressed to someone in particular. Brown pushed a pen with her fingertip and it rolled against another pen, and all the pens fell off the table. How was she supposed to do this if she didn't know who she was doing it for? It was ridiculous.

After about twenty minutes, she heard scrabbling at the door and leapt to her feet.

But whoever it was, they weren't coming into the room, they were just pushing a piece of paper under the door.

It read:

Write the stories.

'Stories?' Brown howled. 'What stories?'

She ran through the rooms of her house, looking for the person who had ordered stories. She ran downstairs and watched the street. It could have been anyone. Anyone. How could someone have slipped in and slipped out again without her knowing? Perhaps they'd followed her in . . .

Brown returned to the desk and picked the pens up off the floor. She wrote down the words: *Once upon a time*, and then she stopped. She looked about her. There was something missing. There was something wrong. She found a mirror and turned around in front of it with her arms held out in front of her. She was all there, all in one piece. Then what? What had she lost?

Brown wrote down a list of things that had been stolen from her, things she had lost, both replaceable and irreplaceable. Umbrellas, gloves. Expensive tubes of mascara. Cheques. Earrings; one out of virtually every pair she had ever owned until she had had to leave off wearing earrings altogether. Several jackets, left at cafes and parties. A diary, once—a year's thinking. What else . . . a television and a cat, from the time she had lived by herself and left her front door unlocked one day. The thief had left a ransom note for the cat; she'd considered responding to it, but hadn't.

Another piece of paper came in under the door: *WRITE THE STORIES*.

This time Brown didn't bother searching for the person who wanted stories. She would not be toyed with, and she would not obey. Instead she went out into the city, to look for what she had lost. There was no guarantee that she would recognise it even if she found it, but trying felt better than sitting at that strange and awful desk. Everything seemed like a clue. The glances of strangers, the first letter of every street sign she passed—she tacked them together and created the name of a street that was impossible to reach. She didn't give up. She went looking every day.

And every day there was a note or two. *Write the stories*. And sometimes there was money, so that she could eat.

People began to call her Madame la Folle. One day she passed a man who stood playing his guitar on a corner of the Boulevard St-Germain, his back to the churchyard railings, and she realised he was singing about her—Madame la Folle with your money falling out of your pockets, trampling your own bread underfoot, leaving a trail of letters you meant to post . . . what else have you lost?

The list in her notepad grew and grew. As she read it she turned a ring round and round her finger. It was made of cheap brass, and it was slightly misshapen, as if unable to withstand the heat of her body. She could not recall exactly how she had come by the ring, or when she had first put it on. She pulled the ring off her finger and felt pain, which surprised her. She looked up at the map on the ceiling, inspecting continents through the brass circle she held in her hand. Seen through the ring, the borders of each country throbbed and blurred.

'Where are you?' she murmured. 'Where are you?' She wanted the question removed from her with forceps at white heat, leaving a clean cavity behind. Then, perhaps, she would be able to perform her task. She was beginning to feel that she owed it to whoever was keeping her alive.

There were moments in which Brown forgot her search. She came across a flock of red balloons once, tied to railings, and since no one was watching she popped them, one by one, with her sharp fingernails. And she enjoyed avoiding light. It made her feel triumphant. She made night-time trips to Sacré-Cœur, darting around the glare of the floodlights that the boats flung out as they passed along the river bank. When she reached the basilica she crept down its steps and jumped high where the bottom step sat directly on the hill. She jumped as high as she could and she closed her eyes and made believe that she had fallen into the city's arms. Madame la Folle.

* * *

Blue's man kept her waiting while he tried to get Brown back. He put up posters with photographs of Brown all around Paris, asking if anyone had seen her. But the wind blew the posters away into the Seine, or he saw people take the posters down and make off with them—a different person each time, and he would give chase, shouting out for an explanation. But no one explained, and no one helped him. He knew it was all coincidence—he told himself it was coincidence, because it was horrifying to think that, having made a decision, he was now being actively prevented from changing it. Blue was by his side at all times, and she was devoted and affectionate. Instead of asking annoying questions while he was working, she attended to her own affairs. Brown began to seem like a strange dream he had had. She would never come back, and it was perverse to chase her like this. Blue . . . Blue was no trouble at all. So he turned to her.

It didn't work. He kept it up for a couple of years, saying: 'Yes, I'm very lucky,' to anyone who complimented him on his improved circumstances. But it didn't feel like luck. It felt arranged. Blue was a stranger, and she never became a friend. One evening the man stood by the fireplace in their living room, looking at a photograph in a magazine. It accompanied an article about Blue and himself, a profile of them as an artisan couple. The man tried to read the article as if he were someone else, someone who didn't know them. The couple in the photograph complemented each other beautifully; her glossy head on his shoulder, his arm tucked around her with his cuff drawn up over his fingers, so he held her through the linen of his sleeve. That was how precious she was to him—she couldn't be touched with a naked hand. He built doll's houses and she peopled them with dolls. Film stars and sports stars bought them for their children. The couple in the photograph hoped for children of their own soon. Quoting a poet, the artisan man said that their love was a lifelong love, a love for all the lives they might ever have had. He read that again. Had he really said that? He repeated the words aloud. Then he threw the magazine onto the fire and didn't stay to watch it burn.

Blue was in her studio making eyes for her dolls, letting a single drop of dye fall from a pipette into each glass ball, watching it until it soaked through. She didn't greet him—she was lost in detail. He picked up a brown eye and was impressed, as always. The dye floated in the centre of the sphere, surrounded by clarity.

He handed the doll's eye back to his wife, a woman his friends gazed at with awe and admiration, a woman whose flaws were far outbalanced by her virtues, and he told her: 'Leave me.'

She looked up. 'I beg your pardon?'

'Go,' he said. 'Leave me. Please.'

'For how long?'

He turned away, so as not to have to look at her shock, so as not to have to watch her patience take form. He knew that he was bringing ruin upon himself.

'You're talking nonsense,' she said, to his back. 'We work well together. We have a life together.'

'I know,' he said. 'But if you don't leave, I will.'

'Is this about . . . her?' She didn't ask angrily. She sounded . . . curious, wistful. 'Still? After all this time?'

'No,' he lied.

'I don't understand you. Her love was bad. You told me so yourself.'

When he turned to face her he saw that she had

picked up her pipette and returned to work. Drop after immaculate drop.

'Whatever you're feeling now, it will fade. I'm not leaving. And neither are you,' she said.

'I see,' he said. And he nodded. He went to his own studio, where he fell into a stupor he couldn't wake up from.

* * *

Brown thought she might be grieving for someone who had died. She walked around Père Lachaise, looking for a name that meant something to her alone. The cemetery watchmen pitied her. When she hid in the cemetery just before closing time, the watchmen all looked the other way. She was harmless. And perhaps the additional hours would help her find the right tomb at last. She passed the first few hours of the night surrounded by tall green fragrance. Lavender buds tickled her arms and back as she went up and down the tree-lined paths, looking at names carved in stone. Her hands were tucked into her sleeves in case of stinging nettles, so her torchlight kept faltering. Dormice shook the lavender with their paws and tails, caught Brown's reflection in the dark shine of their eyes and ran away with it. White-flowered shrubs thickened around her and so did sleep; it directed her limbs. Lie down now, sleep said, sweetly. Lie down. These are the secret hours of the day, the time that owls and bats take to themselves, the stars change places now; let them. You lie down.

She stopped walking when she saw the name Étienne Geoffroy for the fourth time. The cemetery was smaller than she had thought it was.

Or there were parts of it that couldn't be brought to light, not by her torch, not even by the moon. She came to a path that divided into two, and she shone her torch to the left, then to the right—

She saw a man. He was standing on the other side of the path, half-hidden by a sapling. For a fraction of a second, less than that, she saw him. He darted out of sight; the rattling of branches deafened her. Her throat froze. Move, she told herself. You must move. *But if I take the wrong path—if I go deeper in—*

She listened for some sign, tried to find out where he was, but there was so much calling amongst the tombstones, croaking and chattering and echoes. *I must move. I must move.* After the first step the rest were easy, the way was sure, left, right, left right, and she fell down and cut her hands on stones because she heard him calling her. 'Madame la Folle! Madame la Folle? A word in your ear, if you please. Just a moment of your time . . .' She had lost her torch. A loud cracking sound nearby—him? Where was he? Everywhere. His voice was behind her, ahead of her, above, below. She rolled into a ball against the exposed roots of a tree for a moment. Then she raised herself up onto her knees and crawled, slowly, slowly, so slowly, *Cover me, leaves, cover me, earth, don't let him find me.*

Hands plunged through the leaves, seized her wrists and dragged her up. She screamed then. She screamed and screamed, first at the sky, which was whirling like water, then she was screaming into a hand clapped over her mouth. She looked into eyes too wide to be sane. He released her once she was quiet. A man with a shock of white hair and a face painted like a harlequin's, dead white with black diamonds around his eyes. His features were very hard. Skeletal.

'Why won't you just write the stories?' he said. 'You've been asked nicely.'

Fear pressed her tongue against her gums.

'Fear not, Madame,' the man told her. 'I am Reynardine. And I can get you whatever your heart desires.' He sat down upon a tombstone and patted the space beside him. What could she do? She joined him.

'The stories are for you?'

He shook his head. 'One moment.' He cleared his throat and his gaze grew shadowy, as if something dark had spilt into him. When he next spoke, it was with an accent that was familiar to her, but in a voice that was not. It was deep—more a vibration that came through the ground than a voice.

'Who is it?' she whispered.

'Can you see us?' And for a moment she saw and felt them all, crowding her. Faces she recognised from family photo albums, some she had never seen before, old ones leaning on walking sticks. They were all familiar. They all knew her, and she knew them. Then they relented and faded away.

'We're here,' they said, through Reynardine's lips.

'What do you want?'

'You are Yoruba.'

'Am I?'

'So you think your accent fools us . . .'

'But I can't even speak Yoruba!'

'That doesn't fool us either.'

'All right,' she said. 'I know. But look—I'm in Paris at the moment.'

'Don't interrupt,' they said. 'You might want to get away from us. You might feel that we crowd too close, that we want too much. But we like you. We think you're spirited. And we're trying to listen.'

'To what?'

'To what you won't tell us. We want your stories.'

'I don't have any. I don't know what to write.'

'Tell the stories. Tell them to us. We want to know all the ways you're still like us, and all the ways you've changed. Talk to us. We're from a different place and time . . .'

'I'm not lying to you,' she said, shaking her head. 'I really can't do it.'

'You can and you must,' they snapped. 'Those stories belong to us. It doesn't matter what language they're in, or what they're about; they belong to us. And we gave them to you without looking at them first. So now it's time to see what we've done.'

After a long moment, the harlequin returned to himself and began speaking reasonably. They weren't asking for very much, were they? he asked. Just a few words on paper, anything she liked, anything that came to mind, nothing that anyone else need ever read. It didn't even have to be good.

He honestly expected her to believe that she could make a bad offering and her ancestors wouldn't mind.

'What's your part in this?' Brown demanded.

'Favours are a useful currency,' said Reynardine.

'You're working for them because favours are a

useful currency?'

Reynardine yawned clownishly, and rubbed his eyes. Black paint came away on his knuckles. 'I work for myself,' he muttered. 'I'm freelance.'

Brown looked down at her hands. She had never been good at anything. There had never been any work that she'd been able to make her own. She raised a hand to the moonlight and the brass ring winked at her.

'I want what I lost,' she said.

'You should do this just because they asked you to. You came from these people. You owe them everything,' Reynardine pointed out.

Politely, she disagreed. She was vastly outnumbered, she knew that, but that didn't mean she would budge. There's a reason the Yoruba were famed as warriors.

Reynardine was amused.

'Do this and I'll restore what you lost,' he said.

Brown was suspicious. 'How? Why?'

Reynardine stood, and looked down at her. His gaze was very wild indeed; it seemed to have no focus. She came very close to flinching.

'How?' she asked again. 'Why?'

Reynardine made some answer, but it was muffled because he was walking into the ground; the earth covered his head.

* * *

Brown worked for days. She didn't know how many days—afterwards she would only ever be able to recall that time as a pause between two breaths she took. In between she ran through the twelve fountain pens. More appeared. She ran through blocks of paper, and more was provided. Occasionally she would feel a hand, a hand that was not her own, passing over her hair, as if blessing her. The words didn't come easily. She put large spaces between some of them for fear they would attack each other.

She'd thought she didn't have any stories, but in fact she had too many.

She put down things she didn't know she knew. She wrote about a girl who babysat herself while both her parents worked and worked for not enough pay. The girl didn't answer the door or the telephone because no one was meant to know she babysat herself, and besides, it might be the Home Office, and then they'd all be deported. So that she would not be scared, she pretended she was a spy and wrote secret spy notes on pink paper. She posted the spy notes out of the living-room window; she sent them spinning down onto the heads of passers-by, who picked them up and didn't understand them. They'd look up, but the girl had disappeared from the window—no one was supposed to know she was there.

Brown wrote about another girl who lived in a city that men were forbidden to enter. This girl knew nothing but the city and the stern stretch of coast that surrounded it, and she thought that men were just a funny story, and she didn't expect that she was missing much.

She wrote about an Okitipupa village boy who was nobody's boy, and earned money for himself by taking care of other children. She wrote about the afternoon nobody's boy returned to the village in despair, having mislaid four of his ten charges and roped the remaining six boys to his waist with a long piece of scarlet rope and a great many strong knots. He had spent two hours looking for those four boys, and was just on his way to the first of the boys' parents to confess what had happened when, in a moment like a nightmare, the missing boys jumped up from the shallow pits they'd been lying in, boy after boy shaking the earth with unearthly cries.

There was more, much more, and she put it all down, though she didn't see what good it could do. She put it all down for the ones who had said, Tell us. *Here are your stories, then. Have them back.*

Reynardine came then, and he smiled at her, and he took all her stories away.

What did Reynardine leave behind?

A man she knew.

He slumped against the wall of her room, with his legs stuck out in front of him. His eyes were open, but when she spoke to him, he didn't look at her. He didn't breathe. His heart didn't beat. His lips were blue. Brown lay down with him, and she tried to give him breath, and she asked him if he was dead.

'I don't know,' Reynardine answered, from the doorway. 'Probably.'

And Brown turned to him and cried out: 'Reynardine! Reynardine! What have you brought me?'

Reynardine tutted. 'I brought you what you lost.'

'But he's still lost! You tricked me.'

'Listen,' said Reynardine. 'Have you considered joining him?'

Brown sat listening, thinking. She held her man's hand, and she didn't feel able to let go just then.

'I dare you,' Reynardine said, 'to be lost together.'

She wasn't as worried as she could have been. She had recently been visited by people long deceased. They had seemed well enough, and had even been so bold as to make demands of her. She accepted the dare.

Reynardine snapped his fingers, and she stopped living.

* * *

Stiffly entwined in each other's arms, the two lovers were moved to Père Lachaise—*sans* coffins, and at dead of night. Reynardine took care of that. He was owed favours and he made the arrangements. It's said that Reynardine is monstrously cruel, but sometimes, to a woman who takes him at his word, he can show kindness.

The first moment in the tomb was the most forbidding. The silence, the stillness, the dark.

Then they realised: they were together, and there was no one else. She felt his lips tremble against her forehead. After that he became courageous and brought his arms down around her. He kissed her closed eyelids and he kissed her mouth and he kissed handfuls of her hair and he kissed her elbows. She placed her brass ring on the palm of his hand and closed his fingers around it. He opened his hand and the ring was gone. It had not fallen, unless it had fallen through him, and if so, it had left no mark. No more counting kisses.

Reynardine had thrown a candle and a box of matches in with them. They didn't need the candle . . . in the darkness they learnt to waltz. Then they lit the candle anyway—why not? And they let its flame warm their stone house for a little while as they danced on behind their locked door.

Mary Foxe saved my life once. She has a vested interest, of course—if I go, she goes. But she didn't do it as if she had a vested interest. She did it as if she cared. It was nine, maybe ten years ago. Before Daphne. I was working late at night, trying to get something down about a boy at war; he'd signed up to be a hero and had all sorts of ideas about standing aloof from both his equals and his superiors. I couldn't yet tell whether this kid's stupid ideas were going to get him killed, or whether he was simply going to be slapped down and made useful in some minor way. It was not a story about me—in France I learnt to do exactly what I was told. I'm talking about the Marne—frontal assaults; don't blink, don't think, just do. I looked around my study and everything was just too damn cosy. The anodyne calm. The gentle, sputtering dance of the fire, and the books that towered all around me, their spines turned out. I couldn't write down the echo of an exploded shell. I couldn't smear the smell of the trench across the page. I couldn't do this thing so that anyone could see what I meant. The things that had happened—things I laughed at when they crossed my mind—you can't hold onto them too long, unless you want to go crazy. The dead don't trouble me—dead is dead. It's the ones who took impact and lived. Joe Persano: shrapnel put his left eye out, and he refuses to wear an eye patch; a glass eye rolls slightly in the crumpled hole left for it. Tom Franklin has no hands. Ivor Ross's right trouser leg is empty and half his mouth is puckered up for a sour, perpetual kiss. And here I am, whole. It got so I had a pistol to my head, there in my cosy study, and I wasn't at all sure that I'd taken it out of my desk drawer myself. I must have been holding it, but there was no feeling in my fingers; the gun seemed to be floating, held up by Joe's ill will, Tom's, and Ivor's. The gun's nozzle pushed at my skin, as if trying to find the correct part of my skull to nestle against. Death like the insect, menacing the tree . . .

'Shhh,' said Mary Foxe. She reached over my shoulder, prised my fingers loose one by one, and took the gun. Then she stuck a pipe in my mouth. I watched tobacco trickle into the bowl. I watched her hand, tamping the tobacco down. Tap, tap, tap, and the pipe moved between my clenched teeth. Tap and pour, tap and pour. She lit a match, and I watched the flame circle the bowl once, twice, three times, before it took and a mist rose.

'I know you think you're going mad,' she said. 'But you're not. Don't be perverse. Celebrate.'

She poured some scotch from the decanter on my windowsill and pushed the glass towards me. Between that and the pipe my sense of perspective began to return. I opened the desk drawer and the gun was in there, looking innocent, as if it hadn't had an outing this evening, or ever.

Mary sat down and set the decanter at her feet. 'Say something, you,' she said, warningly.

'Mary,' I said. 'I seem to have a memory—false, I hope—of you being my wife at some point.'

Mary stirred in her seat. 'Oh yes?'

'Yes. My loving wife. I did all I could for you. But you weren't happy. You said I didn't listen to you and that I treated you like a child. You moved out of the nice house I was working overtime to pay for, the house I bought because you said you liked it. I waited a week—everyone told me to give it time, that you'd come to your senses. I was always home on time, and never ran around on you. On weekends I drove you all over town like I was your chauffeur, took you to see the friends you wanted to see. I took you to the opera on your birthday, for crying out loud. I hadn't put a foot wrong. But you didn't come back. Your friends had lent you money and you'd moved into some tiny one-room apartment. I found that out by visiting a friend of mine who was married to a friend of yours. He said he didn't want to get involved because his wife would raise hell for him if she ever found out he'd told me. So I turned on the waterworks. It shocked him so much he told me where you were and said he hoped I got you and my manhood back . . .'

I stopped for a while, because it was strange. The more I said, the clearer the memory became. I didn't think I was going to be able to say any more—I just wanted to watch the thing play out in my head. Mary poured me some more scotch. That helped.

'I went round at dusk. I was drunk as drunk—that was my preparation for the possibility that there might be another guy there with you. I knocked on your door—I knocked with my head and my elbows, like I was trying to dance with the door. Amazingly, you opened the door, with this resigned look on your face that said you'd been expecting me. I said: Honey, and something else, something like Honey, look at me, can't you see how it is? Come home. And you looked kind of sorry for me. But I saw that you had a chain on the door, and you kept it on even when you saw that I was just a wreck, and begging. When I saw that you had that chain on, I knew I was going to hurt you. I was going to get in there and hurt you. It was kind of like caging up an animal—something—the bars, the boundaries hard and cold like that—it just makes the animal as mad as hell, even if it was just a fluffy little lapdog before. It becomes another thing altogether. I stood up straight and I lowered my voice and, I don't know how, because I was out of my skull drunk and could barely move my tongue, I began to talk to you as if I was sober and possessed of reason. I spoke warmly and with understanding and had some soothing response to every objection you made to letting me in. You let me in, and I almost fell in through the door, but I told myself keep it together, keep it together, you still love her. There was no one else there, you were all alone. I was so glad. I was so glad. I tried to hold you, to get a kiss from you. And you said: "St John, you're hurting me." I only wanted to kiss you—how could that be hurting you? But you kept saying that I should "stop it". I'd slapped you a few times by then. Trying to make you quiet.'

She dimpled at me. 'Go on,' she said.

'Well . . . things went on like that between you and me . . .'

'Went on like what, exactly?'

'I kept hitting you, I guess. I picked up a chair and I backed you up against a wall and started slamming it on either side of your head, just to scare you, at first. "Shhh," I said. "Shhh." You got too scared, or not scared enough. You kept putting your hands up to protect your face—I just grabbed your arm and punched you until you were on the floor. I stomped on your hands.'

Mary nodded, as if going over a mental checklist.

'I kicked you in the head.'

She nodded again.

'Then you must have worked out that I kept going for you because you kept moving. So you kept still. I walked away and watched you from across the room, to see what you'd do if I gave you room. You didn't do anything, just lay there. I walked towards you again and you held your breath. I stayed close to you and you didn't exhale; you tried to die.'

'Go on,' Mary said, wanly. She wasn't smiling any more.

'I crouched down and I talked to you. Just some things in your ear. No idea what I was saying, nonsense probably. I was just talking to calm you down. While I was talking I slit your throat. Messily, because I couldn't walk in a straight line, let alone guide my hand from ear to ear without stopping. It was a real mess. A real mess.'

Mary didn't shudder, or look shocked. She looked polite, if anything. Somewhere between polite and bored.

'It couldn't have happened. I'd have got the chair for that.' I wasn't really talking to her—more thinking aloud.

'Yes. You would have. But too late for me. What made you do it?'

'What made me—'

'Yes. Why did you do it?'

'You're asking me why, in my false memory of our marriage, I killed you?'

'I'm trying to help you think.'

I made a few brief guesses—I was in a killing mood, I was afraid of time, I was fooled by some inexplicable assurance that I was merely dreaming out my revenge, making myself safe for the daylight hours. Love fit in somewhere, I wasn't sure how—disbelief that it had gone away, trying to force its return, trying to create an emergency that would scare love out of hiding.

'You did it because of love? Because you loved me too much?' she asked, jovially. Her merriment was giving me the creeps. The whole conversation was giving me the creeps—talking like this about something that hadn't really happened. I shouldn't have started it. She'd seemed so interested, though, and that was rare. Maybe she was trying to be nice in her own way.

Mary pulled the stopper out of the scotch decanter and took a long swallow. 'Okay, never mind about love,' she said, wiping her mouth. 'You hated me. Because I wouldn't come back and I was making you hate yourself, making you think there was something wrong with you.'

'No . . . I already told you. It was because of the chain on the door.'

'Mr Fox.' Mary toyed with the cut-glass stopper. 'Is this a joke?'

'You found it funny?'

'That you just recounted one of your stories to me as if it was something that you really did?'

'Hm,' I said. 'You're right. I'll write it down.'

'You already did,' she said, her forehead creased.

I waited blankly while she searched my stack of notebooks and picked up number six. She licked her finger and opened it up near the end. There, in my handwriting, was the tale I had just told her. As soon as I saw it I remembered writing it, and I was flooded with relief. Thank God it wasn't me. Thank God I wasn't capable of doing such a thing. It was cold, but I was sweating. When I put the book down I saw that I'd left moist ovals on the paper.

'*Now* I'm worried,' Mary said.

the training at madame de silentio's

Madame de Silentio takes in delinquent ruffians between the ages of sixteen and eighteen and turns them into world-class husbands by the time they are twenty-one. You're admitted to Madame de Silentio's Academy if you answer at least 85% of her entrance exam correctly, and you graduate with a certificate that is respected in every strata of polite society. No one can ever remember any of the questions that were on Madame de Silentio's entrance exam. I know I can't—I tried my best to fail the exam. I preferred not to be educated, fearing it wouldn't suit me. Of course, I know better now. I won't lie, it took me half a year, but I now realise how lucky I am to have this opportunity to become a man of true worth, to have the man I will be intercept the boy that I was.

What is her secret, you may ask. How did

Madame de Silentio attain her ranking amongst the great educators of the modern world? It's simple. Madame de Silentio knows what's best for young people. She knows what's appropriate. She refrains from cluttering our minds with information we don't need to know. Here at Madame de Silentio's our textbooks get straight to the point—European history is boiled down to a paragraph, with two sentences each for the histories of Africa, Asia and the Americas. Australasia doesn't count. Young men at Madame de Silentio's Academy learn practical skills that set us in good stead for lives as the husbands of wealthy and educated women. Here is a sample of the things we are taught:

Strong Handshakes, Silence, Rudimentary Car Mechanics, How to Mow the Lawn, Explosive Displays of Authority, Sport and Nutrition Against Impotence.

It says in the prospectus that Madame de Silentio's students eat, sleep and breathe good husbandry. That's true. We're taught to ask ourselves a certain question when we wake up in the morning and just before we fall asleep: *How can I make Her happy?* 'Her' being the terrible, wonderful goddess that we must simultaneously honour, obey and rule (she'd like us to rule her sometimes, we're told)—the future wife. In our Words of Love class we learn all the poems of Pablo Neruda by heart, and also Ira Gershwin and Dorothy Fields lyrics. Love Letters, a compulsory extracurricular course of study, involves a close reading of the letters of Héloïse and Abelard. Our Decisive Thinking examinations are conversations conducted before the entire class, and your grade depends not on the answer you give, but on the tenacity with which you cling to your choice. You earn a grade A by demonstrating, without a hint of nervousness or irritation, that you are impervious to any external logic. You earn an A+ if you manage this whilst affecting a mild and pleasant demeanour.

We sleep eight to a dormitory, and our dormitory bedsteads are iron, with shapes from the end of days twisted into the headboards—lions lying alongside lambs, children caressing serpents. Some of the boys sit up in these dormitory beds and scream in the night, but then the matron comes with a cup of warm milk and puts a few drops of her special bittersweet medicine in it, and the screaming boy drinks deep and the trouble goes away, far away. Madame de Silentio understands that becoming a man of true worth is a difficult process. And we understand that once we're in the academy we've got to stay here for as long as it takes—there's no recourse to parents or guardians, as they've signed their rights to us away in their contract with Madame de Silentio, and it's our own stupid fault for having been so unmanageable. Eighteen is the age at which any student is free to leave the Academy, but by then we've become used to the place. This is no philanthropic institution, mind you—the families of heiresses pay Madame de Silentio considerable sums of money, sums that we students can only guess at and whisper about, to ensure that they get the perfect husband for their precious Elaine, to ensure that their wayward Katherine is settled with the right life-partner. The Academy is in many ways a business, but there's nothing wrong with that. Madame de Silentio has found her niche, and the way of the world is such that if she did not demand recompense for her efforts she would receive none. So, good for Madame de Silentio.

Having recently been made Head Prefect, it's my duty to write a new chapter of the handbook that each new pupil is given on their first day, that awful first day when you just think you're not going to be able to stand it. The handbook provides some company. I take this responsibility very seriously, just as seriously as I take keeping the juniors in order and being a good ambassador for the Academy when we have to leave the grounds to round up the runaways. I've consulted the annals of school history, and I found mention of an act of disobedience committed by two moderately promising students—it happened twenty-five years ago, and the consequences were quite grave. I conducted interviews with Madame de Silentio herself, and with those teachers who remembered what had happened, and I've pieced together a narrative that I'd like to try out on you. I think it makes an invaluable cautionary tale for any new boy who is thinking of defying our headmistress.

* * *

Charles Wolfe and Charlie Wulf met in their second year of studies at Madame de Silentio's, when they were assigned neighbouring beds in the same dormitory. Charlie, at seventeen, was Charles's elder by a year. By all accounts the boys took notice of the fact that they essentially had the same name. In diaries, and in correspondence intercepted by staff, each boy declared that there must be meaning in the similarity between their names. They felt they were brothers. Interesting, because they were very different.

Photographs reveal Charlie Wulf to have been a bit of a pretty boy. Eyes like great big puddles, Byronic waves of hair, the spare frame of a long-time drug addict—before joining the student body he had been forcibly and abruptly weaned off opium in our soundproof music room, which was placed off-limits for three weeks. It seems favouritism brought Charlie to the Academy. I refer to the letter written to Madame de Silentio a full year before he was admitted, in which his mother and father, taking turns to write a word each, explain that in the silence of the heart every parent chooses a favourite. In Mr and Mrs Wulf's case they chose the same one, much to the jealousy and rage of their other nine children. Siblings always detect these things, but without proof there's not a lot they can do. Charlie seemed to have been born an escapist; at the age of seven, having complained of a boredom that made him 'feel sick in his tummy', he broke into his father's liquor cabinet and drank himself into a state of catalepsy. By the age of fifteen he was seeking oblivion in opium dens, and since his wealthy parents made him a separate allowance twice the size of that allotted to each of his siblings, Charlie was able to buy almost as much oblivion as he desired, running through a month's allowance in less than a week and beatifically starving until the time came for the next instalment. The letter from Mr and Mrs Wulf also lists certain diseases Charlie had contracted and been treated for, ending with a deadly scare that was the last straw. He'd been sent to rehabilitation clinics and boot camps and each time he had escaped with the aid of his captors. Mr and Mrs Wulf believed Madame de Silentio's Academy was the only institution without a trace of indulgence at its heart, and therefore the Academy was the only place that could clean their son up. They would give custody of their son over to Madame Silentio if it would save his life. *Charlie's life shall be saved*, Madame de Silentio assured them. *Better than that—his life shall be made useful.* Charlie Wulf was weak of character, consistently receiving D grades or lower for his Decisive Thinking. He was also a cheat when it came to exams, and a plagiarist when it came to essays—he was punished for the latter two faults twenty-seven times in his first year alone. These faults aside, he was well liked for his easy manner and the way he successfully avoided snitching on others, even when it was easier, perhaps even advantageous, to do so.

Charles Wolfe was fair-haired, and secretive. His features were crooked and unattractive. Much less is known about him, much more conjectured. Charles's father was a government official in India; his household included several guards and a poison taster, all of whom were present at every meal. Major Wolfe's very brief letter to Madame de Silentio, referring to Charles simply as 'the boy', indicates disgust at Charles's habit of stealing things. '*Blue things—always blue things—the boy seems to reckon there isn't enough blue in the world. See what you can do with him.*' Mr Curie, one of our science teachers, recalls seeing Charles Wolfe leaning against the Academy railings during recreation, drinking Coca-Cola through a blue straw, with such a tough look in his eyes that no one dared mock the dainty way he took his refreshment. Mrs Engels, one of our English literature teachers, recounts her suspicion, unsupported by any documentation, that it had taken Charles Wolfe much longer than normal to learn how to speak. He seemed to have learnt to read long before he learnt to speak. Mrs Engels says that she sometimes remarked on the unusual way Charles Wolfe formulated his sentences, and when she did he fell silent and seemed ashamed. Charles Wolfe held grudges. He wrote in his diary that he would like to kill Mrs Engels. It seems Charles Wolfe was capable of hating with a single-mindedness that sometimes took him into trances. *Subdue this*, he wrote several times in his diary. *Subdue this*. Charles Wolfe took every prize and passed every test and exam with distinction. He was going to make a first-rate husband. The teachers weren't sure about him, though. They kept an eye on him. There had been incidents in the first year—there had been no evidence that the incidents were connected to him. But still. We won't blame them for their vigilance.

The grounds of the Academy are extensive. One asset we used to boast, but are now denied access to, is the lake. A thirty-year-old prospectus shows a group of prefects boating on the lake as a treat, but the lake has a dark and forbidding aspect, and the prefects don't seem to be having much fun. The boys were allowed to boat occasionally, but they were forbidden to swim. And Charles and Charlie seem to have been magnetised by the lake. *The water is very green and has a sweet taste*, both boys wrote in their diaries, at different times.

Exactly the same phrase at different times. Charles Wolfe goes on to conjecture that it's a vial of the lake water that the matron carries around with her and uses when someone needs medicine in their warm milk. He notes that after a few mouthfuls of the lake water you 'feel fine. Like a king.' He also notes that Charlie Wulf guzzled the lake water in a manner that worried him slightly. If you're wondering about the diaries, Madame de Silentio insists that we keep them, and that we write full accounts of our thoughts and our days. Then she spends all Sunday reading them. It's a tricky business, writing the diaries. Madame de Silentio doesn't want to be acknowledged in our diaries, so we have to write them as if we don't know anyone's going to read them. It's like prayer, somehow. She never comments or acts on what she reads in our diaries, no matter what's in there—that makes it even more like prayer.

In his diary, Charlie, a weak swimmer, records the afternoon he leant too far into that sweet green taste and fell: '*Into the shock of the water. My mouth opened and the lake rushed into me, a strong, cold, never-ending arm rammed down my throat. I didn't know you could fall like that inside a body of water, that when you fall it's as hard and helpless a thing as falling through air.*' Charles Wolfe dived and retrieved his pathetic friend, and they both saw something incredible. I say incredible even though during my interview with her Madame de Silentio shrugged and spoke of it as something quite commonplace. In swimming to shore, the boys stirred the water with open eyes, and beneath them they saw a bed of silt and rock with a shape pressed into it. Each stroke was firm and clear, even the gap between the emaciated thighs. It was a man down there. A man trapped at the bottom of the lake, wrapped round and round with a great, rusty, padlocked chain. His face seemed very white and stiff to them at first, then they realised that a mask had been forced over it—a commedia dell'arte mask, with its thick ivory grimace. Under the weight of all that water, the man was alive, and he saw them seeing him, and he struggled, and struggled. 'Yes, I had a prisoner out there,' Madame de Silentio says. 'Thought it was the safest place, but no. Reynardine was his name. No use dwelling on all that, though. Won't do a blind bit of good.'

The next seven days of each boy's diary hold the dutifully scrawled lines: 'Nothing today', the bare minimum required to meet Madame de Silentio's demand that we record something every day. Matron Seacole, who has since retired, very kindly responded to my written enquiry with the recollection that Charlie Wulf kept the dormitory up three nights in a row with the shouting and kicking he did in his sleep, and had to be dosed a total of ten times. Charles Wolfe was wakeful, but didn't fuss and said he was fine. The boys wrote notes to each other, in a code that I have been unsuccessful in cracking. I can draw no firm conclusions as to what was happening inside the heads of these boys during the seven days of what they described as 'nothing'. Charlie's schoolwork slipped badly. Charles's schoolwork remained at an excellent standard.

On the eighth day, both boys meticulously recorded a 'conversation with a prisoner' in their diaries. They had learnt the prisoner's name, and they had learnt that he had been a prisoner a long time, longer than he could remember. They had learnt that Madame de Silentio had imprisoned this man, and that the man wished to be freed. And they wished to free him.

Madame de Silentio, Charles wrote in red ink, beneath that day's diary entry. *Why did you do this to Reynardine?*

Madame de Silentio stuck to her policy of not responding to diary entries.

The teachers suggested keeping a close watch on the boys, but Madame de Silentio insisted that they were intelligent boys undergoing a thought experiment, that they were not seriously planning to do anything.

The teachers kept the boys under close observation anyway.

Charles and Charlie didn't return to the lake for quite some time. If it were not for the fact that they knew the man's name was Reynardine, I would say the 'conversation with a prisoner' recorded in their diaries is a fabrication, and an artless one at that. It looks fake to me; the tone of the exchange is almost unbearably stilted. But then the entire situation is unusual. And if the conversation was indeed a fabrication, it's difficult to establish where else they could have got the name Reynardine from.

The boys must have developed some system of passing notes that made them feel safe—perhaps they found a hiding place: either way, they stopped corresponding in code. Flurries of extant notes are filled with guesses at the relationship between Reynardine and Madame de Silentio and, oddly, a semi-serious argument about Reynardine's face beneath his mask. *He must be like a freak—a fish,* Charles wrote to Charlie. *He can breathe down there. He can speak.* Charles writes to Charlie of having swum down with a diving light between his teeth and spoken face to face with the prisoner, of having held the padlock that bound him in both hands, of testing the mechanism inside with a fingernail while Reynardine breathed bubbles in his ear. This in the darkness of 3 a.m., while the rest of the school—including the heavily dosed Charlie Wulf—snored . . . I can't imagine.

I reckon he looks like you or me, Charlie responded. *The question is, which?*

What do you mean by that? Charles wrote back to him, in very precise, very black lettering, the handwriting of hostility.

Thinking that the boys had been reduced to mere squabbling over aesthetics, the teachers relaxed. That was their mistake, because when the staff relaxed, the boys struck, bribing three first-years to report a sighting of rats in a first-floor broom cupboard and locking Madame de Silentio and Miss Fortescue, the deputy head teacher, into the broom cupboard when those two worthy ladies went marching in to investigate. After that Charlie stood guard outside Madame de Silentio's office. Within, it was the work of a few minutes for Charles, the experienced thief of small items, to unobtrusively comb Madame de Silentio's belongings and pocket two keys. He knew his padlocks, but was too pressed for time to exercise proper Decisive Thinking—all he could be sure of was that one or the other of these keys would free Reynardine.

When imagining such relationships—prisoner

and gaoler—you'd imagine that the gaoler is always aware of the whereabouts of the key that gives her her power. You—or I, let's say I—imagine her stroking the key and gloating over it, taking it out nightly and admiring it. Not so. Madame de Silentio says she'd just tossed the key into a drawer somewhere and hadn't looked for it for years. She didn't miss it. Her office was in the order she'd left it in, and the baffling time spent in the broom cupboard was brief enough to be passed off as minor mischief on the part of the first-years, all of whom she punished with a severity disproportionate to the crime. 'Can't be slapdash with these things. Got to let them know it's not on.'

And so Reynardine was freed. That simply, that easily, because Madame de Silentio was unable to believe that she could be disobeyed, Reynardine was freed by a boy who conspicuously asked for a dose and let the milk run out of his mouth and soak his pillow once the matron had walked down to the other end of the dormitory.

Reynardine rose up amongst the loose chains, his legs twitching, as he had forgotten how to walk. Neither of the boys record this; that's just how I think those first few seconds of freedom were. He told Charles he would be gone by morning. He flexed his hands in a way that worried Charles, but gave a gurgling laugh and said: 'You have nothing to fear from me, boy.'

He told me he won't forget what we did for him, Wolfe wrote to Wulf.

By the middle of the next day, Madame de Silentio knew that Reynardine had been released. This wasn't due to any psychic connection; it was due to the local news. ‘The thing about Reynardine,’ Madame de Silentio explains, ‘is that he is a woman-killer. He doesn’t do it joyously—oh no, he does it with dolour and scowling. Women upset him. He said to me once that he hates their Ways, that from the moment he encounters one of them he’s forced to play a Role, and he won’t stand for it. Paranoid nonsense.’ The night he was released he passed through Greenwich, killing and killing. Forty women gone between 2:30 and 4 a.m., and he went quickly on throughout the country, doing more. Worse, in the days that followed, other killers, killers of children and aged parents and love rivals and husbands, they, too, swelled the murder rate, as if inspired. A bad week in time, an awful week of red shivers, the streets empty of civilians and full of police.

Madame de Silentio called the boys into her office and took the key back from Charles. Useless now, but still, it was hers. The boys didn’t know what they’d done, they didn’t connect this red week with Reynardine, until Madame de Silentio explained it to them.

For the rest of their time at the Academy they were in hell, without her even laying a finger on them or saying another reproving word to them. The two boys went around together, always together, without speaking to each other, their hair limp, their eyes bulging, their faces the faces of drowned men. Each day brought news of Reynardine’s work in the world. *He didn’t look like what he was*, Charlie Wulf wrote in his diary. That was his last entry before all the leavers’ diaries were handed in. Charles Wolfe didn’t mention the lake incident again.

Upon their graduation, Madame de Silentio sold Charles to a beautiful woman named Helene. She had blue eyes, which it thrilled him to look into. He believed that the petty thievery of his childhood had simply been impatience for the day when he would have two blue eyes like these to adore. But Helene was haunted by her past self. She'd been a fat child, even her ankles had been fat. In a letter to Madame de Silentio, Charles wrote that Helene had a serious fit of the hysterics when she saw him making supper for her—he was frying fish fingers in oil. She was unable to accept a hot meal as a gesture of love; she was convinced Charles was trying to make her fat again. He was able to soothe her—our training covers all emergencies, but he wished he hadn't had to draw upon it. Helene didn't like introducing Charles to her friends, either, because she found him ugly. She left him at home, or if she entertained at home she left him skulking around in the kitchen. As a test, Charles went missing for two weeks, roaming London, sleeping under newspapers on park benches. When he came home, Helene spoke of a party she'd recently been to, running rapidly through a list of anecdotes connected to names he didn't know, and she looked irritated when he asked her to slow down and explain who was who. 'I already told you,' she said. She hadn't noticed that he'd been gone. She'd probably come home from her parties and chattered away to thin air, believing that he was hidden in it somewhere, listening attentively. She hadn't been worried at all during his fourteen-day absence, hadn't looked for him.

'How can I be a better husband?' he asked her,

humbly.

Helene gave Charles Wolfe a mask to wear. A white mask. Not flat white; rather a colour suggestive of earth, brilliant but faintly fibrous, as it is beneath the skin of a pear. The mask's expression was neither happy nor sad. Its lips ran in a straight, geometric line, a humanly impossible one. It was a heavy mask; it changed the way Charles held his head, and, by extension, it changed the way he moved. As long as Charles wore the mask, Helene allowed him to escort her to dinners out, friends' weddings, etc. Helene's friends tried to act as if her masked husband didn't bother them, but he bothered them tremendously. I suppose it's hard to find a face friendly if you see it every day and it never smiles at you.

Charlie Wulf . . . Charlie Wulf was sold to a plain-looking woman. Plain, but wholesome and good-hearted. Laurel. She turned her back on the frivolous pursuits of her class and trained as a nursery-school teacher. She wore long skirts and always found a kind word and a hug for even the most tiresome of the children that played at her feet. Charlie had absorbed more training than anyone had credited him with, and he had no trouble speaking Words of Love to his wife. Laurel didn't like to hear them. It was all too insincere. She worried about how they looked as a couple—on the street, in their home. She turned all the household mirrors to the wall. She heard people making fun of her, even though Charlie assured her that she was imagining things. She became jealous if he appeared to take too much of an interest in conversation with her female friends. Laurel wrote Charlie tear-stained letters, turned him out of the house again and again, arrived unannounced at his hotel room in the early hours of the morning, just to check that he was alone. She couldn't believe in him.

At his wits' end, he asked her what he could do to help her believe.

And Laurel gave Charlie a mask to wear . . .

Reynardine might have come to the rescue (that would have been unfortunate for Mrs Wolfe and Mrs Wulf). But favours aren't always returned. Charles and Charlie don't seem to have communicated at all after graduating. Not a word, not even an attempt at a word. They no longer had need of each other.

Or—

I realise I'm reading very finely between the lines here, but maybe those two had fallen in love, and wanted to spare each other the anxiety of speaking with subtext, each wondering what the other wanted. A boy of weak character and his strong-minded friend; neither would have been likely to declare themselves first. It's not impossible, is it, that what I'm saying could be true? It's the abruptness more than anything. In the first place they seem to have chosen each other to confide in, out of all the boys in the academy, when actually it would have been safer to do as most of us do and confide only in our diaries. For many months these two found something to say to each other every day. Then they married, and nothing. There are feelings of some kind in this matter, even if I don't know what they are. The lake deeper than either of them had supposed, Charles kicking for shore with Charlie in his arms, the seconds without light or breath before both heads rose up and claimed them . . .

I'm surprising myself. I'm not a romantic.

At any rate I've derived some interest from finding out about my father's time at the school. Before this I had been looking for answers. I'd wondered about the cloud that seems to hang over my name when it's called in the register, and I'd wondered why the murder rate is so high nowadays, and I'd wondered about the mask, and about the difficulty my father had in looking at me and speaking to me. My mother didn't speak to me either—she was always busy, she sat on committees and things. Only after years of schooling do I talk as others do. Even now Mrs Engels sometimes looks more thoughtful than usual when I volunteer an answer in class. And I wondered, of course, why I was sent here when I hadn't done anything wrong. It must have just been Decisive Thinking.

Mr and Mrs Fox were hosting a dinner party. Downstairs, a motherly looking woman with fat grey pin curls laid the table and checked on the various items being cooked in the kitchen. Upstairs, the Foxes were engaged in a dispute. Mrs Fox had left her dressing-room blinds up, and Mary Foxe stood on a block of air and observed the scene with interest. Mrs Fox had a lot of nice things, and she was careless with them—perfume bottles with plush atomisers peeped out of embroidered pillowcases. Silk stockings tangled themselves around ivory combs shaped like castles.

A gleaming sable fur rippled in the light. Mrs Fox seemed to be using it to protect the carpet from her pots of face cream. The lady herself sat at her dressing table, her hair swept up into a chignon, her eyes downturned. She spoke, then her husband spoke, then she spoke again, with stubborn emphasis, and all the while she toyed with a brooch, a pink and white gold fox, complete with filigreed brush tail. Its eyes were two garnets.

Mrs Fox pinned the brooch to the collar of her dress, stood and made for the door, which Mr Fox promptly closed and leant against with his hands in his pockets.

Mrs Fox said something sarcastic. Her husband looked into her eyes and said nothing. Mrs Fox laughed nervously until the gaze ended. Then Mr Fox saw Mary. He grimaced slightly, and winked. Mary grimaced and winked back.

'What do you care whether I wear it or not? No one will notice.'

'You know what our friends are, D. Everyone will notice. So shut up and put it on.'

'What did you say to me, St John Fox?'

'Shut up and put it on.'

'You can't tell me to—'

'Shut up and put it on. Or I'll 'phone round and cancel.'

'Appearances,' Mrs Fox said. 'Got to keep up those appearances, haven't we?'

'What do you want, a slap?' He made his offer in a tone of flat pragmatism, like an expert barterer at market; it was as if he was saying: *Let's face it, you'll be lucky to get a slap*.

'Ha ha!' Mrs Fox's voice rang out scornfully. 'Go ahead!'

He took a step towards her and she ducked behind a standing mirror. He moved it aside and scooped her up in his arms. Within moments Mr Fox was pacing around the room with his lady wife over his shoulder, kicking ineffectually.

'I can't wear it,' Mrs Fox said, breathlessly. 'I told you.'

'Yes, you said it gives you a rash.' Mr Fox exchanged disbelieving glances with Mary.

'It's true.'

'Why now? You've had it a while.'

'I don't know. Maybe because you don't love me.'

'That's a ridiculous thing to say,' Mr Fox said, in a voice that was both hearty and hollow.

'What's ridiculous is you bullying me like this. Put me down, please. I'll wear the stupid ring—I'll wear it, I said, even if it makes my finger swell up to the size of my head. Then you'll be sorry.'

Having been set on her feet again, Mrs Fox caught sight of her disarranged hair and wailed. Mr Fox went downstairs and, as he spent a few minutes charmingly obstructing the caterer's efforts to finalise preparations, Mary watched Mrs Fox pick up her wedding ring and slip it onto her finger. Mary watched Mrs Fox rub at her ring finger as she redid her chignon, pushing the gold band first above, and then below her knuckle, until at last she yanked it off and crossed over to the sink in the next room, where she plunged her hand under a running tap, so relieved by the cold in the water that she fell to her knees and splashed her face and her dress. Mary would have liked to speak to the woman, to try and offer her some kind of assurance that she would be happy at a later date.

The urge to do so became overwhelming, so she left. Mr Fox was out in the garden, smoking his pipe. He murmured a pleasantry, which Mary ignored.

'Mr Fox. You're not going to change, are you?'

'I don't think I will, no.' His tone was light, but measured.

'For example—you're working on something at the moment, aren't you?'

'Of course.'

'Tell me what it is.'

He looked at her, considering. 'You really want to know?'

'I really want to know.'

'Well. It's about a man who works hard as an accountant all day and likes to go out driving late at night, to . . . to relieve his stress. And one night he's driving so fast he doesn't see a woman who's trying to hitchhike from the side of the lane, and he knocks her down. But he keeps going because he's afraid he killed her and would be arrested and go to gaol and all sorts of unpleasantness like that. The next night he stays at home. But the night after that he goes driving again and, well, he more or less deliberately knocks someone down. Over six months he makes a real career of it, knocking down pedestrians; mainly hookers . . . it really relieves his tensions—'

'Stop,' Mary said, brusquely.

'But I haven't even told you the best part yet.'

'You'll always refuse to see—or refuse to admit—that what you're doing is building a world—'

He smiled slightly, and she amended her words: 'What you're doing is building a horrible kind of logic. People read what you write and they say, "Yes, he is talking about things that really happen," and they keep reading, and it makes sense to them. You're explaining things that can't be defended, and the explanations themselves are mad, just bizarre—but you offer them with such confidence. It was because she kept the chain on the door, it was because he needed to let off steam after a hard day's scraping and bowing at work, it was because she was irritating and stupid, it was because she lied to him, made a fool of him, it was because she had to die, she just had to, it makes dramatic sense, it was because "nothing is more poetic than the death of a beautiful woman", it was because of this, it was because of that. It's obscene to make such things reasonable.'

He shrugged. 'These are our circumstances. I'm just trying to make sense of them,' he said.

Mary was silent.

'Everyone dies.' He smiled, crookedly. 'I doubt it's ever a pleasant experience. So does it really matter how it happens?'

'Yes!' She put a hand on his arm, trying to pass her shock through his skin. '*Yes*.'

'I'm sorry I've been wasting your time,' Mr Fox said, softly. The darkness in the garden absorbed the blue-black mane of his hair and made it look as if the sides of his face and the top of his head had been chiselled away.

He asked her: 'Do you want to stop playing?'

Mary began to answer him, but the guests arrived, in pairs. Three couples in all, and each brought wine, even though their hosts had plenty waiting. A blonde woman called Greta was very huffy with Mr Fox, refused to surrender her cheek for a greeting kiss but somehow made a joke of it. Her husband, a sleek blond man with a strong jaw, touched Mrs Fox's arm as he kissed her hello. The blond man's accent had the slightest hint of the foreign to it, and everyone called him by his surname: Pizarsky. Even his wife called him that. Pizarsky . . . Mary recognised the name. Her eyes widened.

Pizarsky looked at Mrs Fox often throughout the evening, and each time he looked it was for a moment longer than was casual. His gaze was hesitant. Almost meek.

Nobody seemed to notice this but Mary, who saw it all from her place outside the window, her heels grinding into the flowerbed. Should Mr Fox fear this Pizarsky, as a rival? The man was so quiet that it was impossible to tell. The other husbands vied endlessly for the most outrageous comment of the evening, planned a forthcoming fishing trip in great detail and addressed Mrs Fox with elaborate compliments on the food. Mrs Fox, pale-faced, accepted their tributes without a single guilty blush. She displayed her wedding ring for five minutes or so, then kept her hand beneath the tabletop. She and the other women spoke of ascending and descending skirt hems, and how difficult it was to hit upon the right length. Their eyes danced with the satisfaction of secret-society members talking in code. They interrupted each other. 'Do you remember . . .' they said. 'Do you remember when . . .'

After dinner, the six of them moved to the withdrawing room. Mr Fox had a dab of sauce at the corner of his mouth—Mrs Fox removed it with a swift, affectionate gesture and the corner of a very white napkin. Mr Fox kissed Mrs Fox's hand. When the teasing started up he mildly remarked that he thought a man might kiss his wife in his own drawing room on a Sunday evening if he felt like it. The others laughed hysterically. They'd started out sipping genteelly from glasses, but as they got drunker the drinking grew more lavish, and was done straight from bottles. They played charades, very badly, and were unable to establish who had won.

To Mary it looked like a great deal of fun.

what happens next

There was a death on the plane back to London. It was the woman beside me. I didn't know it could happen like that. I mean I knew, but I didn't believe it.

We pushed our seats back at the same time, our eyes met, and we laughed. We'd both ordered vegetarian meals. 'I hate this food,' she said. 'But I like getting it before everyone else.' Her name was Yelena. She was from the Ukraine, she told me, and I reminded her of her younger daughter. She was fifty-something, I think. Late fifties. Her fuzzy brown hair, her round, shiny eyes. She reminded me of a duckling, a greying duckling. I'd only just met her, but I liked her. I don't know. We talked about New York. She'd been visiting her eldest daughter, a journalist for a fashion magazine. 'You don't know how far she's come,' she said. What else . . . she showed me a group photo of her eldest daughter, her son-in-law, and her grandson. They looked happy and wealthy, suntanned in winter. I told her that I'd just been visiting my mother. 'Good daughter,' she praised. I shook my head: 'Only child.' She asked me what my mother does and I said she's a yoga teacher. I almost always lie about my mother. This woman, Yelena, started watching a sitcom and giggling, so I put on my noise-cancelling headphones and drank three-quarters of a bottle of cough syrup. I like it because it wears off faster than sleeping pills. I licked my lips. My stomach felt full; it seemed to sigh. When I looked out of the window sleep came down over it, steadily building black, softening my neck so that my head lolled, gathering me up in its vapour so that I drifted above the cramped angle of my seat. At some point my neighbour began to drum a fist upon my arm, then she began to groan and gripped my wrist; I shrank away and turned my face deeper into the flight cushion. I was dreaming.

I dimly recall hearing a beeping sound, and another noise, like a toy rattle being shaken. But they might have been in the dream. I love sleeping. Waking is more and more hateful the older I get. I say this as if I've lived too long. I'm twenty-two.

I woke as they were taking her away. Everyone was talking—everyone, in every seat. I felt their voices through my back and in my hair. There was still daylight in the cabin, but the overhead lights were on. Two male flight attendants carried Yelena away down the aisle, wrapped in blankets. And a balding man with a stethoscope walked behind them. I kept my head very still and just took my time to look and listen, without saying anything. Yelena's arm kept trailing; her palm touched the floor, and the attendant who had the upper half of her kept catching her arm, but couldn't keep it aloft. Not to worry, said the flight attendants, and the man with the stethoscope said something similar with every step. They were taking her through to first class, which was almost empty, something Yelena and I had complained to each other about at the beginning of the flight. Someone asked if Yelena was dead. The flight attendant said something about her having been 'taken ill'. But you've covered her face, someone else said. A beige silk scarf had been laid in a floppy triangle over Yelena's eyes, mouth and nose. Someone behind me started praying, in Latin, and rattling beads. People kept looking at me, and at the empty seat beside me. There was Yelena's handbag, beneath the seat in front of us. Her tray, with the remains of her meal on it, had been hastily pushed on top of my own tray. Her seat was still warm. The sitcom was still running on the little screen. I kept listening to what was being said: I heard the words 'cardiac arrest'. I should look after Yelena's handbag. When would they come back for it? Should I take it up to the front . . .

The stares from the other passengers grew fixed, and I realised that my lips were moving, so I stopped moving them. Someone asked me if I was all right. Yes, I think so, thank you. Someone else asked me if I was all right. Yes, I think so, thank you. She seemed fine. Maybe she wasn't well but didn't want to say so . . .

I shouldn't have drunk so much of that cough syrup. A quarter of a bottle would have been sufficient. Half at the most.

The people around me kept asking if I was all

right. Their voices were very kind, filled with concern, as if it was I who needed their concern. I couldn't see exactly who was talking to me—it all seemed to be coming from every direction at once. My nose ran. Tears fell; they stung, like hail. Sorry, I said. Sorry. Eventually someone came and took me away, and I scooped up all my things and Yelena's and followed behind the air hostess, dropping books and bottles and passports. Leave them, leave them, Miss Foxe, the air hostess said. I'll bring your things along for you in a minute. I had a moment of bewilderment—*who is Miss Foxe?*—then I just let everything go and went to First Class, which is where they wanted me to sit so that I could tremble out of sight of my former cabin mates, so that I wouldn't distress them, so that I wouldn't complain later about how I'd been treated after the incident. Yelena was six seats away from me. There was an empty row in front of her and an empty row behind her. They'd arranged her in the seat as if she was sleeping—her face was still covered, but it looked better now that she was upright; it looked as if covering her face was something she did just to help her sleep. Her hands were folded on her lap. I know it sounds strange, but I calmed down a bit once I could see her. She looked lonely, but I didn't want to join her. The air hostess put Yelena's handbag beside her and brought me some gin. I huddled up under a blanket, dipped my thumb into the glass and sucked it. Yes, it was like that . . .

I closed my eyes and tried to do some stupid breathing exercises.

'Only two hours until landing,' a man's voice said. It seemed he had addressed the words to me, so I opened my eyes. He was sitting to my right, his whole body turned toward me, his chin on his fist as he studied me. I hadn't heard or felt him draw near. He was older than me, but I couldn't guess how much older. He was good-looking. Enough to make me feel uncomfortable. Tall and dark, etc. There was room between his eyes for a third eye of the same size—I've read that that's one of the standards of classical beauty. He was wearing a black suit, but it looked as if he'd slept in it for a week straight—wrinkles within wrinkles. 'I'm glad to hear it,' I replied.

'That woman over there is dead,' he remarked.

'I know. I—I was sat next to her.'

'What happened?'

'I think she had some sort of massive heart attack.'

He said, 'I see,' and spent a second or two thinking about it. 'Did you know her?'

'No.'

'Your eyes are just like a cat's,' he told me. His voice was husky. There was gravel in it, and waves. I blushed. It was the way he looked into my eyes, unfalteringly into my eyes as he spoke to me and heard my replies. As close and as direct as the look exchanged when standing face to face after a kiss, or at the peak of a bad fight. Worse than that, actually. Closer than that.

He lifted a lock of hair away from my face. 'Why is this part white?'

'I was struck by lightning when I was little.' A lie I tell everyone. It made him smile. I liked that he didn't believe me. I liked that he didn't question the story, but let it stand. We talked a bit more. His name was St John Fox. (St John . . . I thought that had died out as a first name centuries ago. Posh. He was definitely posh.) We made a half-hearted fuss about having almost identical surnames, wondered about being distant cousins. He'd just presented a paper at a psychiatry conference in Manhattan. I made a joke about him being Dr Fox and he said, seriously, that he preferred 'Mr'. I asked him what the subject of his paper was, but he said it wasn't particularly interesting. Which meant he thought I was stupid. I wished I hadn't told him that I model. To make up for it I told him about my psychology degree, and he said, 'I've got one of those too.' We talked until the plane landed, and then I broke off and stood up when the economy-class passengers started filing through the cabin, whispering and staring. I didn't want them to see me lounging around in First, chatting with a handsome doctor. I waited around to see what would be done about Yelena—the aeroplane staff told me they had to get everyone off the plane first. St John waited with me, though I hadn't asked him to. I spoke to the doctor and a representative from the airline; I answered their questions and told them all I could think of. We waited until they asked us to leave. That made me think they were going to do something bad. Stick Yelena on a trolley with some luggage, something like that. There was no wheelchair waiting. This worried me.

St John stepped off the plane. I didn't follow. He stopped and looked behind him, with an expression of mild surprise. 'It'll be all right, Mary. Let them sort this out. She's gone. We should go, too.'

We talked all the way through passport control

and baggage reclaim. He wasn't wearing a wedding ring, but that didn't mean anything either way. I have married friends who don't wear rings. My parents were married and didn't wear rings. I finally got him to tell me about his paper. He was interested in fugue states. A fugue state is the result of an afflicted consciousness, he said. A person in a fugue state is somewhere between waking and dreaming, with the mere appearance of functioning normally. An already fragile man might suffer strain from some extraordinary life event at nine o clock one night, then wake up at seven o'clock the next morning and just walk away from his home, his family, his life. He might take a bus or a long train ride, or a flight, and once he is elsewhere he becomes someone else. He'll take a new name and forget his old one. His handwriting might change, the way he speaks and behaves changes subtly but significantly. He has no memory of his old life—until, abruptly, the fugue wears off, and what's left is a frightened, exhausted human being, miles and miles from home and unable to recall what he's seen and said and done since the evening of his dreadful shock.

'You said it wasn't an interesting subject.'

'Most of these cases are historical. It's been argued that fugue states are a nineteenth-century malaise, convenient for central European men looking for work in other countries, a disguise for individual attempts at economic migration, that sort of thing.'

'But you don't think so.'

'No.' His eyes were very bright; they'd been like that since he'd begun talking about his subject. He looked like someone in love. Well, in love the way people were in old movies.

'Are you working with fugue-state patients right now?'

'If I was, I wouldn't be allowed to discuss it.' He wheeled my suitcase up to the taxi rank. He only had a light-looking hold-all himself. 'My car's parked down there. I'd offer you a lift, but . . .'

'But?'

'But you shouldn't drive off with strange men you only just met on the plane.'

'Of course.'

(I would have gone with him.)

'It was nice to meet you, St John. Thanks—' I had no idea what I was thanking him for. He was gazing at me again, with that overwhelming concentration. I seemed to interest him very much—as an artefact, almost.

He drew a business card from his wallet, a pen from the top pocket of his jacket and rested the card on top of my hard case. 'Look—you've had a bit of a shock today. And I have some concerns,' he said, writing a phone number on the back. 'It's because your eyes are like a cat's, you know, and you were struck by lightning. If you don't phone I'll assume the worst.'

'Bold,' I said, accepting the card.

He touched my wrist. Lightly, and with just one finger, but I shivered. It wasn't that his hand was especially cold. I think it was the subtlety. If I hadn't been looking, I wouldn't have even noticed what he'd done. *He took my pulse*, I thought. *Stole it*.

'Too bold?'

He walked away from me, backwards.

I didn't know how to answer. I think I just

shrugged awkwardly and turned away.

* * *

I don't do anything I don't want to do. Not even for curiosity's sake.

For example: there's the time I went to Berlin to see a man I liked, a stage magician I'd done a shoot with to promote something or other. The visit went badly. I'd turned up at his door as a surprise, and he didn't like surprises. If I'd thought about it I would have realised that—a magician must control his props and the space in which he orchestrates his tricks—it looks like play, but the magician's mind must be as strict as an iron brace. We went for a walk and he told me that I didn't make much sense to him outside of the photographs. He seemed to be trying to tell me that I was a creature of chaos. I said: 'Okay, I'll go home today.'

The magician said: 'Thank you for understanding.' He turned homewards and I stood still.

'Aren't you coming?'

'No, I'm going home.'

'But your things—'

'Throw them away. I'll get new things. There are so many, all around.'

'You're angry.'

'I'm not. I swear I'm not.' I really wasn't angry. I did want him to go away, though, and quickly, so that I could begin to forget about him. So I smiled, and hugged him, to show that I wasn't angry. He left, calling after me that I should phone him if I changed my mind about picking up my things. I kept walking. Under a bridge in Prenzlauer Berg I came across a man playing a violin; he was wearing a top hat and dinner jacket and his notes were apple-crisp. Because he was playing so well I looked at him. At first I thought my sight was sun-spattered, but once my eyes adjusted to the tunnel I saw that the scars were really there—harshly moulded welts that gripped half of his face. They crowded his left eye, forced its corner to travel down with them. I stopped walking.

'Wunderbar,' I said. 'Wo hast du gelernt?'

He didn't change the pace of his playing. Nor did he look up.

'Schläfst du hier?'

No answer. Sunset lanced through the tunnel, cutting our shadows off at the knees. I found my purse, took out a note and let it flutter into his violin case. I liked his indifference. I respected it. He finished his piece and packed up his violin, shaking the money out of the case first. It blew away, but I stomped and trapped it under my foot, still watching him, wondering, I suppose, if he would acknowledge me before leaving. 'If you want to talk to me you can talk to me,' he said, as he snapped his case shut. 'But not here.'

And he leapt to his feet and sprinted away, through the tunnel and across the smooth lawn of the park, through the rose-covered trellises that flanked its gates. He crossed over concrete and, at a mad, desperate dash, through the traffic that whirled along a broad avenue. And I followed, chased briefly by my flying ten-euro note, colliding with pedestrians, knocking handbags off shoulders and newspapers from people's hands. The violinist's hat fell off his head and I picked it up and ran harder, shouting, 'Entschuldigung!' and shaking it joyfully. Near the end of a dimly lit alleyway my quarry knocked on a door in a complicated manner—a series of knuckle raps and open-handed slaps—was abruptly admitted and tumbled inside. I drew the line at that. I approached the door, which looked like any other door, and placed the top hat to the left of it. Then I went off in search of something to eat. The running had made me hungry. I hope he recovered the top hat—it wasn't a cheap one.

I've wondered, I have wondered, what that chase was all about, but I've never regretted leaving the matter at that. I didn't want to follow the violinist into the company of persons unknown to me. So I didn't do it.

I decided that I would not be calling S.J. Fox—there was something married about him. So I left his business card in the back of the taxi. I've left purses and cameras and mobile phones in the backs of taxi cabs and have never once been called back to collect them before the cab drove off. This time the driver called out: 'You've forgotten something, miss,' and I had to go and pick the business card up.

* * *

I liked to go home. I'd worked hard on the place, repainting a room a month, stencilling bright butterflies in corners, building little galaxies of light with crystal lampshades, pouring gauze over the windowpanes. There was no darkness where I lived.

I let myself in, picked my letters up off the

doormat and walked through two weeks' quiet, the floorboards soft under my feet, a gentle path to my unmade bed. It looked storm-tossed, just the way I'd left it, just the way I liked it. I lay down, opened letters, and listened to my answer machine. There were hardly any messages. A couple from my agent, about jobs.

As I listened to the messages I looked at an invitation to a fancy-dress party; really looked at it, held it close to my face. The words were printed alongside a picture of me, looking too silly for words. They'd done my hair up in Victorian ringlets and dressed me up in a grey wolf suit and a red cape. The snarling wolf's head was hung around my neck, sharp teeth and bright gums. In the background there were soft multicoloured lights that were supposed to suggest fantasy and imagination. It was for charity. The party was due to start in an hour, and the venue wasn't far from my flat—not by taxi. I could still go. It seemed wrong not to take a chance to meet people.

There was a shepherd's crook leant up against my bathroom door—I'd got it on the Portobello Road a few months ago. I considered going to the fancy dress ball as a saucy shepherdess. Or Christ. Or I could go as a saucy shepherdess and when people asked me if I was a shepherdess I could say, 'Christ, actually.'

I moved on to the last letter in the heap, the only one addressed to Miel Shaw. It was a dove-grey envelope addressed in thin dark purple print. Which meant that it was from my father. I had one hundred and twenty-seven other envelopes like it, many of them unopened because they'd arrived on days I knew I couldn't cope. The letters were all in a shoebox under my bed. My hoard. I opened the new envelope little by little, sliding a nail along under its sealed flap, from one corner to the other. It took a long time.

The letter was upsetting, so I'll try to paraphrase it. It had been written by someone else on his behalf—dictated, it seemed, and sent without editing. My father apologised for writing to me—he said he knew that I didn't like him to. But he had been taken aside and told terrible things about what was happening inside his body. He was dying of colon cancer. He had gone through chemotherapy, and he was still dying. There was a smell in the air—a sweet smell that terrified him and was with him always. He thought it was coming from his stomach. He asked me to visit him at the prison hospice. You've never seen such a place, he said. *You couldn't know that a place like this exists. Come and see me. Just quickly, just once.* Or if I telephoned, if I wrote back—just to show that I was there, that there was someone. He said that he'd seen me in a magazine, but that I'd just been paint and porcelain. Are you really there? he asked. Are you?

I folded the letter, put it back in its envelope and added it to the others in the box. *I don't care. I don't care.* He hadn't put my name in the letter, and that made it easier for me to refuse the letter—it had not been written to me.

I thought I heard something in the next room,
a footfall.

I paced through the flat with the reassuring weight of the shepherd's crook in my hand, checking that all the windows were locked. They were. I was alone. Safe, alone.

All the times I've been frightened because of my father. My need for night-lights, my inability to sleep in a room unless I'm able to clearly see all four corners from the bed—and dreams, bad dreams like messengers he sent. All the times he's frightened me. Die, then, I thought. *Die*. And I wondered when he would be gone.

I phoned my lawyer, and I phoned his lawyer, and left messages. Long messages. Part of the reason I changed my name was so that my father wouldn't be able to contact me. Yet somehow he has always been able to find me. His secretary used to send me cheques twice a year, cuts from my father's investment yield that he instructed her to pass on to me. But I've never cashed them, not under any circumstances. When I moved house I left a post-office box as my forwarding address, and I haven't checked it since. You have to be like that when there's a person like my father in your life; when you leave places you mustn't look back or you'll find him there.

'S.J. Fox, psychiatrist,' I murmured. 'S.J. Fox, psychiatrist.' Whilst thinking I was looking at his card. I'd placed it on my bedside table. The card was so plain, so black and white and uncreased, that it made everything around it, the frosted-glass lamp that shone light on it, the framed photograph of my cousin Jonas and me, look insubstantial. I was interested in his work, this St John Fox. Did he know, could he tell, when a fugue state was coming on? The clinic he worked at was in Cornwall, and that was far away. I covered the card with my letters. There was no point invoking psychiatry in this matter. I am sane and it's well documented that my father is sane. He seemed fully aware of what he'd done, and he was sorry, so sorry. My father is eloquent and sensitive, fair-haired and fair-skinned. His facial expressions flow into each other with mesmerising transparency, grief, anguish, scorn. 'He gets so worked up,' my mother used to say. She said it lovingly. Then she took to saying it in a puzzled way, then with contempt.

There was always something strange about the three of us together. Little things that might have been fun, but somehow weren't fun. One sunny morning my father made my mother lie down—she was laughing, and she said she wanted to do it, but she was an actress, can you trust an actress and a sunny day?—he made her lie down in the garden in her bikini and he wrote all over her. I can't remember what he wrote; it was a long poem, in blue ink, an original poem, maybe. I was ten going on eleven. I didn't like what was happening and I didn't know why. He wrote on her back first, kneeling beside her, then he made her turn over and wrote all across her front, pressing hard, and the letters were big and ugly, but she pranced around afterwards holding out her arms and saying things like: 'Am I in the poem? Or is the poem in me?' And he just sat in a deckchair as if exhausted by his work and watched her. I thought, something very mad is going on, she doesn't like this, but she'll never say so.

I was taken to a theatre matinee for my twelfth-birthday treat; that should have been fun, too. We had the best seats possible, because that's what things were like with my father. My mother was playing Juliet, and the first two scenes dragged—blah blah, said one actor—Romeo, I presumed. Blah blah blah, said a second actor; some relative of Romeo's. Asking him something; merry, but concerned. Blah blah blah blah, Romeo said, looking downcast for a few seconds before proceeding to jump around and climb things. My father stared into space and I felt my eyes begin to close of their own accord. Until Juliet made her airy appearance, soft and slender—'How now! Who calls?' and suddenly we were listening, Father and I, watching, our heads tilting to take her in, as if we'd never seen her before. The stage makeup exaggerated her eyes, but her mouth was still larger, very much larger. Something from the distant past—a great-grandfather who was an African. She was self-conscious about her mouth and called it her clumsy flytrap, but my Aunt Molly told me that that's how it should be—when a woman's lips are larger than her eyes it's a sign that she's warm-hearted. Her hair was a bright mass of crinkles, a lion's mane. Romeo embraced her and she gave herself over to him with eager, trembling bliss. There were quite a few embraces, and my father became conspicuously still and watched with startled pain. I was uncomfortable because I'd never seen her like this before, but he'd seen her perform plenty of times. It's only acting, I thought. *Is he always like that when she acts?*

After the matinee my parents took me to lunch, and the strangeness was there with us. It was there in the powdery smell of the velvet on the restaurant chairs and it was there in the palm fronds that tickled my head. My mother and father talked politely about things they had read in the newspaper, and changed the subject whenever it seemed they were about to disagree. As usual, my father ordered something that wasn't on the menu, just because. He told me to order whatever I liked, and I did. My mother drank martinis and said sharply: 'Three whole courses! What a pig you are, Miel.' And I was so surprised I almost cried. It was my birthday. And she'd never said such a thing before. My father and I were silently against her for the rest of the meal, sticking to our plan to order ice cream even though she wasn't having anything and was ready to leave.

I wish I hadn't ever been bad to my mother. I see that afternoon again and again. She had acted wonderfully, she had been Juliet, and then we'd met her at the stage door and treated her as if she had done something wrong. We hadn't said 'well done' to her, or much of anything. My father had just pushed a bunch of flowers into her arms.

Just over two years later, my father killed my mother. She was running away from him down some stairs and he seized her by the hair at the nape of the neck—he must have lifted her onto her tiptoes—and he forced a knife through her chest. From behind. Then he called the police, and waited for them. I was at boarding school, and everyone there knew, because it was in the newspapers, and some of my friends went and lit candles in the school chapel. I found that deeply bogus. All the newspapers were kept away from me so I wouldn't see what was being said. I didn't need to read about my mother—I knew her well—we spoke every day until he killed her. She'd moved out of his house and she was living with her new boyfriend, Sam. She went back to the house to get some things. She had his permission, as long as he didn't have to see her. So they'd settled on a weekday afternoon—he was supposed to be at the office. But he wasn't.

He said that she had been turning me against him (this isn't true: my father always frightened me. If I had been allowed to testify I'd have said so). He had a lot of explanations that I wasn't really able to take in at the time. He said he couldn't take it any more.

'It'.

What is 'it'? Sometimes I think he killed her to show us something, to show us what 'it' is. She was my best friend, and she knew almost everything—if she didn't know she made outrageous guesses. She made me laugh and I made her laugh. When I spoke to my mother I was the funniest, cleverest, most interesting girl alive. Other people's mothers told them to 'be good' or to 'take care'. Mine told me to be bad and wicked and not to worry. While waiting for her to phone me at school I'd feel seconds bursting inside me and leaving clouds. That won't come again—it can't. I'll never have that with anyone else. I'll never even come close.

So. When I say I've been visiting my mother, that means I've been visiting her grave. I bring her foxgloves; her maiden name was Foxe. At her funeral she was hidden away in a closed casket because she was no longer beautiful. He'd done other things before he stabbed her—no one would tell me what. I suppose I could have insisted on seeing her, if I'd really wanted to.

I had counselling, which helped. I discovered cough syrup as an aid to sleep, and that was even better.

* * *

I didn't go to the charity ball that night. I couldn't face it. I called Jonas instead—he's the closest thing I've got to a brother. His parents took custody of me and paid for the rest of my schooling and my food and clothes. And because I was academically advanced and they thought it would be wrong for me to be kept back, they put me through university at the same time as Jonas—I was a drain on their resources. I kept a tally of the running costs as best I could and paid them back when I got a big enough contract. They were very angry, because they love me, and Uncle Tom tore the cheque up, and we never spoke of it again. They are such good people and I owe them so much that I can hardly look either of them in the eye. Jonas's mother, Molly, is my mother's younger sister—they used to tease each other about their Anglophilia, two American girls who married British men and developed a keen interest in the goings on at Ascot, Wimbledon and the Henley Regatta. Their older sister, Jane, is the one who still lives in America, and the one who had my mother flown out there to be buried. She's an odd one, Aunt Jane. I don't think I like her. Jonas isn't keen on her either. It exasperates him that she uses his name so often whilst speaking to him; it gives the impression that she's trying her hardest not to forget who on earth he is. She does that to everyone. She's always careful to call me Mary, so I find her constant repetition of my name sinister, as if she's reminding me that I'm not who I say I am.

Jonas is a seminarian—in four or five years' time he's going to be a priest. I've never been inside his seminary, only glimpsed the grounds. A silence in the centre of London. The main entrance is a glass door set between grey pillars, and when I wait for Jonas on a Friday afternoon, sexy, soberly dressed men of every nationality pour out onto the street. Sexy because they belong to God and will never more be caressed by human hand. A strange thing, because I remember when we used to French kiss, Jonas and I. We'd French kissed all over the house while his parents went to concerts and galas and dinner parties. It was my idea. He said he'd never kissed a girl, and I felt sorry for him. So I showed him and showed him and showed him. 'This isn't right,' he stammered. 'We're related by blood.' But he liked it, and he was good at it. Very good at it, actually. Gentle, but subtly demanding, too, the way he'd pass his hand through my hair, his lips moving over my mine, slow, savouring. He was talented, at an age when other boys were horrible kissers, just horrible and sloppy. I was fourteen then, and he was sixteen. When Jonas came to the phone I asked him if he remembered that we used to kiss. 'I remember,' he said, tersely. 'Is that why you called?'

I meant to tell him about the letter from my father, and to ask what to do. But I could already hear him telling me that I'd have to go to the prison hospice, that place of marvel my father promised me. So I ended up telling Jonas that someone had died on the plane, and that her name was Yelena. He didn't ask me if I was all right. He listened. He let me tell him what happened again and again, in more detail as the details came to mind.

'Why are you laughing?' he asked, abruptly. It

was true, I was—and not quietly, either. I managed to say that I had to go, and hung up. So he was dying! My laughter rose in pitch to equal a scream.

Maybe the letter was a trick, like my father hiding in the house, waiting for my mother to come home without fear. I'd know tomorrow, when the lawyers phoned me back.

Dinner was vodka, such a lot of vodka. And *Swing Time* was on TV, so I watched that.

'Listen,' Ginger Rogers said to Fred Astaire, 'no one could teach you to dance in a million years!'

That dried my laughter up immediately. I turned the TV off and went to bed, to the sleep that I loved.

* * *

In the morning I Googled S.J. Fox, and found a sad story—a eulogy he'd written for his wife four years ago. It was tender. Very tender, and I stopped halfway through—I had no right to be reading it. There was no mention of the word 'suicide', but it was clear to me that that was what he was getting at. Someone from his wife's family had posted the full order of the funeral service, including the hymns sung and the psalms and Bible passages read, and they, too, pointed to suicide. Oh, you broken, broken soul, they seemed to say. There is a balm in Gilead, etc. I studied the photograph of her. Daphne Fox. She was sitting on a mossy boulder with sunshine all around her, wearing a picture hat and holding on to it at the crown so it didn't blow away. She'd been a PE teacher at the local comprehensive school, and given it up when she'd married him. Like someone from another age. She was a bit plump, and she smiled shyly. Not at all the type I would have expected to see with someone like S.J. She seemed to like butterflies. She was wearing a pair of butterfly earrings and a butterfly pendant. I also made out a butterfly bracelet; the wings closed around her wrist. The life of a butterfly is very short. The German word for butterfly is *Schmetterling*. These were thoughts I had while avoiding the fact that Daphne Fox looked familiar to me. She was a redhead, like me, but that wasn't it. I must have just looked at her for too long.

*   *   *

Having ascertained the facts, the lawyers returned my calls. Their voices were serious and low. The letter wasn't a trick. My father was very ill.

Jonas said, Go to him.

Aunt Molly said, Go to him. So did Uncle Tom.

Aunt Jane said, Go to him, Mary.

There was something morbid about their insistence. He was going to die soon, so now his words were important and had special meaning. That's what they wanted me to believe. It was disgusting . . .

I pretended my mother spoke to me. I pretended she said, Don't go to him, he's evil. Don't forget, she said, that he had that folder full of newspaper clippings. Don't forget how he made you look through them. Don't forget that some nights he kept you up until you had read through all the clippings again. He'd test you. He'd watch you wilt.

Why was Fatema Yilmaz buried alive under a

chicken pen?

As punishment for talking to boys. She wasn't allowed to.

Who punished her?

Her father and her grandfather.

How deep was the hole they dug?

Three metres.

Three metres? Are you sure?

No—no. Two metres.

Correct. Why was Medine Ganis drowned in a bathtub?

Because she wouldn't do as she was told.

Elaborate, Miel. Elaborate.

Her father chose a man for her to marry and she said she wouldn't do it.

Who was there when she drowned?

Her father was there, and her two brothers were there, holding her down. Her mother was there, but she took no part in it.

Where in the article does it say her mother took no part in it? Don't embroider. Silence is consent.

But it doesn't say her mother was silent—

Enough. Why was Charlotte Romm shot to death in her bed?

Because her husband didn't want her to know that he'd spent her parents' life savings. But, Dad—

Yes, Miel?

He shot their children, too. And her parents.

I know. But I didn't ask you about them. Don't answer questions you haven't been asked.

My mother would tell him to stop it—I passed these stories on, with gruesome embellishments, to other kids at school and their parents complained—but he said that the world was sick and that I should know I wasn't safe in it. My mother told me not to listen to him, but it was impossible not to. I kicked open cubicle doors in public toilets, so expectant of discovering an abandoned corpse that for an instant I'd see one, slumped over the toilet bowl, her long hair falling into the water. I saw them in the dark, the girls, the women yet to be found. I counted their faces, gave them names and said the names, as if calling a class register. Here's what I learnt from the clippings: that there is a pattern. These women had requested assistance. They'd told people: someone is watching me, has been following me, has beaten me up before, has promised me he will kill me. They'd pointed their murderers out, and they had been told 'it won't happen', or that nothing could be done, because of this and that, etc. I was jumpy in those days, expecting something terrible to happen to me at any moment, without knowing where it would happen to me, or why, or who would do it.

My father sent press clippings to me at school, from prison. As if to say, your mother wasn't the first and won't be the last. Maybe I could have shown all the clippings to someone and somebody would have looked at his sanity again, tried to get him treatment. But that might have reduced his sentence, or they might have hospitalised him. My father, out in the world again—a thought I couldn't think. Not ever.

* * *

A box arrived in the post, forwarded from the agency. I signed for it, and sat down on the sofa with it, afraid that it was something my father had sent to me. Then I reminded myself that his letter had come directly to me—he knew my address. Still, my hands shook as I unwrapped a brass-handled magnifying glass and a tiny book about half the size of my thumb. I turned the pages—there were only three, and each had a word written on it in a fine, light hand. Trying to breathe, I held the glass over each page and read:

You

didn't

call . . .

He'd included another card inside the box, allowing me the excuse of having lost the first one. He answered on the third ring, as if he'd been waiting.

'It's me,' I said, stupidly.

I thought he couldn't hear me clearly, and was about to add: 'It's Mary Foxe,' but he spoke just a heartbeat before I did. 'Are you seeing anyone?'

'No.'

'Will you see me?'

His voice in my ear. It did interesting things to me. It curved my back and parted my lips. I felt lazy and feline, and he wasn't even in the room. 'Yes. When?'

'I'm in town next week—I do a couple of days a week at a private practice.'

'Call me next week, then.'

'I will.' He paused. I paused.

'I'm sorry about your mother,' he said, at the same time as I said: 'I'm sorry about your wife.'

I recovered first. 'Thank you for saying that,' I said, without emphasis. He must have found one of those stupid and unnecessary 'she isn't doing too badly for a girl whose mother was murdered' articles. He'd have had to dig deep, though. It was such a long time ago.

'Likewise,' he said.

'I'm sorry I snooped.'

He made no reply. He'd already ended the call.

'Soon, then,' I told the dial tone.

* * *

I stopped talking to Jonas and Aunt Molly and Uncle Tom and Aunt Jane. It wasn't easy. I missed them. Especially Jonas. I attended foam parties and tube parties and hedge and highway parties. I took every job my agent could get for me. People looked at my contact sheets and told me I was doing my best work yet. I couldn't see what they meant—the pictures looked the same as always.

It was at another charity fundraiser that I remembered where I had seen Daphne Fox. Light hummed in crystal chandeliers. Jonas, decadent Catholic that he was, would have loved the party. Men in dinner jackets and starched white collars, throats pulsing with laughter. Yards of oyster-coloured silk, and diamonds, diamonds, garnets, rubies. One old man had a walking stick topped with an emerald the size of an egg. I holed myself up in a corner with a couple of girls I knew from jobs I'd done, and we listened to the speeches and stood there drinking and looking at everything through our sunglasses, waiting for something to happen. The room was in half darkness, raked by a roving spotlight. Every now and again someone who had only been a silhouette suddenly transformed into a pillar of flashing jewels. I hadn't thought to wear any jewellery, and when the spotlight finally fell on our group, I stepped out of it. It didn't take much to make my head spin just then—the sudden change from blinding light to dusk made my hands clammy. That and the cough syrup and the cocktails and the wine. I excused myself and weaved out of the ballroom, towards the toilets; a crowd of women emerged and momentarily surrounded me. 'Come back,' I wanted to tell them. 'Don't leave me alone in here.'

But they had, and I walked up the row of cubicles, kicking doors and watching the mirror while a tap dripped bleakly and muzak floated in through the speakers. I kicked the last door open and clenched my jaw against a scream—the image of a dead woman flashed fiercely, just as I used to when I was eleven; exactly like that.

It was the same woman I conjured up each time, sprawled in the cubicle with wet, dangling hair, and that bashful, almost apologetic expression—*sorry about this*. The face was Daphne Fox's. That was my last clear impression for a while.

*   *   *

Some time went by. A night, a very late night, I think; street lamps spiked the dark, and no one was out. Whatever I was doing, wherever I was, I was most aware of the grinding of my teeth—the sound and the feeling. The supple clicking was a comfort.

At first I was alone, then I was with S.J. Fox, at a restaurant—potted plants as tall as trees, fancy bread rolls, tapenade, and out of a window I saw

Cleopatra's Needle dividing the sky. I was very nervous. Close up his skin was weathered and held frown fractures so fine and deep that he seemed made of them. I still couldn't guess how old he was. I didn't listen too closely to what he was saying. His expressions changed suddenly and completely—a frown would chase a boyish grin midway through a sentence; not even my father had switched masks so quickly. And that was what all the expressions felt like—masks. I didn't believe them. They were too thorough, too nuanced, they were never at odds with his subject matter. He probably had to be like this because of work—he had to show people what normal, balanced emotions looked like. But that's just not how it happens. People move from comic to tragic with the remnants of a smile left on their lips. Natural expressions linger. There was someone behind all S.J.'s masks, someone who stared mockingly and dared me to say that I knew he was there. And that was the one I wanted to meet. The unprofessional.

It took a lot of concentration not to mention his wife. *I never met Daphne, but I've seen her in my head . . .*

We walked out of the restaurant and down the street, to the hotel he was staying in. His arm was around my waist. I moved deeper into the curve of his arm as he collected his messages at reception. In the lift he gently pushed me away and made me stand on my own, facing him. 'You have a gap in your teeth,' he whispered, and he filled it with the tip of his tongue. He looked at me as he did it, and I looked at him. This was no silver-screen kiss, we were in each other's wide open eyes, and I dared not flinch. It was a long way up—the lift kept stopping, and other people entered it and left—I couldn't see them, only felt them, like clouds drifting around us.

His hotel room was cream and burgundy. He drew the blinds and sat down on the chair by the dressing table. I sat on the bed.

'I loved Daphne,' he said. He studied my reaction—I had opened my mouth, but I said nothing. He went on: 'I did. But in the last few months she was worse than a child. She lit fires on the carpets and she threw coffee tables through locked windows. She always had to be watched.'

I couldn't look at his face any more, so I looked at his long-fingered hands, the way his knuckles jerked as he opened and closed his hand around the room key.

'I see. She was too much trouble—'

'That's not what I was saying—'

'So you killed her?'

There, it was out.

'Do you always talk like this?' he asked, calmly.

'Did you kill her?'

He answered with a smile. The darkest and most malignant I had ever seen, too strong to be voluntary. The door, I thought. The door. But I didn't dare turn to it, in case it wasn't there. His smile stayed. It stayed and stayed, until it became meaningless. It calmed me. So lightheaded I stopped trying to sit straight. I dropped onto the floor, and he watched me approach, on my knees. I didn't stop until I was looking directly into his eyes, deep in their hollows. His face tightened—he was barely breathing.

'Oh, you,' I said. 'You are a man I've been

waiting to meet.'

I took his hands. I arranged them around my throat, closed my own hands over them, tight, like a choker. 'Did you kill her and get away with it? How did you get away with it?'

'She killed herself.'

I moved so that they pressed together, the four pairs of hands. I let go, then pressed them together again, made my breathing fold like bellows. It felt good. It felt like forgetting.

'Stop it,' he said. But he didn't move his hands.

'Did you kill her? Did you kill her?'

'I said stop it.'

'And me? Do you want to kill me? Is that why you look at me the way you do?'

'What do you want, Mary?'

I offered my lips to be kissed. He didn't move his head, though he stayed close.

'Kiss me,' I said.

He took a deep, rattling breath. 'You're . . . a strange girl.'

'Kiss me.'

He did. My hands worked at the buttons of his shirt, carefully, slowly. He peeled my dress away from my shoulders. Then we were on the floor together. I was pinned beneath him at first. Our open mouths. Our heat. I hooked my legs around his, drank his skin, strange salt that ran like water; my hair swept across his bare chest; I was astride him by then, and I took him an inch at a time, ('Wait,' I said, 'wait,' pulling away every time he tried to take too much) an aching delay between each movement that brought him deeper. Such pleasure when he finally steadied me above him, his hands where my waist softens into my hips, such pleasure when he filled me.

'I'm sorry I said those things,' I said, when we lay together afterwards. His lips brushed my forehead.

'It's understandable,' he said. 'I understand. The lightning . . .'

I hated the kindness in his voice—where did it come from? It wasn't why I wanted him. I wanted the look in his eyes when I'd asked: 'Did you kill her?' The moment in which he had hated me.

'You shouldn't work out of hours,' I said.

He laughed softly. 'Then don't make me.'

He left me sleeping—when I woke I held out my arms to him and there was nothing, not even a note.

Another day passed, and another night, I think. Without him. Then there were a lot of people, and I didn't know who any of them were. There were so many of them. Why so many? I realised that I was in public. I had to stay there, in public, because I didn't know how to get home. Every direction looked exactly the same to me.

Someone took my mobile phone. Someone else took my purse. It wasn't robbery, exactly—I must have just been sitting there, on a park bench after dark holding out my purse and my phone, my hands like weighing scales, and then they were empty. I didn't worry about it. I thought it was summer. 'It's summer,' I said to myself. And I saw ants troop past my feet in single file. I wondered about ants. I wondered whether within each ant there is another and another and another until finally you reached a cold small chip of the universe, immovable and displeased.

Then Jonas was there. I don't know how he found me. We went into McDonald's, because it was nearest and I was almost frozen. Ha! Not summer after all. I said I wanted onion rings and he bought me onion rings, which I didn't eat. No, I tried ring after ring on my heart finger. Wedding rings. None of them fitted, but they didn't fall apart, either. Jonas watched me and he rubbed his head all over, as if searching for a thought, then raked hair out of his eyes. His dear face—his thrice-broken nose, his summer eyes. He had bought me onion rings; he wasn't going to take anything from me. I didn't really have anything left, anyway, apart from mascara and my door keys. I was happy when he put his arms around me. I hid my face in the lapels of his jacket and my frame loosened, lava-like, beneath my skin. I don't know how I didn't scald him. Jonas's heart beat steadily, not fast, not slow; its order restored me. He drew back.

'Where have you been?' he said. He was Old Testament angry, calm and wild at once, like a prophet come down from the mountains with a storm under his tongue, holding it until it was time.

'When?'

He stared at me, and I said quickly: 'I went to a party.'

'Are you sure?'

'Yes. A big one. There were probably photos in the paper. It was at . . . oh . . . at—'

'The Athenaeum?'

'That's it.'

'Three nights ago.'

'Three . . . really . . . ?'

'Yes, really.'

'Oh . . .'

He counted days off on his fingers, his face stony. 'So there was yesterday night. And the night before that. And the night before that. We've been trying to reach you.'

'Have you . . .'

'Roger died on Friday. They were going to cremate him day before yesterday, but we've asked them to hold on until we could reach you.'

'Reach me? Why?'

'So you can see him,' Jonas said, simply. 'If you want to stop being afraid, Miel, you'll do this.' He pulled me up out of my seat. I fought him, but he merely locked his arms around me and contained me. I stomped on his foot and his grip didn't loosen, but his touch became gentler; he brushed his nose against my cheek: 'Sh, sh . . .'

'No,' I said. 'I can't.'

'I'll be there.'

I hoped someone would intervene, but everyone else in the vicinity just stared down into their cartons of fries. They must have thought we were having a lovers' tiff.

* * *

Jonas took my keys and opened the front door, talking on the phone as he did—he was cancelling my credit cards for me, asking me for information. Jonas is a good boy. I don't deserve him. He unzipped my dress, which had wine all down its front, and dragged the satin down over my waist, my hips—it might have been erotic if he hadn't been so businesslike. He chose a new dress and pulled it over my head, leaving me to wriggle into it. Jonas isn't afraid of me. God knows I've tried to frighten him in my time, jumping out from behind doors and screaming shrilly, prank-calling him when I knew he was at home alone, bookmarking his favourite psalm with a Tarot card—the hanged man. He's never been scared of me, so he'll never run. I'm glad, so glad of that. I've tried to show gratitude. But what can I do for Jonas? Last summer I spent almost an hour blowing dandelions off their stems towards him, so that he had a chance to wish for everything he wanted. He was very polite about it, but it can't have meant much to him. Jonas thinks about eternity and other things that make wishes seem tiny and silly.

* * *

The morticians had done well with my father. He didn't even look that stiff. There was a waxiness to him, but it was more like that of a new doll's. It was almost eight years since I'd last been in the same room as him, and he looked even younger than I remembered. The sickness had made him small in his suit. I hadn't expected to be able to see that he had suffered. Now he looked cordial; it felt impossible that he could have done anything terrible, could ever have felt or thought or planned . . . if you didn't know, you could believe that this man had never done anything at all but lie there, patiently waiting for whatever happened next. His cheeks so rosy I almost laid a hand on one, for warmth. I have my father's nose. I have his ears. I touched my nose and ears. Soon they would be ashes.

Beside me, Jonas began to pray. I don't know how I knew he was praying, since he didn't speak, and his lips didn't even move. But he was praying. For a moment I tried to see this situation from Jonas's perspective. But I couldn't do it at all. I will never think the way you do, Jonas. You see, my father is a murderer, and yours is not.

Father, in my life I see
(Father in my life I see)
You are God who walks with me
(You are God who walks with me)

I looked back at my father, to see what he thought about Jonas praying. My father was amused, and I followed his lead.

*   *   *

I think I'm going to have to go—

I think I'm going to have to go.

'Go where?' S.J. asked. He was at the other end of the line. I phoned him, at home, at 4 a.m., and he answered.

'Where do you think you have to go?' S.J. asked again.

Where indeed . . .

My family was a mistake, I think. The three of us.

I'm the only one left.

I think I'm going to have to go.

'Will you come and get me?' I asked him. 'Please.'

'Now?' We were talking about a seven-hour drive through the dawn, and through rush hour. If he started now, he'd be here at about noon. Anything could have happened by noon. They were going to cremate my father at 9 a.m. It sounds amazingly stupid, but I was convinced I'd burst into flames with him. I'm bound to my father. How did this happen? I've been running from him.

'I'll come,' S.J. said.

'No.' It scared me that he was so willing. I know I'd asked him to, but his 'yes' was impossible to decipher—what was it supposed to mean?

'I want you here. For observation.'

'Haha. I'll take the train,' I said.

'All right. I'll take a couple of days off.'

'You can't. People need you.'

'So do you,' he said. 'Call me when you're on the train.'

I nodded, and I very carefully wrote down the address he gave me.

When I sat down at my computer, checking e-mail before bed, I saw that I had opened twelve identical windows, and Daphne Fox smiled coyly at me out of each one.

* * *

I'm no good at train journeys. Half an hour of scenery (which I try to admire), half an hour of the sound of the train on its track and I have seen and heard enough—my legs begin to jiggle frenetically entirely of their own accord. I began to fall asleep, but the empty seat beside me made me watchful. I didn't want to fall asleep and wake up and find someone sitting there looking at me. Yelena, Daphne, anybody. The dead are capable of creeping up on you when you aren't looking, just as capable as the living are.

I kept myself awake with phone calls—to my agent, to explain that I'd be away for a while.

'What? How long for, exactly?'

'I don't know. My father died.'

'Oh . . .' He didn't say that he was sorry—honest man, my agent: 'Take all the time you need, darling. Call me if you need anything.'

He got off the phone quickly. I called Jonas next, and told him where I was going, in case he was interested. Jonas was suspiciously enthusiastic.

'Sounds promising, Miel,' he said.

'Does it?'

He sighed.

'And it's Mary, by the way,' I said. People shouldn't think that they can call me Miel just because my father has gone, as if I'm a little girl who was hiding from an ogre. Now they're all walking around calling out that I can come out now. Well it's too late.

It took almost as long to get to Brier Moss by train as it would have by car. Six and a half hours later I climbed out of a taxi cab and walked up to a house that stood alone behind a large flat whorl of a garden, almost out of sight of the road. Grasshoppers ticked away in the bushes as I knocked on the front door. S.J. answered, in pyjamas, barefoot, and carrying a towel. Drops of water clung to his lips and ran down his chin, and as I followed him into the house he ducked his head beneath the towel and emerged with his hair standing on end. The hallway smelt strongly of polish and paint; its walls were a very strong and spotless white. No stand for coats and hats, no mat for wiping muddy feet, no carpet, even. The other downstairs rooms were unfurnished and painted the same white as the hallway, until we came to his study, which was walled with shelves that stopped only at the ceiling. There was a ladder attached to the shelves by a wooden claw, the sort of ladder I'd only seen in bookshops—on it you could move around all the books and climb, touch all of them, pluck the exact book you wanted out from amongst the rest yourself. They all looked medical—gynaecology, psychiatry, neurology.

He was watching me. 'What do you think?'

I set my bag down by the door and walked around, looking.

'Cosy.'

There was only one chair, and that was behind the desk, which faced the French doors and the late afternoon. I could see how someone would want to live only in this room and abandon the others. But nobody actually does that. You have to at least have something to look at or sit on in the other rooms, even if only for form's sake. I told myself I would wait a little while and then point that out to him. There was a plate on his desk with three squares of iced cake on it. Each had been firmly and largely bitten into just once, and then left. It seemed a strangely dainty thing to do.

'Wait here,' he said, and disappeared.

I looked out through the French doors and said to myself: 'What . . .' It was such a bare garden. Nothing flowered. There was just green grass levelled low in every direction. It was the sheer effort of maintaining these conditions that amazed me. Because things grow. Wherever there is air and light and open space, things grow. So much cutting and uprooting must be done to keep a place like this bare.

My phone rang in my pocket. It was S.J.

'Have you left the house?' My voice pitched

higher than I'd have liked it. But I hadn't heard him leave. And I didn't want to be alone in this house. He tutted.

'I'm on the roof,' he said. 'Meet me up there.'

'How—'

'Go round to the side of the house—not the side where the cedar tree is, the other side. There's a ladder. Climb up.'

I hung up and did as I was told, leaving my bronze pumps on the grass and stepping quickly into the sky—not quite running; there was dew on the soles of my feet, and the iron frame beneath me creaked a little too much for my liking. But I went up with ease, the walk was easy, and I didn't look down once.

He was waiting for me at the top, as he had said. He took my hand and pulled me off the top step and onto the flat tiles. There were two chairs ready, with a single lantern set between them. The chairs faced north, looking out over rooftops and hills and the roads dipped deep in them. The view made me dizzy; the same scene endlessly multiplied. It could have been a trick done with mirrors, vast ones. Dusk was only just falling, and I heard moths stun themselves against the lantern, the hard flicker of their wings as they sprang away again. S.J. poured whisky from a jug into shot glasses and toasted me. 'Here's to visions,' he said.

I drank, and realised it wasn't whisky. It started off like liquid gingerbread, then lingered on the tongue, deep and woody, the way I imagined tree sap tasted.

'What's this?'

'Non-alcoholic. Nutmeg, mostly.'

'Nutmeg? That's meant to be an aphrodisiac,

isn't it? It tastes nice.'

'Yes. And in large doses, it's a psychotropic agent.'

I spat my drink back into the glass. I never want visions. They're not fun.

'Mary,' he said, suddenly.

'Yes?'

'I didn't do anything to Daphne.'

'Okay.'

'I tried to take care of her—to help her. And I couldn't.'

His voice was completely steady, but he was crying. 'She slipped through my fingers every time.'

I wiped his tears away with my hands.

'Okay,' I said. 'Okay.'

'I didn't speak to anyone for three days after I found her. I mean I didn't speak to anyone who didn't have to speak to me. Nobody called. They knew what had happened, but they didn't call. I stared at the phone. I understood what was going on—I've done it myself. When someone's bereaved you think they want to be alone, or that they don't want to talk, or that they only want to talk to someone close to them. Someone closer than you are. So you don't phone. You assume that the poor bastard is being inundated with calls from other people, and you don't phone.' His voice grew halting. 'They were—long days. I wanted to talk. To anyone. I didn't want to be alone. I wanted to be with people. But mostly I stayed here. I tried not to go too far from the house, because I thought that if I got too far away I might decide not to come back. And it would be a shame not to come back. The house is all right. It didn't do anything wrong—'

'People should have called,' I said. I was angry. Why wasn't he angry? 'Even if they tried and it was engaged they should have kept trying. They didn't even try. I would have called.'

'Really?'

'Yes. And I'd have said anything that came into my head. I'd have read you the weather forecast. We should have known each other back then.'

There was something childish, something timidly happy about the way he smiled as he listened to me. As if he had been promised something so good that he was trying to manage his hope, trying not to believe it until he saw it with his own eyes.

* * *

Later he showed me where I would sleep. The room was crammed with a four-poster bed hung with grape-coloured velvet, which I gaped at as I walked around it. I heard the creaking of a rocking chair, but couldn't find the chair itself at first—the space was complicated by folding screens and empty vases and trinket boxes. I began counting the different vases, lost count, began again. At some point this room must have been bursting with flowers. Five foxgloves stood up like spread fingers in one of the vases. There was a dressing table and chair in there too, and a kind of mirror closet—it was a box of mirrors that had a latch and pulled open so that you could stand surrounded by every possible view of yourself whilst dressing.

Daphne's room. Daphne had been gone for four years. This was the state of things, him living in two rooms—just his study and a bedroom, the one next door to this. I tried not to show that it made me sad.

We undressed. He turned the light out and lay down beside me. He kissed me, and parted my legs with the stroke of his hand. He was gentle at first, and rocked slowly, then he pressed all the breath out of me, little by little. At first it was good, and then it wasn't good. Our bodies were cold and it hurt when he moved inside me. I didn't wince or cry out. I kept my eyes firmly closed.

(He'll stop once he feels that it's hurting me.)

But he didn't; he stopped when he was finished.

'I can't stay here,' he said, and he left, stumbling over things—shadows, slippers, whatever was on the floor.

Minutes pricked shallowly, like thorns. I shivered in my chemise. I'd never slept in a four-poster before—my dreams came framed by the purple velvet of the canopy. I kept waking up, or thinking that I did—I couldn't tell. This was Daphne's bed. Daphne Fox had lain here, looking up into this canopy. How had she lain? What had she looked at? Was it here that he had found her? The pounding on the door, the footsteps rushing towards the bed, the sound he made when he found her dead. He'd have shaken her, I imagine, slapped her, tried to revive her, dragged her about, knelt over her with his mouth pressed desperately to hers. Now, in her bed, I tried to find her. I lay on my front, but it was too suffocating, so I changed and lay listlessly on my side, my head on my arm, pretending to be a woman who didn't want to live. Then I turned onto my back, and cold surged all along my body. My hands followed it. How full my breasts were, how soft my stomach; in death everything froze. But my thighs were warm, and the bedclothes were soft against my back, and there was the smell of the foxgloves . . . my bones moved with suppleness under my skin as I pushed my hips upwards, rocking against my fingers . . . it became almost too much. Who is touching me? Me, it's only me, only me. The heavy wetness on my fingers, as if I'd smeared them with honey. When it was over, goosebumps forced themselves up from every patch of bare skin.

And the handle of the bedroom door clicked as it turned from the outside, and the door swung open.

I shot upright and jerked the bedclothes up around me. But no one appeared in the doorway, and when I marched up to it, there still wasn't anyone there. I looked up and down the empty passageway. In a very small voice I said: 'S.J.?'

His bedroom door was closed.

I closed mine, too, and returned to bed, only to be jolted from sleep by the sound of the door opening again. It was not a dream or any sort of reverie. There was something terrible about watching the door come open the second time. It opened all the way, and with such force that I don't know what stopped it from slamming against the wall.

I didn't call out. I closed the door again. There must be something wrong with the doorframe, or the way the door had been set in it when the place was built. It happened, doors popping open of their own accord, bad builders taken to task. The third time the door opened it felt as if I was being told very sternly to go. But go where? Get out, clear out.

I stood, half asleep, and held the door closed for two hours or so. It began to feel as if I was shaking a small, cold, smooth stump that had been proffered in place of a hand. When I'd had enough of that I sat, then lay on the blue carpet, hardly aware of what I was doing, or where I was. The door opened again as soon as I let go of the handle. Let it stay open then, let it stay open. I heaved myself back into bed as a collection of parts, concentrating on getting my arms up over the edge, torso, legs.

* * *

The next time I opened my eyes it was very early morning. I put on a pair of slippers that were beside the bed. They were just my size. Which gave me something of a jolt. But they were warm, so I left them on. I went down to S.J.'s study. The plate with the squares of cake on it was still there on his desk, and I wanted to get rid of it. It jarred me. I found it feminine. So I opened the French doors and stepped outside, showering moist crumbs amongst some finches and sparrows who were already pecking at the grass outside. There were seeds in the cake, and it smelt of rum. I hoped the birds wouldn't get too drunk. I wiped my hand on my skirt. Then I stood near the twisted cedar tree, staring. There was just enough light for the leaves to glow. I imagined touching a branch and watching it rise, followed by another branch and another, the trailing leaves parting so that I could step into the space the tree guarded, the secret place it hunched over for safekeeping from the sun.

S.J. came out of the house and stood beside me.

'Morning.'

Tentatively, without looking at me, he held out his hand. I took it and held it clasped to my chest. I didn't look at him either. We were eyeing the cedar.

'Morning.'

'What shall we do today?' he asked.

We went out walking, wrapped round in scarves and jackets. We tramped down lanes and places in the earth that seemed to have been dug and rubbed until granite came through, then abruptly left. We passed signs with names like 'Merrymeet' and 'Tremar' and 'Saint Cleer' written on them, and by the time we crossed a low stone bridge with its feet in a shallow pebbled brook our landscape was three-quarters blue. I began to step gingerly, even though I could see that the ground was firm all around me. There was so much sky that it felt as if we were on a precipice—there was not enough grass to stand on, it was so thin and flat by comparison. We walked around a barrow that rose from the long earth in the shape of a taut shoulder. Every now and again a bird coasted overhead, spreading shadows with the flap of its wings, and I would move uneasily, thinking that it must be coming for us, since there was nothing else for miles but flat tors and, in the distance, a hill so vast that it looked both broken and smooth as the eye tried to absorb its image all at once. I ruined my boots in what felt like an unending series of turf pits that had stored the previous week's rainfall. I struggled in the last pit, thinking I was sinking, and S.J. crooked his arm and stood still on a safe spot, so I could take his elbow and step out. We came to a halt by a lake that seemed to have clouds in it even though it was a clear day. The moor swept on after the water interrupted it, and looking at the other side I felt doubled; without turning I could see what was behind me. S.J. told me stories about the lake. He was a good storyteller; matter-of-fact, convincing. Excalibur had come out of this lake, he said, and I saw no reason to disbelieve him. I saw kites go up. Small figures rushed along up the hill, their wrists and fists leashed to the bright creatures in the sky. I want to stay here, I thought. I want to stay.

In the evening S.J. worked, even though he'd said he wouldn't, sat in the study with huge books opened up all around him, underlining bits of the case studies he was taking notes from. I looked at some cookbooks for a while, then left him and went upstairs, to the blue room. With dramatic bravado, I switched all the lights on and went through Daphne's things, moved them around recklessly, daring her. If I was afraid that something bad would happen, why wait? Why not make it happen now?

Some papers had been folded into a square and pushed into a corner at the back of one of the dressing-table drawers. The words were written in faded, grainy pencil strokes—I had to hold them under the lamp to make them out properly. There was a lot of crossing out. They were the same few sentences, over and over. Different drafts. The last one read:

I've drunk quite a lot of bleach. Enough to kill me, I shouldn't wonder. I did it on purpose.

Daphne

I put my head down on the desk because I felt

braver with my head supported. In the corner of the last note, written in small letters and lightly, was *L 11: 24–26*. Without lifting my head, I dragged a King James pocket Bible, covered in white leather, out of another drawer in the dressing table. I set it in front of my nose and looked through it.

Leviticus . . . Lamentations . . . Luke . . . well, it couldn't be Lamentations, because that only had five chapters.

The Leviticus passage was incomplete; the first sentence of it referred to the sentence before it, and the last sentence was an admonition against eating pork and mutton.

Luke said:

When the unclean spirit is gone out of a man, he walketh through dry places, seeking rest; and finding none, he saith, I will return unto my house whence I came out.

And when he cometh, he findeth it swept and garnished.

Then goeth he, and taketh to him seven other spirits more wicked than himself; and they enter in, and dwell there: and the last state of that man is worse than the first.

My gaze snagged on two parts of the passage again and again:

I will return unto my house whence I came out

Seven spirits more wicked than himself.

I read the passage aloud. I couldn't help it. Better that than keep it as a thought.

As I said the last word, the rocking chair groaned behind me.

Exactly as if someone had sat down in it.

And the chair began to rock.

I changed my mind—I didn't want her there. I didn't.

I ran, leaping three steps at a time, coming down so hard I almost turned my ankle.

S.J. looked up when I re-entered the study, breathless.

'What is it?' he asked. There was a note in his voice—as if he knew.

'Nothing.'

I lay down at his feet, my breasts against the rug. I turned the pages of a cookbook and pretended to read, but really I was imagining him walking across my back; his heel grinding into the base of my spine, the next step pushing the vertebrae away from each other; by the time he reached my neck I'd be in pieces. He wouldn't do it, but he could—he had the ability. With his lips and hands he refigured me, coaxed me into moving so closely with him that we disappeared and left a trail of sighs behind us. Not just in the bed. Against walls, across tables, on floors with my heels dancing the same pleading two steps over his shoulder blades. But we didn't go into the blue room again.

'Where's all the downstairs furniture?' I asked him, in the morning.

He looked wary. 'In the cellar,' he said.

There was a little platform immediately inside the cellar door, and a staircase leading straight down. It was gloomy once the door had closed behind us.

'You first,' S.J. said in my ear.

So I went first, sending a torch beam ahead of me with one hand and feeling my way with the other. S.J.'s hands collided with mine, and I heard him breathing behind me. There were a lot of chairs and tables packed into a very small amount of space; it was like climbing out into a sea of brocade and velvet padding. Insects wriggled around between the armchairs, and chair legs fell apart as I moved them out of my way; I picked bits up and saw they were worn through with holes. Woodworm. We stayed down there until we'd identified some pieces that were salvageable, taking turns sitting on each chair and leaning against each table to be sure. It was a slow, airless hour, full of rustling, like someone whispering through cloth. From time to time I trained the torch on S.J. He kept looking at me, looking away, then back at me, quietly surprised that I was still there.

We dragged the whole pieces out and arranged them in the rooms they belonged to. The place began to look less like an austere puzzle. I tampered with his placement of the sofas and armchairs and side tables and vases, and he tampered ceaselessly with mine. When we caught each other in the act we pretended we hadn't seen. Those were the rules of playing house.

*　　*　　*

The next afternoon we went down to a cove in the opposite direction from the one we'd taken to get to the moor. It was only a little cove; it sloped down to the water smoothly. Gravely, as if guiding me into the deep of his secrets, S.J. showed me the markings on the stones he collected. Darkness fell and we stripped down to wetsuits and walked into the sea. When we tired of swimming I just floated and span in the gloss of the water and he bobbed beside me. We were top and tails; he held my ankle so I didn't float away too far.

I texted Jonas: *Happy*.

And he sent the word back to me: *Happy*.

I ignored my agent's phone calls and deleted the threats he left me via voicemail—I was smiling in a way that felt new, so fresh it was like another face, and I didn't want to stop. Not even for the moment needed to take one of those pictures people said were so good, the ones in which a girl with blank and shiny eyes stood on one leg, looked over her shoulder, was an acrobat, was no one.

* * *

The day S.J. went back to work I dashed around Brier Moss, buying things to cook for a dinner party in the evening. He wanted me to meet some of his friends. Two female friends and two male friends. They were all single, so he was also hoping to set them up. I bought candles and flowers and artichokes and steak and braced myself for a frosty reception from the single female friends. It wasn't unlikely that they had stayed single in the hopes that he might suddenly fall for them. When I came back from town I went into S.J.'s study, to fetch a cookbook. He'd left the French doors open, and in going to close them, I almost trod on a finch. The bird lay on its back in between the doors and didn't take fright at my drawing so near. Its beak and feet pointed at the sky, blackened, as if blasted by flame. It had died with its eyes open and some liquid in them congealing. And there were more just outside. I stopped counting after ten. They were all in the same condition. There were more birds chirping from somewhere, there were still birds, still singing, but I couldn't see them. *They must be very high up.* For a moment I thought I'd be sick, but I wasn't sick. The majority of the bodies were congregated in an uneven half-ring around the cedar tree. *Oh* . . . my eyes flickered closed—for a moment I saw myself standing on the grass, cake flowing from my hand like sand—my eyes opened again. I used a rolled-up magazine to push the bodies towards each other, into a heap. I wanted to dig, so that I could bury them, but I had nothing to dig with. I tried a little with my hands, and it took a long time to make even the slightest pocket in the ground. I had to cook the food, I had to get ready for guests. I didn't want people to arrive and find me here, scrabbling in the earth with my fingernails. I just had to leave the birds where they were.

I went into the kitchen and stood beside the Aga, staring at the wall. It was on; it had been on all morning. I'd laughed at it when I first saw it, but it gave off serious warmth. Dinner would be ready, possibly even burnt, in no time. And then I would have nothing to do.

I think I'm going to have to go.

I grasped gratefully at that thought. I became busy. I chopped the steak and made a marinade for the artichokes. I closed the kitchen door and lined the bottom of it with tea towels. I opened the oven door and knelt down and breathed blue, dancing gas. I coughed, but without urgency. I was dizzy and the heat around me was not unpleasant; it was like being lost in a fog when you had nowhere in particular to go. It didn't matter. I collapsed onto my stomach and looked to the side, not that there was anything to see, apart from grey-coated metal.

I began to choke. I couldn't move. I wanted to, but my head wouldn't do it—the fog was in it.

I heard a distant sound—a dial turning.

The Aga shut down. No more blue, just gaping blackness.

Someone was crouching near me. She put her hand on my leg. My skin shrieked. I can't explain how it felt. There was movement beneath her fingernails.

'You're an idiot,' she said. Her voice wasn't at all the way I'd imagined it. It was clear and firm.

'Nothing's wrong here. Can't you see that? Nothing's wrong. Next time just don't feed the birds with cake that's been experimentally laced with pharmaceuticals. You listen to me, Mary Foxe, or whatever your name is. Stay here. There's a decent man here who will probably fall for you if you don't make a mess of things. He'll take care of you. And you take care of him. No point having any more death.'

My mother. My father. I couldn't speak.

'Yes,' she said. 'I know. But you're what happens next. That's all I wanted to tell you upstairs, but you ran like—like the Hound of the Baskervilles or something.'

'Thank you, Daphne,' I whispered.

'Oh, yes, you owe me one. So you'll tell him?'

'Tell him what?'

'That it's not his fault about me. Because it's not.'

'I'll tell him.'

'Don't just say it. Make him believe it.'

'How—'

'*Make him believe it.*' She squeezed my ankle.

'I will!'

'I'm tired,' she said. 'I'm going now. Be bad. Be wicked. And you should worry. But don't.'

Mary stayed out of my way for a couple of weeks. I was busy with Daphne, trying to get her to like me again and call off the death threats from her friends. I began teaching Daphne to drive. She was fearless—a little too fearless for my taste—and she learnt fast. She'd bought a pair of driving gloves specially, and her hands rested serenely on the wheel when it was her turn to try taking a corner. We drove down to the pheasant farm I used to shoot at when I was coming up—fifteen minutes away, but it took us thirty-five with Daphne driving. She brought a pheasant back with us and cooked it up for dinner—it was the worst meal I'd ever encountered, but I choked it down and appreciated it. She was trying, and I was trying. It'd be wrong to say my wife hasn't got any go in her. On our honeymoon she spent the best part of a morning leaping around a rock garden, bouncing from ledge to ledge like a lunatic and singing some almost offensively sugary song. She slipped, and twisted her ankle, but she didn't howl about it. She bit her lip and she cried a little, because, she said, she didn't want to pretend it didn't hurt. And she hobbled around good-humoredly, taking snapshots and studying the gaudy little paintings for sale on the streets just as solemnly as if they were up in a gallery. Remembering that she'd cried, I got a doctor to look at her ankle for her when we got back to the hotel. It was a sprain. I'd have understood if she'd howled.

Another day we drove down to the state park. It's called the Devil's Hopyard. That was a pretty good afternoon. Close to the waterfall each tree quivers as if trying to shake itself awake from a bad dream without waking the others up. And the stones all around the waterfall itself are half hollowed out—we looked at stone after stone for almost an hour. The hollows were definite, as if someone had come along with a scoop and removed the heart of each stone.

'These are the reason this place is called the Devil's Hopyard,' I told Daphne. 'People round here used to say the devil himself made the marks in the stones with his hooves as he walked over them . . .'

'It's the only explanation,' Daphne said, solemnly. I found myself playing with her hair—just sort of mussing it and walking my fingers down the strands until they fell back into place again.

'How's Mary?' she asked me, almost straight-faced. Almost.

'Mary who?' I asked.

That night, after love, she rolled away from me and sat up in her own bed. I was falling asleep, but she sat in a way that demanded I look at her. She had her hand on the top of her head, as if trying to keep something in.

'What is it?' I asked. I stretched out an arm. 'Come back!' She stayed where she was.

'I've just got to go and—you know.' She was whispering as if she didn't want to be overheard. Even though we were the only ones in the house.

'Oh—okay, honey. Good thing you remembered.' Daphne sponged with Lysol disinfectant to keep from getting pregnant. It worked, too. She hadn't wanted a kid when we got married, and I hadn't argued.

I closed my eyes. Daphne didn't move. I felt her weight a few inches away, warm and still. I opened my eyes again. She was looking at me and her smile had crumpled.

'What? Have we run out?'

'No.'

'What is it, D?'

'You want me to? You want me to go and—you know?'

'You don't want to.' I was alarmed, and I sounded alarmed. It wasn't the thought of a baby, per se. It was just the sudden change; she might as well have pulled the mattress right out from under me.

She smiled. Falsely, brightly. She scrambled out of bed. 'Okay. Thanks for letting me know how you feel.'

'D. Hold on. Hold on just a second—'

She vanished into the bathroom. I went up to the closed door and heard nothing. The taps didn't turn on. She might have opened the cupboard and reached for the yellow bottle that sat between my razor and her set of heated curlers, but if she had, then she'd done it with infamous and unnecessary stealth. After a few more minutes I became convinced she'd climbed out of the window and run off into the night. I knocked on the door. 'D.'

'Yes, darling.'

'Are you going to come out?'

'Yes, in a minute.'

There are things I should have said to her then, but I didn't say any of them. I thought I'd tell her when she came out. She didn't come out. She was still in there when I fell asleep. I woke up at some point before dawn and she was there in bed beside me, nestled up against me. She'd taken my arm and put it around her. And I was grateful. Pathetically grateful. Next time the matter came up, I would say the things I knew I should say.

Very early the next morning we walked down to Cloud Cove and walked out across the sand to the island; it was accessible on foot when the tide was out, and I wanted to show Daphne the lighthouse. I own it—I mean, I inherited it, and just like my father, who inherited it from his father, I don't know what the hell to do with it so I just make sure it gets a good spring-cleaning from top to bottom three times a year and keep some books there. My great-grandfather won the place in a game of cards. I always think I might go over there to work, but I never do.

Daphne and I didn't talk much on the way over. We picked up bits of driftwood, shells and pebbles, and arranged them on the ground when we felt we'd carried them too far away from where we'd picked them up. The wind nipped us through our clothes.

'Oh God,' Daphne said, as the lighthouse came into view. She said, 'Oh God,' again and again with every step we took towards it. 'It looks *evil.*'

It wasn't evil. It was just a white tower with long slits for windows. Not even a particularly tall tower. She liked it better when we were inside and she saw that it was spick and span and modern. I took her up to the lantern room, and she stared at the lantern through the glass panels. It was the size of a man, and covered in dust. I pointed out the lenses that surrounded it, and explained how they refracted the light from the lantern and made it fly out in all directions the way she'd seen it in movies. When I took her to the watch room she insisted on turning the handles that rotated the lamp lenses. We heard the lenses whirring—not a comfortable sound to have above you—like huge wings flapping in place—but there was no kerosene in the lamp and even if there had been, it was morning, so the whole thing was a pretty pointless exercise.

'You must have loved this place as a boy,' she said, as we came down the spiral staircase. 'It must have been like a four-storey playground.' She'd brought some log books down with her, clutched against her chest, even though I'd warned her that all she'd find written there was times and dates and comings and goings and observations on what direction the wind was coming from.

'Not really,' I told her. 'I didn't see the point of it.'

'All right, well—normal kids would love it . . .'

She'd brought a flask full of coffee and some rolls, and we had those at the kitchen table. She looked over the log books, lost interest after about four pages, as I had predicted, but soldiered on. I left her at the table and went to go and pack up a few books I wanted. I dragged a couple of crates over to the back door, so I could look out at the sea while I searched—the tide was high, and choppy, but not so that I couldn't see across the cove. I looked from my books to the water, from my books to the water—sunlight flashed once, twice, three times on the waves. The fourth time I saw that it wasn't light. It was a hand, raised up at the end of an arm, and it was waving at me. Gradually, Mary Foxe walked out of the sea and paced across the sand towards me. She wasn't smiling. Her hands were behind her back. She looked as if she had a lot on her mind. Once she was standing directly before me, she dropped a curtsey.

'Mary.'

'Yes, Mr Fox?'

'I think I know what we're trying to do with this game of ours.'

'Tell me.'

'We've been trying to fall in love—'

She raised her eyebrows. 'With each other?' she asked, coolly.

'Would you let me finish?'

'With plcasure.'

'We've been trying to fall in love—yes, with each other—but we've been trying to take some of the danger out of it. So no one ends up maimed, or dead. We're trying for something normal and nice.'

Mary folded her arms. 'That is *not* what we're trying to do.'

'Oh. What, then?'

'Your wife loves you. Turn to her. Properly. Stop fobbing her off and being a counterfeit companion. It would be good if, after all this, just once you wrote something where people come together instead of falling apart. Just show me you can do it and I'll leave you alone.'

'But I don't want you to leave me alone.'

She turned to face the sea. The wind whipped her hair around. Her hair is a miraculous color, like autumn leaves shaken down around her shoulders. She looked wild and lovely.

'Mary. If you were real I'd run away with you for ever.'

I went to her; we faced each other. She said: 'You're cruel, Mr Fox.' Her voice, her eyes. She was weary.

My heart was doing that jerking thing it did when I'd thought Daphne might leave me, but worse. Much, much worse. Almost unbearable. I was about to go off like a bomb or something. It actually hurt.

(Please don't let me keel over on the sand at this woman's feet.)

'I would like to have breakfast with you,' Mary Foxe said. 'And I would like to have you defer a little to my tastes and habits—at present I have none, because you haven't given me any. I'd like to go to dinner parties with you and play charades. I'd like to have friends to lend me books and tell me secrets. I would like to have nothing to do with you for hours on end and then come back and find you, come back with things I've thought and found out all on my own—on my own, not through you. I'd like not to disappear when you're not thinking about me.'

She enunciated her words very slowly and carefully. As she spoke I saw that I'd proposed the impossible.

'So if you *did* find some way for me to be real and for me to be together with you, then I wouldn't mind that. I wouldn't mind at all.'

'Honey,' Daphne called out. 'Shouldn't we go before it gets dark?'

Mary wasn't there any more. She'd never passed

out of my sight so abruptly before.

I was shaken, and Daphne mustn't know that I was shaken. I'd told her she had nothing to worry about where Mary was concerned. I'd said it wasn't 'like that'. Had I lied? To Daphne? Or just now, to Mary? I'll say anything to get out of a spot. I counted to ten, holding my chest like a fool, like Young Werther guarding his sorrows, then I went to Daphne. She was sitting on the front steps with a paperback. It had to be *War and Peace*—it was thick enough. The title was in Cyrillic, and so were all the contents.

'Is that . . . Russian?' I asked her.

She answered in words that left me stone cold. Russian, I presumed.

'Daphne!' It made her laugh, the way I was looking at her.

She winked. 'Don't worry, I'm not possessed. I said I'm just brushing up. I've been taking a correspondence course. You've got a lot to find out about me, my friend.'

She looked a little cold, so I put my jacket around her shoulders and we strolled down to wait at the post where the ferry came in. And she leaned against me, and it was all right.

hide, seek

Once, in Asyût, east of Cairo, a boy was born to a market-trading family fallen on hard times, a family too poor to keep him unless he had somehow been born full-grown and ready to work. The boy's tiny mother had given birth to five big, healthy, noisy boys before him. But the first thing this particular boy did when he was born was cough quietly, and turn a blind, bewildered glare on his brothers, who elbowed each other and watched him closely. This new boy was far too small. He had to be spanked six times before he proved his lungs to the midwife, and even then, his cry wasn't lusty enough. He was limp and wouldn't cling to a finger when it was placed in his palm. He refused his mother's breast, wrinkling his nose at the knotty brown bud of her nipple with slow bafflement.

Yet his eyes said that he needed something.

The boy's mother saw into the future. Her mind hunkered down in the midst of her tiredness and spread the dead circle of her nerves until it overlapped into her next life, her next fatigue. The boy's mother saw that she wouldn't be able to coax this son, to coddle him, to silently cherish him, to let him fall and find no help, to do all of the things that it would take for this boy to survive into his strength as a man.

(She looked into his eyes—they were like a famine. Seeing them sent hurt and light through her. His eyes kept asking, asking, and she knew that a person could die trying to love him.)

If it hadn't been certain before, the decision not to keep the boy was now absolute.

'He will not be strong,' the boy's father winced, when news of the birth was brought to him at his sand-blown stall. 'He will not be of use.' He didn't tell the other men whose threadbare robes jostled his at market because it was not a good thing to have to send a child away.

'He will not be strong,' the midwife said, averting her eyes from the child's. She left as soon as she could, with promises that she would tell all the doctors she knew about the child, in the hope that they knew of some infertile couple.

Sunset on the outskirts of Asyût brought clarity.

Even from the narrow side-streets where damp sand beads and breathes, any window can tell you why they say here the world began with a brother and sister locked in a beautiful circus trick. In Egypt, like everywhere, the land is made to fit the sky; but here it is more so. Here it is possible to say 'this is land' and point, and 'this is sky', and point, but the eye can't discover the dividing line. Nut cranes her neck over her long lithe blue back to kiss Geb, and Geb cradles her, careful, because she is nothing, less than nothing, but if he should drop her it would be the end of everything. The boy's mother was comforted by sunset, and she closed the shutters and began preparing her new son's cot.

The next day's noon came like a blazing hoop, and the sun spat razorblades through it. People did what they had to to keep from wilting. Slim women waddled; fat women crept close to the ground, barely taking steps. Amongst them came a tall, ramrod-straight woman in pure black; she parted the jostling knots of people in bounding spurts, like a dark thought. She was accompanied by the boy's midwife.

The woman took the market traders' son away with her because, she said, she needed a seeker, and this boy was one.

The woman's voice was soft and you had to listen hard for it, otherwise you thought she was trying to speak to you with her eyes alone. The atmosphere around this woman told of books and fine rugs. The boy's mother cried and held herself, held her leaking breasts as the woman took her son away. But she didn't change her mind.

* * *

A girl was born in Osogbo, in a small hospital a few feet away from a stone shrine to love. The girl was a heavy baby, with features that were pleasing because they were fluid and made her simple to look at, as if she was carved all of a piece. The girl was very quick learning to walk, speak in both English and Yoruba, eat solids, use her potty, smile in a certain way that brought maturity down like an axe on her face. At six years old, she prostrated herself before her elders unasked. She clambered over her milestones with unassailable, businesslike calm. No cute lisping, no unusual habits. It took the girl's parents a long time to realise that their daughter's docility and sweetness was in fact vacancy, a kind of sleepiness and an instinct for ease that translated itself to her entire body. The girl's hair grew soft and light so that combs flashed through it without tangling, so that it sat well in plaits. Blemishes fell away from the girl's skin with simple soap and water. The same question put to this girl two times in a row would yield two different answers, depending on who asked the girl the question, and in what tone. The day that he saw that it was enough, the girl's father was chauffeuring a sweaty, bearded oil executive to the airport. The girl's father looked away for a moment from the well-fed face, from the firm, confident mouth of his passenger in the rear-view mirror, and saw his daughter following a street vendor home, nodding and smiling in the shade of the bush-lined thoroughfare, a sack of the street vendor's rice piled across her shoulders with a sturdy, troubling grace. The girl's father bundled her into the car without ceremony or apology to his passenger, and at home he thrashed her with a walking cane. He held her head down on the kitchen table as he beat her, and his fingers dug into her scalp, but he did not feel her neck tensing against him, and she didn't make a sound. He kept on hitting her because he wasn't sure whether she was feeling this or not. The neighbours came en masse, some with their fingers entwined in the fur at the scruff of their goats' necks, and they remonstrated with him. Women pulled off their head wraps and wrung their hands. 'It is too much,' everyone told him. The girl's father stopped when he was tired of hammering on her bones. He watched her breathing; her shoulder blades rose and fell with her head turned away from him and into the table. When she lifted her head she said unsteadily, 'Sorry, Daddy.' Blood welled from the space between her lips.

* * *

The boy grew up with a hard smile and a complicated manner that was at once condescending and eager. He developed a gait that made him seem arrogant. These were attempts to counteract his eyes and their treacherous tendency to ask. He wasn't handsome, or talkative, but his adoptive mother made sure that he dressed well, in English tailoring and American denim. And his sadness was luminous. Girls his age gave him kisses and held his hand even when they shied away from other boys. Women offered him honeyed pastries, confidences, concern. He walked the markets and puffed pipe smoke in corner tea houses, breathed in the spice-pod musk of men and took their advice with throwaway thanks.

The woman who had adopted him was a widow, and it was possible that her bereavement had made her mad. The boy's new home terrified him, because the downstairs was bright and softly pastel-coloured and air-conditioned, but the upstairs was cordoned off. If he looked hard enough, he could make out doors and bare floors, but that was all. At night he slept on a couch beside the woman who had adopted him; the woman herself slept on a boat-shaped chaise-longue, it took to her body in a way that he would never see again, let her sleep with grace although her arms and legs were bunched up and her feet were hanging off the end of the couch. It didn't seem to matter very much that the woman didn't grow older as he grew older, either, though he suspected that something about the woman herself slowed him down, bathed his thoughts in perfume, set his dreams afloat so that his mind was abuzz with stranger things than her age, or her solitude, or the silent upstairs.

The woman insisted on being called mother.

(Which the boy called her, but with a secret hiss that came from a place inside him that he did not understand—inside his head her name became *motherhhhhhhh*, smothered myrrh.)

She was an art collector, but she only collected art that was body pieces, one considered piece at a time, painstaking finds because she was looking for a collection that, when put together in a room, would create the suggestion of a woman, a woman who crammed the room from wall to wall. The boy took telephone calls and messages left for his new mother by her contacts all over the world. He travelled Egypt with her and observed cemetery graffiti as she did, so closely that she almost inhaled it—in hundreds of perfumeries they watched glass-blowers torture air between their hands, force it to become solid.

Always, as they travelled, she pointed and asked him, 'Do you like that? What do you see there?'

He told her the truth, and she always listened to him. She said that he chose well.

But when they got home, the boy did not ever feel anything in the presence of these well-turned ankles and smooth calves, these arms and shoulders captured in shade and the moment of motion. They were a collection, not a woman.

Then the boy and his mother got a face for their collection. The face was a photograph. The photograph was of a girl who had died with her family one night when her neighbours smashed the door down and took an axe to all the living inside that house. The neighbours did this because a radio broadcast told them to. The radio broadcast advised them not to wait for the evil that lived next door to grow and get the better of them. And so it was done. But after killing the family, the neighbours had not touched anything else in the girl's house, which is how the boy and his new mother, picking over this room at the end of a series of devastated rooms, found the girl's picture. At first the boy thought that it would be wrong to take the picture. But it was a picture unlike any other. It had been taken in the back yard of the house, at some point between the sun's disappearance and the illumination of the moon. The girl's smile did not seem to correspond to the presence of the camera, or even to a joke told off-camera. Her smile was unnerving because it had no reason. They took the picture home, even though the boy's new mother complained that it wasn't art. Then the boy's new mother asked him what he thought of their almost complete collection, waved her arms at all the fineness and said, 'You want someone. Is she here?'

He said, 'No.'

'We need a heart,' the boy's new mother said, and when she looked at him, in that moment, she seemed to him so high. It seemed that her feet connected to the ground only tenuously and it was her shadow that bore her up. The boy thought in that moment that this woman must be beautiful, no of course she was; fine eyes, wide-curved lips, and cheekbones like slanted hooks. But at the same time he thought that his new mother must be a spider.

*　　*　　*

What nobody knew about the docile girl from Osogbo was that her heart was too heavy, and that almost from birth she had felt its weight, a gravitational pull that invited her to her grave. Her heart was heavy because it was open, and so things filled it, and so things rushed out of it, but still the heart kept beating, tough and frighteningly powerful and meaning to shrug off the rest of her and continue on its own. People soon learnt that they could play on her sympathy, and, because she was terrified that one day this unasked-for conscience of hers might kill her, she gave away whatever money she earned, gave away bread and went without. The girl tried, several times, to give her love away, but her love would not stay with the person she gave it to and snuck back to her heart without a sound. What people didn't know about this girl was that the ancestral dead kept her company—they came to find her at bathtime and sat four at a time in the bathwater with her, cooing wistfully and using their wasted, insubstantial hands to wash her hair. The girl urged them to take care of their own children, but they refused. Her head lolled at these times and she was overcome with gratitude. At bedtime the dead took her with them, and in her dreams, she visited their graves.

At first, in rebellion against her heaviness, the girl thought that she needed to be thinner, and she took to reading imported women's magazines on credit from a bookstall owner. The magazines talked about calories and saving calories and keeping some back so that you could have a glass of wine. One day at the dinner table, the girl asked her mother for an estimate of how many calories there were in the fried stew that bubbled at the bottom of her bowl beneath a layer of *eba*. There is no Yoruba word for calories, and so her mother just looked at her and said musingly, smilingly, in English, 'Calories,' as if she was trying to understand a punchline hidden in between the syllables. Then the girl didn't ask any more and just sat looking at the food, which was bottomless and made to sink hunger.

The girl decided that she had to hide her heart somewhere until she was big enough to keep hold of its weight. One night the dead helped her, some stroking her hair and soothing her while others hooked their fingers into her and carefully lifted a strand of steam from her chest. The girl took her heart, and that cool night she was frightened even though she walked amidst a crowd of other people's ancestors. The shrine was a rectangle of stone arches that spoke of other kinds of love—strange, ugly, smoke and choking sort of love, carvings of cruel hands that killed candle flames to break refusal in the dark, women thrusting out hard breasts and genitals. Also in the carvings was the kind of love that wakes you up from nightmares. And also there was a sundial of wise children's faces. The shrine was the kind of place where a Valentine's heart would have trembled and wilted. With her fingers the girl scratched a place for herself in the north wall and slipped her heart through into the dry moss behind the stone.

And she walked away, and she walked away, and that was that, and that was that.

*   *   *

Because he had been told to, the boy looked for hearts. He examined unusual playing cards and alabaster chess pieces and went to London with his new mother to examine posters plastered onto the walls of public-transport stations. On the boy's twenty-first birthday, his new mother took him to the west coast of his continent to view a shrine, a shrine where, one of their contacts had told her, you could hear and feel a heart beating when it grew dark. They stood, amidst a small crowd of other curious people, and waited for sunset, which came with a slow earthquake that sent the ground slipping away, until they realised that the sensation was the legendary heartbeat. The boy, now a man, stood a little apart from his new mother, who listened intently, and the heartbeat said things to them both, things that made the boy smile with all of his soul in his face, things that made the new mother suck in her cheeks and look suddenly pinched and old. They stayed long after everyone had gone, and fell asleep at dawn with their heads laid on rocks converted to pillows with thick shawls.

When the next morning came around, the asking in the man's eyes was so powerful that no one could look at him without offering, offering, offering.

*   *   *

The girl was lighter without her heart. She danced barefoot on the hot roads and her feet were not cut by the stones or glass that studded her way. She spoke to the dead whenever they visited her.

She tried to be kind, but they realised that they no longer had anything in common with her, and she realised it, too. So they went their separate ways. Other people became closed to the girl, and she enjoyed it this way—at the market place she handed over her bread and exacted the correct payment for it with a slight pressure of the hand and an uncaring smile. When the girl moved amongst people, she felt as if she were walking in a public place at an hour of the night when it was too dark to come out, or at noon, when it was too hot to be outside, and all the doors around were closed and barred. The girl felt this solitude to be an adventure. She moved away from her parents and went to live by herself on the ground floor of a tenement, even though this was frowned upon. When she was not working or wandering, she listened to the white noise inside her head, or she sat on her bare floor and listened to people arguing, romancing, accusing, the people all around her, she let their words fall into her body like coins into a bottomless well. Sometimes she thought about her heart, and wondered how it was doing without her. But the girl was never curious enough to go and find out.

Except once, when she almost went back to see.

Except once, when she woke up one morning convinced that she was in love. All over her, her skin felt softer even than her breath, and her eyes felt wider, clearer, dreamy, lashed and lidded with an unknown stuff that had drawn a man in. For a week, she washed and dried and rubbed cream into her body with a special, happy care, and she realised that she was preparing her body for caresses. She found a taste for cold things that released their sweetness slowly—ice cream that slid down her throat before she could taste it, tinned peaches in chill syrup.

But there was no heart there in her chest.

When the girl remembered this, she forced herself to eat a bite of mashed plantain, and the first swallow was hard. But after that, life stepped straight again.

* * *

The man's new mother told him, 'That heart, that heart in the shrine, it's the heart that we must take for my collection.' And then the art collection, the beautiful woman, the new mother's obsession, would be complete. 'If only we can locate the heart and take it with us,' the man's new mother said, watching her new son closely.

The heart had told him, it had called to him, *Come. Take from me, I am inexhaustible.*

But the man said nothing.

'I know that you know where that heart is,' the man's new mother said, and she bared teeth as sharp as daggers. 'You are a seeker, you find things. Bring it to me.'

The man told his new mother to give him five days. He ground valerian root into her tea to make her sleep, and the new mother slept with a beauty like rose and earth, and her bitterness was a weed whose roots were scourged by her sleep, and so her bitterness fell away.

The man moved the collection, in carefully packaged batches, to the Osogbo shrine. It was a cry to the owner of the heart, this offering; he would not take the heart from the walls of the shrine until she came. He looked at all the love carved into the stone, and it was a lot of love, and he believed that it must be enough; he had to believe that it was enough. He arranged the fragmented woman as best he could, and sometimes he felt as if unseen hands helped him, propped a canvas in such a way that the light enhanced it. The man was desperate now, and he asked the heart to call to its owner, for she was the strength that he had somehow been born separately from.

The heart called.

The heart called.

The man called.

The gathered woman, scattered across sculptures and glass and photographs and scraps of paper, the gathered woman became complete and almost breathed.

Almost.

The man waited for five days. He thought that he must surely die under the sun and the pain of this disaster. But he didn't die, because the shrine stones protected him.

When on the sixth day the man saw that the heart's owner did not come, he left that place.

I don't think my husband likes me. And I don't know how to make him. I try talking to him about books, and when he replies he won't look me in the eye, and sometimes his voice is muffled, suppressing a coughing fit . . . or laughter. I think it's important to be able to laugh at yourself—I hate people who are always offended. But when you've got to be prepared to laugh at yourself every single time you open your mouth . . . well, that's just depressing. I asked Greta for advice and she gave this tiny scream, as if she'd just heard the funniest words ever uttered, and she said: 'Oh, did you marry him for the intellectual conversation? You didn't even finish college, Daphne.'

I took her point, even though it was unfair of her to bring that up. College was a near-fatal bore. I had some really serious nosebleeds just at the thought of going to lectures. Gush, gush, gush, and afterwards I had to sit still for a couple of hours on account of having lost a lot of blood—doctor's orders. Philosophy! I must have been crazy. I only did it because they told me at school that I was smart, and gave us all these thrilling speeches about the privileges and responsibilities of women in higher education. I can learn things, all right; I don't deny that I can learn things. But I can only learn them when it isn't important. If someone tells me something and then says: 'Well, you'd better remember that, because in three months' time I'm going to make a decision about you based on whether you've remembered or not,' then it's all over and there's nothing I can do about it. Pops says he loves me just the way I am, but not everyone in the world is like my father. Maman, for example. A difficult and dissatisfied woman. She made me learn flower arranging and how to walk properly—books on my head, the whole bit. These things ruined me for life. Now it sets my teeth on edge when I see flowers carelessly flung into a vase, and I'm forever looking at other women in the street and thinking, 'Sloppy . . . sloppy.' And I know I shouldn't care, and I want to poke myself in the eye for caring, but I care anyway, so thanks for that, Maman. I guess most mothers are difficult and dissatisfied, though. I haven't heard of any easy-going ones, unless they're dead and everyone's being nice about them. But even then they don't say: 'She was real easy-going,' they talk about her sacrifice and how she had time to get involved in everyone's business. Anyway. My mind is wandering. I know that's because I'm thinking crazy thoughts and I don't want to be thinking them. I liked St John because he's different from the boys I grew up with. Nothing like John Pizarsky or Sam Lomax; they just shamble around like they always did, only in nice clothes they buy for themselves now. I can't take them seriously. Now St John could have been born into his elegance. It's a dangerous kind of elegance—he doesn't raise his voice, he lowers it. Sometimes he says something funny and when I laugh he looks at me and asks what I'm laughing at, as if he'd genuinely like to know. And he's a solitary type . . . but when he comes back from wherever he's gone he can look so glad to see me . . .

Ordinary life just swerves around him, though, and I run off the sides like an ingredient thrown in too late. I can't stand the way he talks to me sometimes; very simply, as if to a child. The other day I suddenly realised, mid-conversation, that we two had spoken of nothing that morning but the matter of whether we ought to have calling cards made up for ourselves, to be left for friends who chanced not to be at home when we visited. Are calling cards too old fashioned, he wondered aloud. And what is the correct design and texture, and should we be Mr and Mrs Fox or St John and Daphne Fox, our names linked in the middle of the card or printed on separate sides of the card. He told me to consult my Emily Post, but I said I didn't have any of her books. He looked kind of surprised (I have several editions) but I lied because I don't like him thinking that these are the only things that interest me. The way he talks to me. I thought it was just his manner—I didn't mind that he never said anything romantic, not even at the very beginning—I was relieved about never having to wonder whether he really meant what he was saying. But now I'm starting to worry that this simplicity is contempt, that he picked me out as someone he could manage. I don't like to give that thought too much air, though. It'd be hard to go on if I really thought that was true.

I wish there was some level ground I could meet him on. Say he liked baseball, I could educate myself about that quite easily; just hang around while my dad and my brothers are waxing lyrical. That's easier than books. With books you've got to know all about other books that are like the one you're talking about, and it's just never-ending, and it's a pain. But this situation is fifty per cent my fault. When I was a lot younger, maybe fourteen or fifteen, I had ideas about the man I wanted. I remember a piano piece my music teacher played as part of a lesson. It was the loveliest thing I'd ever heard. People talked and passed notes all the way through it, and I wanted to shut them up at any cost, just go around with a handful of screwdrivers slamming them into people's temples. I waited until everyone had gone. Then I laid my notebook on top of the piano the music teacher had closed before he'd walked away, and I wrote his name, wrote his name, wrote his name, and underlined each version. I vowed that I wouldn't have a man unless he was someone I could really be together with, someone capable of being my better self, superior and yet familiar, a man whose thoughts, impressions and feelings I could inhabit without a glimmer of effort, returning to myself without any kind of wrench. Music. Sometimes it just makes you want to act just anyhow. I wasn't in love with the music teacher, I only wrote his name because it was a man's name.

I met St John at Clara Lee's soiree—she was great friends with my mother and at that time I had to keep meeting people and meeting people in case one of them was someone I could marry. Clara Lee basically threw this soiree with the almost express purpose of helping me, I mean, helping my mother. So there were ten or eleven clunking bores, two or three very sweet men who didn't think me sweet and a couple who obviously had something sort of wrong with them and the something wrong was the reason they were still bachelors. And then there was Mr Famous Writer; St John Fox. He must not have had anything else to do that evening. He had a terrible sadness about him. It's highly irregular for that to be one of the first things you notice about someone. I looked into his eyes, and realised, with the greatest consternation, that he was irresistible. He took me out on Sunday afternoons, and it was just calamitous—after about three of those I was done for:

So the simple maid
Went half the night repeating, 'Must I die?'
And now to right she turned, and now to left,
And found no ease in turning or in rest;
And 'Him or death,' she muttered, 'death or him' . . .

I didn't want someone I could understand without trying—I didn't want that any more. I wanted St John Fox. It turned out that he felt the same way about me. Then they lived happily ever after . . .

No. I don't think I was really that naive, thank God. I know I've got to work at this.

He went someplace this afternoon—research, he said. He didn't say where he'd be, but he did say he'd miss dinner—and I kissed him at the door. I wore a jewelled flower clip in my hair. He gave it to me himself a week ago, but today he said: 'That's pretty,' as if he had never seen it before. Oh, I don't know, I don't know. At least the dropped phone calls have stopped. They stopped once I'd told him about them. The last one was such a heavy call. She didn't just drop the receiver when I answered. She made a sound. *Pah-ha-ha-ha.* And I recognised it right away. That's how you cry when you are trying not to cry, and then of course the tears come all the harder. And do you know what I said? 'Don't . . . oh, *please* don't.' And she hung up.

Since then I've just been waiting for him to go off somewhere alone. He told me 'she's not real'—I just smiled and pretended to see what he meant. He's been spending a lot of time in his study with the door locked, but I've been biding my time. She must have written him a love letter or given him some kind of token. And if he's been fool enough to hold onto it, then I'm going to find it, and I'm going to force him to drop her in earnest. We're all better off that way. Things were tough enough without this girl coming between us. And the sound of her crying. Sometimes I try to hear it again. I wonder if it could really have been as bad as it sounded. It made me shudder—my husband is capable of making someone feel like that.

I waited for an hour, to make sure that he was really gone; then I searched his bathroom. An unlikely hiding place, but that could've been just his thinking. Then I searched his bedside drawers—nothing. I looked inside all the books in the drawing room, then went to his study again. He made a big show of not locking it before he left, so I'd know he'd forgiven me for kicking his things around a couple of months ago. I'd already searched his study, immediately after the heavy phone call, but there might have been something I'd overlooked. I sat down at his desk and looked around, trying to see some secret nook or cranny or a subtle handle I could turn. And as I looked I slowly became aware of a hand creeping across my thigh, the fingers walking down my knees.

I pushed the chair back as far as it would go; the legs made ragged scratches in the carpet because I pushed hard. I don't know if I screamed—if someone else had been there I would've been able to tell, I'd have been able to see them hearing it. But I couldn't hear anything.

Then I took my hand off my kneecap. My own hand.

Stupid Daphne. Is it any wonder he feels contempt . . .

I pretended that the past couple of minutes hadn't happened, and while I was doing that I opened his writing notebook—well, the one that was at the top of a pile of them. He'd just started it—it was empty apart from a table he'd drawn on the first page. I saw the letter D and the letter M, divided by a diagonal line. And there was talking, faster than I could follow, all in my skull and the bones of my neck, and I knew I'd found what I was looking for. Proof. But I couldn't understand it yet. I settled down and concentrated.

Under D he had written:

Is real. Is unpredictable. Is lovely to hold. Loves me (says M). Doesn't know me.

Under M he had written:

Is so many things—(too many things?). Is unpredictable. Is lovely to behold. Disapproves of me; wants more, better. There's nothing she doesn't know about me.

I sat with my head in my hands, shaking. Because the situation was so much worse than I thought. My husband was trying to choose between me, his wife, and someone he had made up. And I, the real woman, the wife, had nothing on the made-up girl. We each had five points in our favor. That son of a bitch.

I hate him, I hate him, oh God, I hate him.

I was holding my stomach. I felt sick because I

had been a fool, I'd been foolish. I'd stopped using the Lysol after we made love. I wanted to run upstairs and fix that right away, but then I thought: it might be too late. I could already be pregnant. I have a doctor's appointment tomorrow. I thought if I gave him a child—

But he's been making lists. I'm pretty sure I could have him certified insane. But then she'd win, wouldn't she, this Mary? It'd be the two of them together in the ward. Unbelievable. Horrible and unbelievable. I had to laugh. There's no one I can tell, not even Greta. There's nothing I can do about this. I measured my waist with my hands. He must have imagined her smaller about the waist than me. How much smaller . . . I pulled my hands in tight, tighter, this much smaller, this much. She was taking my breath. Taller than I am, or shorter? Taller. So she could look down on him. He seemed to like her looking down on him. I hunched over the desk with my hands in fists and my wedding ring swung from the chain around my neck.

'But it's not fair,' I said. 'You don't really exist. He could take a fall, or hit his head, and whatever part of his brain you belong to, that could suddenly shut you out. You're just a thought. You don't need him.' The sounds I'd heard down the telephone, the awful sobbing, those sounds were pouring out of me now. So many crazy thoughts kept coming—maybe I could make him take a fall—not a serious one, but it might shake him up, and she'd be gone. Or I could ask him, tell him, to stop, just stop, do whatever was necessary, he could kill her or something—what did that even mean, to kill someone imaginary—why, it was nothing at all. He could do it. He should do it, for me.

I had to get out of his study, go and get the Lysol, do something, before I started kicking his things around again. That was no way to win him over. I could see him adding to Mary's side of the list in his cheery handwriting, all apples and vowels: *She doesn't trash my study.* I stood up. And then I sat down again, staring at the floor. I stood up and sat down, stood up and sat down. There was something on the floor. A shadow that stood while I sat. Long and slanted and blacker than I knew black could be. It crept, too. Towards me. 'Oh my God.' I held my hands out. 'No!'

The shadow stopped. What would have been its hair fanned what would have been its face in long wings. The shadow seemed . . . hesitant. I didn't move. The shadow didn't move.

'Mrs Fox?' it asked.

Its voice was faint, but present. Not inside my head, I heard it with my ears.

'Did you hear me?' The voice was even fainter the second time. If I ignored it, it would disappear. But I couldn't ignore it. I looked at the ownerless shadow on the floor and I saw something that was trying to take form, and I felt bad for it. I felt sorry for it.

'If you can hear me, why won't you speak? Do you know who I am?' I really had to strain to hear the last few words.

'You're—Mary,' I said, as loudly as I could.

And she stood up. I mean—she stood *up* from the carpet in a whirl of cold air, and there was skin and flesh on her, and she was naked for almost a second, and then she turned, and she was clothed. I screamed—that time I know for sure I screamed, because she looked so alarmed, and screamed a little herself.

'You're real,' I said. I don't know why it came out sounding accusing; I just wanted to establish the facts.

She held her arms up to the light and looked at them exultingly, as if she'd crafted them herself. They were nice arms. Nicer than mine, that was for sure.

'Stay back,' I said, when she took another step in my direction. 'Stay back.' I picked up St John's stapler. It was a big stapler, about the size of a human head. If I had to, I'd staple her head.

'Okay, okay,' she said, wide-eyed. She must not have wanted anything to ruin all that peachy skin. He'd said she was British, but her accent was just as New England as mine—maybe even more so.

The doorbell rang, and she scattered. That's the closest word to what happened to her when the doorbell rang. I want to say 'shattered', but it wasn't as sudden as all that.

It was John Pizarsky at the door. Before I let him in I looked hopefully through the spyhole for Greta. Maybe I could tell her after all. What else are friends for?

I could tell her: St John's in a bad way. He says he's fine and he acts as if he's fine, but he's in a bad way. I don't blame him for not being able to tell; he doesn't do sane work for a living. And I have been sleeping with him, eating with him, we took a bath together last Tuesday—so I'm in a bad way too. I've seen and heard a woman he made up. I know what this is a called—folie à deux, a delusion shared by two or more people who live together. It was such a strong delusion, though.

Like being on some kind of drug. Nobody warned me how easily my brain could warp a sunny morning so fast that I couldn't find the beginning of the interlude. One moment I was alone, the next . . . I was still alone, I guess, and making the air talk to me.

Those opium-eaters . . . Coleridge could have said something; he could have let the people know that it could happen this way, without warning. De Quincey could have found a moment to mention this, for God's sake.

Greta wasn't with J.P., but I opened the door anyway. I had to have company. If I didn't have company now, right now, I didn't know what would happen or what I would do.

'What the hell took you so long?' J.P. asked.

'St John's out,' I said. 'And I don't have a number you can reach him on. So beat it.'

(Please stay.)

J.P. stood on the doorstep, looking at me. He looked until I twitched my nose, thinking I had something on my face.

'Say . . . did you ever play croquet?' he asked, finally.

'Never,' I said. 'Come inside and tell me about it.' He stepped back onto the driveway.

'Get your coat,' he said, 'Come outside and play it.'

I had my coat on before J.P., or anyone, could say 'knife'.

It turned out to be the nicest afternoon I'd had in a long time. Greta was at some luncheon or other, so it was just me, J.P., Tom Wainwright and his wife Bea, who's just the right side of chatty and very nice; never has a bad word to say about anybody. So relaxing—we played on the Wainwrights' front lawn. I was terrible at croquet, kept forgetting the rules even though J.P. tried to help and whispered them in my ear. But Tom and Bea just turned a blind eye when I did my worst. And there was sunshine, and cucumber sandwiches, and champagne, and I swung up high on it, higher than heaven, and forgot all about what was waiting for me at home.

my daughter the racist

One morning my daughter woke up and said all in a rush: 'Mother, I swear before you and God that from today onwards I am racist.' She's eight years old. She chopped all her hair off two months ago because she wanted to go around with the local boys and they wouldn't have her with her long hair. Now she looks like one of them; eyes dazed from looking directly at the sun, teeth shining white in her sunburnt face. She laughs a lot. She plays. 'Look at her playing,' my mother says. 'Playing in the rubble of what used to be our great country.' My mother exaggerates as often as she can. I'm sure she would like nothing more than to be part of a Greek tragedy. She wouldn't even want a large part, she'd be perfectly content with a chorus role, warning that fate is coming to make havoc of all things. My mother is a fine woman, all over wrinkles, and she always has a clean handkerchief somewhere about her person, but I don't know what she's talking about with her rubble this, rubble that—we live in a village, and it's not bad here. Not peaceful, but not bad. In cities it's worse. In the city centre, where we used to live, a bomb took my husband and turned his face to blood. I was lucky, another widow told me, that there was something left so that I could know of his passing. But I was ungrateful. I spat at that widow. I spat at her in her sorrow. That's sin. I know that's sin. But half my life was gone, and it wasn't easy to look at what was left.

Anyway, the village. I live with my husband's mother, whom I now call my mother, because I can't return to the one who gave birth to me. It isn't done. I belong with my husband's mother until someone else claims me. And that will never happen, because I don't wish it.

The village is hushed. People observe the phases of the moon. In the city I felt the moon but hardly ever remembered to look for it. The only thing that disturbs us here in the village is the foreign soldiers. Soldiers, soldiers, soldiers, patrolling. They fight us and they try to tell us, in our own language, that they're freeing us. Maybe, maybe not. I look through the dusty window (I can never get it clean, the desert is our neighbour) and I see soldiers every day. They think someone dangerous is running secret messages through here; that's what I've heard. What worries me more is the young people of the village. They stand and watch the soldiers. And the soldiers don't like it, and the soldiers point their guns, especially at the young men. They won't bother with the women and girls, unless the woman or the girl has an especially wild look in her eyes. I think there are two reasons the soldiers don't like the young men watching them. The first reason is that the soldiers know they are ugly in their boots and fatigues, they are perfectly aware that their presence spoils everything around them. The second reason is the nature of the watching—the boys and the men around here watch with a very great hatred, so great that it feels as if action must follow. I feel that sometimes, just walking past them—when I block their view of the soldiers these boys quiver with impatience.

And that girl of mine has really begun to stare at the soldiers, too, even though I slap her hard when I catch her doing that. Who knows what's going to happen? These soldiers are scared. They might shoot someone. Noura next door says: 'If they could be so evil as to shoot children then it's in God's hands. Anyway I don't believe that they could do it.'

But I know that such things can be. My husband was a university professor. He spoke several languages, and he gave me books to read, and he read news from other countries and told me what's possible. He should've been afraid of the world, should've stayed inside with the doors locked and the blinds drawn, but he didn't do that, he went out. Our daughter is just like him. She is part of his immortality. I told him, when I was still carrying her, that that's what I want, that that's how I love him. I had always dreaded and feared pregnancy, for all the usual reasons that girls who daydream more than they live fear pregnancy. My body, with its pain and mess and hunger—if I could have bribed it to go away, I would have. Then I married my man, and I held fast to him. And my brain, the brain that had told me I would never bear a child for any man, no matter how nice he was, that brain began to tell me something else. Provided the world continues to exist, provided conditions remain favourable, or at least tolerable, our child will have a child and that child will have a child and so on, and with all those children of children come the inevitability that glimpses of my husband will resurface, in their features, in the way they use their bodies, a fearless swinging of the arms as they walk. Centuries from now some quality of a man's gaze, smile, voice, way of standing or sitting will please someone else in a way that they aren't completely aware of, will be loved very hard for just a moment, without enquiry into where it came from. I ignore the women who say that my daughter does things that a girl shouldn't do, and when I want to keep her near me, I let her go. But not too far, I don't let her go too far from me.

The soldiers remind me of boys from here sometimes. The way our boys used to be. Especially when you catch them with their helmets off, three or four of them sitting on a wall at lunchtime, trying to enjoy their sandwiches and the sun, but really too restless for both. Then you see the rifles beside their knapsacks and you remember that they aren't our boys.

'Mother . . . did you hear me? I said that I am now a racist.'

I was getting my daughter ready for school. She can't tie knots but she loves her shoelaces to make extravagant bows.

'Racist against whom, my daughter?'

'Racist against soldiers.'

'Soldiers aren't a race.'

'Soldiers aren't a race,' she mimicked. 'Soldiers aren't a race.'

'What do you want me to say?'

She didn't have an answer, so she just went off in a big gang with her school friends. And I worried, because my daughter has always seen soldiers—in her lifetime she hasn't known a time or place when the cedars stood against the blue sky without khaki canvas or crackling radio signals in the way.

An hour or so later Bilal came to visit. A great honour, I'm sure, a visit from that troublesome Bilal who had done nothing but pester me since the day I came to this village. He sat down with us and mother served him tea.

'Three times I have asked this daughter of yours to be my wife,' Bilal said to my mother. He shook a finger at her. As for me, it was as if I wasn't there. 'First wife,' he continued. 'Not even second or third—first wife.'

'Don't be angry, son,' my mother murmured. 'She's not ready. Only a shameless woman could be ready so soon after what happened.'

'True, true,' Bilal agreed. A fly landed just above my top lip and I let it walk.

'Rather than ask a fourth time I will kidnap her . . .'

'Ah, don't do that, son. Don't take the light of an old woman's eyes,' my mother murmured, and she fed him honey cake. Bilal laughed from his belly, and the fly fled. 'I was only joking.'

The third time Bilal asked my mother for my hand in marriage I thought I was going to have to do it after all. But my daughter said I wasn't allowed. I asked her why. Because his face is fat and his eyes are tiny? Because he chews with his mouth open?

'He has a tyrannical moustache,' my daughter

said. 'It would be impossible to live with.' I'm proud of her vocabulary. But it's starting to look as if I think I'm too good for Bilal, who owns more cattle than any other man for miles around and could give my mother, daughter and I everything we might reasonably expect from this life.

Please, God. You know I don't seek worldly things (apart from shoes). If you want me to marry again, so be it. But please—not Bilal. After the love that I have had . . .

My daughter came home for her lunch. After prayers we shared some cold *karkedeh*, two straws in a drinking glass, and she told me what she was learning, which wasn't much. My mother was there, too, rattling her prayer beads and listening indulgently. She made faces when she thought my daughter talked too much. Then we heard the soldiers coming past as usual, and we went and looked at them through the window. I thought we'd make fun of them a bit, as usual. But my daughter ran out of the front door and into the path of the army truck, yelling: 'You! You bloody soldiers!' Luckily the truck's wheels crawled along the road, and the body of the truck itself was slumped on one side, resigned to a myriad of pot holes. Still, it was a very big truck, and my daughter is a very small girl.

I was out after her before I knew what I was doing, shouting her name. It's a good name—we chose a name that would grow with her, but she seemed determined not to make it to adulthood. I tried to trip her up, but she was too nimble for me. Everyone around was looking on from windows and the open gates of courtyards. The truck rolled to a stop. Someone inside it yelled: 'Move, kid.

We've got stuff to do.'

I tried to pull my daughter out of the way, but she wasn't having any of it. My hands being empty, I wrung them. My daughter began to pelt the soldiers' vehicle with stones from her pockets. Her pockets were very deep that afternoon, her arms lashed the air like whips. Stone after stone bounced off metal and rattled glass, and I grabbed at her and she screamed: 'This is my country! Get out of here!'

The people of the village began to applaud her. 'Yes,' they cried out, from their seats in the audience, and they clapped. I tried again to seize her arm and failed again. The truck's engine revved up and I opened my arms as wide as they would go, inviting everyone to witness. Now I was screaming too: 'So you dare? You really dare?'

And there we were, mother and daughter, causing problems for the soldiers together.

Finally a scrawny soldier came out of the vehicle without his gun. He was the scrawniest fighting man I've ever seen—he was barely there, just a piece of wire, really. He walked towards my daughter, who had run out of stones. He stretched out a long arm, offering her chewing gum, and she swore at him, and I swore at her for swearing. He stopped about thirty centimetres away from us and said to my daughter: 'You're brave.'

My daughter put her hands on her hips and glared up at him.

'We're leaving tomorrow,' the scrawny soldier told her.

Whispers and shouts: *The soldiers are leaving tomorrow!*

A soldier inside the truck yelled out: 'Yeah, but

more are coming to take our place,' and everyone piped low. My daughter reached for a stone that hadn't fallen far. Who is this girl? Four feet tall and fighting something she knows nothing about. Even if I explained it to her she wouldn't get it. I don't get it myself.

'Can I shake your hand?' the scrawny soldier asked her, before her hand met the stone. I thought my girl would refuse, but she said yes. 'You're okay,' she told him. 'You came out to face me.'

'Her English is good,' the coward from within the truck remarked.

'I speak to her in English every day,' I called out. 'So she can tell people like you what she thinks.'

We stepped aside then, my daughter and I, and let them continue their patrol.

* * *

My mother didn't like what had happened. But didn't you see everyone clapping for us, my daughter asked. So what, my mother said. People clap at anything. Some people even clap when they're on an aeroplane and it lands. That was something my husband had told us from his travels—I hadn't thought she'd remember.

My daughter became a celebrity amongst the children, and from what I saw, she used it for good, bringing the shunned ones into the inner circle and laughing at all their jokes.

* * *

The following week a foreigner dressed like one of

our men knocked at my mother's door. It was late afternoon, turning to dusk. People sat looking out onto the street, talking about everything as they took their tea. Our people really know how to discuss a matter from head to toe; it is our gift, and such conversation on a balmy evening can be sweeter than sugar. Now they were talking about the foreigner who was at our door. I answered it myself. My daughter was at my side and we recognised the man at once; it was the scrawny soldier. He looked itchy and uncomfortable in his djellaba, and he wasn't wearing his keffiyeh at all correctly—his hair was showing.

'What a clown,' my daughter said, and from her seat on the cushioned floor my mother vowed that clown or no clown, he couldn't enter her house.

'Welcome,' I said to him. It was all I could think of to say. See a guest, bid him welcome. It's who we are. Or maybe it's just who I am.

'I'm not here to cause trouble,' the scrawny soldier said. He was looking to the north, south, east and west so quickly and repeatedly that for some seconds his head was just a blur. 'I'm completely off duty. In fact, I've been on leave since last week. I'm just—I just thought I'd stick around for a little while. I thought I might have met a worthy adversary—this young lady here, I mean.' He indicated my daughter, who chewed her lip and couldn't stop herself from looking pleased.

'What is he saying?' my mother demanded.

'I'll just—go away, then,' the soldier said. He seemed to be dying several thousand deaths at once.

'He'd like some tea . . .' my daughter told my mother. 'We'll just have a cup or two,' I added, and we took the tea out onto the veranda, and drank it under the eyes of God and the entire neighbourhood. The neighbourhood was annoyed. Very annoyed, and it listened closely to everything that was said. The soldier didn't seem to notice. He and my daughter were getting along famously. I didn't catch what exactly they were talking about, I just poured the tea and made sure my hand was steady. *I'm not doing anything wrong*, I told myself. *I'm not doing anything wrong.*

The scrawny soldier asked if I would tell him my name. 'No,' I said. 'You have no right to use it.' He told me his name, but I pretended he hadn't spoken. To cheer him up, my daughter told him her name, and he said: 'That's great. A really, really good name. I might use it myself one day.'

'You can't—it's a girl's name,' my daughter replied, her nostrils flared with scorn.

'Ugh,' said the soldier. 'I meant for my daughter . . .'

He shouldn't have spoken about his unborn daughter out there in front of everyone, with his eyes and his voice full of hope and laughter. I can guarantee that some woman in the shadows was cursing the daughter he wanted to have. Even as he spoke someone was saying, May that girl be born withered for the grief people like you have caused us.

'Ugh,' said my daughter.

I began to follow the conversation better. The scrawny soldier told my daughter that he understood why the boys lined the roads with anger. 'Inside my head I call them the children of Hamelin.'

'The what?' my daughter asked.

'The who?' I asked.

'I guess all I mean is that they're paying the price for something they didn't do.'

And then he told us the story of the Pied Piper of Hamelin, because we hadn't heard it before. We had nightmares that night, all three of us—my mother, my daughter and I. My mother hadn't even heard the story, so I don't know why she joined in. But somehow it was nice that she did.

* * *

On his second visit the scrawny soldier began to tell my daughter that there were foreign soldiers in his country, too, but that they were much more difficult to spot because they didn't wear uniforms and some of them didn't even seem foreign. They seemed like ordinary citizens, the sons and daughters of shopkeepers and dentists and restaurant owners and big businessmen. 'That's the most dangerous kind of soldier. The longer those ones live amongst us, the more they hate us, and everything we do disgusts them . . . these are people we go to school with, ride the subway with—we watch the same movies, root for the same baseball teams. They'll never be with us, though. We've been judged, and they'll always be against us. Always.'

He'd wasted his breath, because almost as soon as he began with all that I put my hands over my daughter's ears. She protested loudly, but I kept them there. 'What you're talking about is a different matter,' I said. 'It doesn't explain or excuse your being here. Not to this child. And don't say "always" to her. You have to think harder or just leave it alone and say sorry.'

He didn't argue, but he didn't apologise. He felt he'd spoken the truth, so he didn't need to argue or apologise.

Later in the evening I asked my daughter if she was still racist against soldiers and she said loftily: 'I'm afraid I don't know what you're referring to.' When she's a bit older I'm going to ask her about that little outburst, what made her come out with such words in the first place. And I'm sure she'll make up something that makes her seem cleverer and more sensitive than she really was.

* * *

We were expecting our scrawny soldier again the following afternoon, my daughter and I. My daughter's friends had dropped her. Even the ones she had helped find favour with the other children forgot that their new position was due to her and urged the others to leave her out of everything. The women I knew snubbed me at market, but I didn't need them. My daughter and I told each other that everyone would come round once they understood that what we were doing was innocent. In fact we were confident that we could convince our soldier of his wrongdoing and send him back to his country to begin life anew as an architect. He'd confessed a love of our minarets. He could take the image of our village home with him and make marvels of it.

Noura waited until our mothers, mine and hers, were busy gossiping at her house, then she came to tell me that the men were discussing how best to deal with me. I was washing clothes in the bathtub and I almost fell in.

My crime was that I had insulted Bilal with my brazen pursuit of this soldier . . .

'Noura! This soldier—he's just a boy! He can hardly coax his beard to grow. How could you believe—'

'I'm not saying I believe it. I'm just saying you must stop this kind of socialising. And behave impeccably from now on. I mean—angelically.'

Three months before I had come to the village, Noura told me, there had been a young widow who talked back all the time and looked haughtily at the men. A few of them got fed up, and they took her out to the desert and beat her severely. She survived, but once they'd finished with her she couldn't see out of her own eyes or talk out of her own lips. The women didn't like to mention such a matter, but Noura was mentioning it now, because she wanted me to be careful.

'I see,' I said. 'You're saying they can do this to me?'

'Don't smile; they can do it. You know they can do it! You know that with those soldiers here our men are twice as fiery. Six or seven of them will even gather to kick a stray dog for stealing food . . .'

'Yes, I saw that yesterday. Fiery, you call it. Did they bring this woman out of her home at night or in the morning, Noura? Did they drag her by her hair?'

Noura averted her eyes because I was asking her why she had let it happen and she didn't want to answer.

'You're not thinking clearly. Not only can they do this to you but they can take your daughter from you first, and put her somewhere she would never again see the light of day. Better that than have her grow up like her mother. Can't you see that that's how it would go? I'm telling you this as a friend, a true friend . . . my husband doesn't want me to talk to you any more. He says your ideas are wicked and bizarre.'

I didn't ask Noura what her husband could possibly know about my ideas. Instead I said: 'You know me a little. Do you find my ideas wicked and bizarre?'

Noura hurried to the door. 'Yes. I do. I think your husband spoilt you. He gave you illusions . . . you feel too free. We are not free.'

* * *

I drew my nails down my palm, down then back up the other way, deep and hard. I thought about what Noura had told me. I didn't think for very long. I had no choice—I couldn't afford another visit from him. I wrote him a letter. I wonder if I'll ever get a chance to take back all that I wrote in that letter; it was hideous from beginning to end. Human beings shouldn't say such things to each other. I put the letter into an unsealed envelope and found a local boy who knew where the scrawny soldier lived. Doubtless Bilal read the letter before the soldier did, because by evening everyone but my daughter knew what I had done. My daughter waited for the soldier until it was fully dark, and I waited with her, pretending that I was still expecting our friend. There was a song she wanted to sing to him. I asked her to sing it to me instead, but she said I wouldn't appreciate it. When we went inside at last, my daughter asked me if the soldier could have gone home without telling us. He probably hated goodbyes.

'He said he would come . . . I hope he's all right . . .' my daughter fretted.

'He's gone home to build minarets.'

'With matchsticks, probably.'

And we were both very sad.

* * *

My daughter didn't smile for six days. On the seventh she said she couldn't go to school.

'You have to go to school,' I told her. 'How else will you get your friends back again?'

'What if I can't,' she wailed. 'What if I can't get them back again?'

'Do you really think you won't get them back again?'

'Oh, you don't even care that our friend is gone. Mothers have no feelings and are enemies of progress.'

(I really wonder who my daughter has been talking to lately. Someone with a sense of humour very like her father's . . .)

I tickled the sole of her foot until she shouted.

'Let this enemy of progress tell you something,' I said. 'I'm never sad when a friend goes far away, because whichever city or country that friend goes to, they turn the place friendly. They turn a suspicious-looking name on the map into a place where a welcome can be found. Maybe the friend will talk about you sometimes, to other friends that live around him, and then that's almost as good as being there yourself. You're in several places at once! In fact, my daughter, I would even go so far as to say that the further away your friends are, and the more spread out they are, the better your chances of going safely through the world . . .'

'Ugh,' my daughter said.

I've grown a beard or two in my time. Long, full, Moses-in-the-wilderness—that type of beard. Mainly as a way to relax, hiding my face so I can take it easy behind my beard. A while ago I went to London, to see a play they'd cooked up out of one of my favorite novels—I couldn't wait the eight months it would take to cross the Atlantic. And in the weeks leading up to the visit I must have just quietly left shaving out of my mornings, so quietly I didn't notice I was doing it, because when I got to London the beard was so bushy it distracted me from the sights. Big Ben and my beard. Buckingham Palace and my beard. The Tower of London and my beard. Caw caw, said the ravens. (Were they making reference to the beard?) I had a great time. No one bothered me that entire trip. Funny to do something and then realise the reason for it afterwards—I'd grown the beard so that no one would bother me. Time to start another beard. If only I could remember how long it took for the last one to grow.

I want to be on my own for a spell. But there's nowhere I can be on my own. I went to the library in town, thinking, it's such a nice Saturday, so fine out, no one will be there—but it was full of bespectacled girls 'studying'. The bluestockings of today. Dressed up just to go to the library, making eyes at a fellow across a room, bold as anything. I like to look, but I don't like it when they look back. All you're doing is taking an appreciative moment, maybe two or three, if she's a serious matter, and she's staring back and thinking, *I've caught his eye. Good. Now what I'd really like to do is keep it until his dying day.* It's some kind of God-awful whim she has. This isn't just talk; I know this type of girl, the type who looks back. I know her all too well. She's the type who's really trying to start something. Rousing at the beginning, the heated command, until you realise she can't get enough attention, and she needs all of yours, every last scrap of it. And then come the ugly scenes. And I don't mean confrontations, but hissed exchanges, half-hours of being kept waiting for her in some lobby or other for no good reason, parties where she bestows one freezing cold glance upon you and then spends the rest of the evening holed up in some cosy corner with someone else; that kind of scene fixes the equivalent of a jeweller's loupe to your eye. You examine your diamond, and find her edges blurred with tawdry cracks; stay involved for a few more months and you'll find she worsens over time. Rapidly, too. All these tactical attempts at mind control; I'm not kidding. It sounds like an exaggeration until someone tries it on you. It's hard to find a woman without tactics. That'll be why I made one up. Then she started a game, had me pursue her through Africa. She cast me as a desperate spinster with an antique sword. She cast me as a fellow who ditched his woman out in some foreign country because he couldn't handle her. Mary Foxe has really been taking a few liberties.

So I'll correct my statement. It's hard to even imagine a woman without tactics.

When the third pretty bluestocking made eyes at me, I left. Libraries always make me feel covered in ink, anyway. Ink on my clothes, ink in my eyes. Terrible. All the body heat in there is bound to make the pages mushy. My parents met in a library. My mother was a junior librarian, and my father's books were always overdue. He asked my mother's best friend what her favorite books were, and he took them out, one by one—*La Dame aux Camélias*. *Thérèse Raquin*. *Madame Bovary*. *Tess of the D'Urbervilles*. *Anna Karenina*. He couldn't make head or tail of them—'Hasty women,' he told me, shaking his head, 'Hasty women.' But he told my mother how much he enjoyed them, and when he got around to asking whether she objected to his calling on her at her family home some Sunday afternoon to continue their discussion, she didn't say no.

I thought briefly about going to see my mother, in her tiny apartment two hours' drive away, but I know she doesn't want to see me, and I know it's not because of anything I've done or failed to do. She doesn't want to see anyone. She's happy like that, I think. Always relieved at the end of a visit. I think she's too old to want to talk any more; she doesn't mind listening, but she's got a radio set for that. She's still in good health, she's still got her wits about her. She had a lot more to say for herself before my father passed away, but then he was a fine man, great company—really great company, actually; let you have your opinions and talked about his own in a way that never put your nose out of joint. And now he's gone she'd rather not talk to anyone else. Solitary people, these booklovers. I think it's swell that there are people you don't have to worry about when you don't see them for a long time, you don't have to wonder what they do, how they're getting along with themselves. You just know that they're all right, and probably doing something they like. Last time I saw my mother she kept nodding and saying: 'Everything's just fine, dear. Everything's just fine.' This was before I'd even made an opening remark—she was in such a hurry to get her part of the conversation out of the way. If I went to see my mother, what would I tell her, anyway?

I drove around instead, just drove around, trying to decide where to stop. As I drove I tried to think of a word, a single word to sum up the way Daphne's been behaving lately. Inscrutable. The woman has become inscrutable.

Take yesterday morning. Daphne was right outside my study, watering the flowers in the window box, warbling to herself—a pretty little racket, and I was somehow enjoying it and getting a little work done at the same time. Then suddenly, she stopped, and said: 'Well, St John . . . you know what Ralph Waldo Emerson says . . .'

I waited quietly, held my pen still to show I was paying attention, braced myself for some cloying scrap of verse she'd just remembered from her high-school yearbook. But she didn't finish her sentence. Nor did she continue with the singing. So I said: 'Go on, D, I'm all ears.'

She made a little moue with her mouth, blowing a couple of stray curls out of her line of vision so that I felt the full force of her stare. 'What do you mean, go on? I don't know what Emerson says.'

'Oh, you don't?' I asked, and I laughed. She didn't laugh with me.

'*You* know what Emerson says, St John. That's why I said, "You know what Emerson says." '

Her sleeves were rolled up and her voice kept going from flat to sharp. I got the distinct impression that she was steaming mad at me for failing to supply her with an Emerson quotation.

'Can I ask—would you mind telling me—where you got this idea that I know what Emerson says? Have I ever mentioned in passing that I know what Emerson says?'

She yawned at me. 'Come on, St John. Don't be shy. Tell me something Emerson said.'

I dropped my smile.

'Did someone tell you that Emerson's a great friend of mine? Did the ghost of Ralph Waldo Emerson call one day when I was out and leave a message for me—*Well now, Fox, my boy—you know what I always say*?'

'I really think you ought to know what Emerson says, that's all,' she returned, without batting an eyelash.

I stood up and went to the window. When I got close to her she looked down at her watering can. 'Mrs Fox,' I said. 'You're a horror today.'

To which she replied: 'Why don't you write a book about it?'

Why don't you write a book about it?

Why don't you—

Speechless, I gestured for her to stand away from the window, then I closed it. We looked at each other through the glass—she had this cool, triumphant smile on. She really felt she'd said something extraordinarily cutting. God knows what I looked like. Then she moved on to the next window box. What the hell am I supposed to make of a conversation like that?

Then there was the picnic D and I went to last weekend—neither of us wanted to go, but my publisher was hosting, and it seemed necessary to show my face. Some of the women had brought their little kids along to run around the meadow, singing their nonsensical songs and making daisy chains. There was this one girl with a pair of angel wings on—she actually had quite a lot going for her. She could whistle around two fingers, and she showed some of the little boys how to skim stones off the stream, and she didn't scream when water splashed her. I wouldn't mind having a kid if she turned out to be like that. Daphne was watching her too, and scowling. At one point the girl with the angel wings bumped into Daphne and said sorry real sweetly. Daphne just ignored her, looked straight ahead, tight-lipped. I told the child there was no harm done, but if I could have gotten a million miles away real fast, I would have. Then my publisher's wife, a new mother, offered to let Daphne hold her little boy, and Daphne looked at me with these eyes of mute suffering as if asking: *Do I have to? Do I really, really have to?*

I don't know what's got into her. Well, I guess I do, but it doesn't justify—

On the other hand, it was presumptuous of Ellen Balfour to think that every woman in the world wants to hold a three-month-old baby just as soon as she catches sight of one. Daphne's right, it was presumptuous. Daphne held the kid, her arms really stiff, as if he could roll out of her arms and bounce off the grass and she wouldn't care. I chucked the boy under the chin a couple of times, and said he was a little prince, and he cried his head off. Then Daphne gave him back to his mother. Mrs Balfour seemed to think Daphne was just overcome with delight and kept saying: 'Oh, bless you, bless you. You'll get one of your own soon, Daphne—may I call you Daphne?' English manners.

Daphne whispered to me: 'That's the ugliest child I ever saw.'

'Bad stock,' I whispered back, less because I actually thought so and more because I've been thinking that Daphne and I should be allies, I want us to be allies even when she's misbehaving. I got a laugh out of her, anyway. Nothing's even happened to us yet—we haven't had a broke spell yet, or watched each other lose people, lose our looks, face down sickness. But D seems to be holding out on me, refusing to go all the way into this thing unless there's a child too. Once I think my way past a lot of stuff that hasn't got anything to do with anything, the thought of being called 'Dad' doesn't give me the jumps—well, not as severely as it used to. I didn't used to think about these things. I must be getting older. Daphne could be onto something, but I won't be hustled into it.

The other day I went on an urgent mission to retrieve my wallet from a jacket pocket before D sent our stuff out to be cleaned. D had left a book on top of the laundry basket: *Happy Husband*, that was the title. And underneath, in smaller letters: *Make him happy, keep him happy!* An advice manual. I took it away, read a few pages, chased them down with a couple of despairing drinks.

There are real books all around the house, everywhere. She could pick one up and in mere seconds she could bc involved in something that makes her laugh and feel nervous and hot and cold and forgive the world its absurdity—Pushkin, maybe, or Céline. Instead she's spending her time reading up on what to do about me. It got me down. The book itself was useless, too—all the advice it offered about the timing of meals and affecting a cheerful disposition and trying to take an interest in the husband's doings even when they're fearfully boring and never saying 'I told you so', these aren't the reasons a person looks with favor upon another person, these aren't the reasons someone stays in love. I put the book back before she knew I'd seen it. If I said anything about it she'd tell me I was taking it too seriously, that she was just looking at it for amusement.

As for Mary, I'd been trying to get her to show up, but she wouldn't. I don't know what that means. Am I drying up? My book about the killer accountant is going as well it can be considering that I hardly know what I'm writing; I'm just jogging along behind the plot like a carthorse, ready to drop it as soon as Mary shows up and it's time to get out of here. But no sign of Mary. She could be staying away deliberately (if so, I didn't know she could do that) or my brainpower's getting weak. Maybe once I'm alone in my beard things will be the way they used to be with her—friendly, I mean. I wrote her name in the steam on my bathroom mirror, as a kind of invocation, and after a couple of slow minutes I added a middle name for her. A kind of incentive, a step towards reality, bait. I wrote Jane. A good, plain, sensible name. Mary Jane Foxe, I wrote. Before my eyes the letters changed; the name grew longer. 'Aurelia'. Mary Aurelia Foxe. This is what it's come to.

I pulled up outside a bar I'd been to a couple of times. I knew I could be kind of alone there, especially during the day, when the social drinkers are waiting for the clock to strike a respectable hour before they start. There were a few guys inside, spaced well apart, one of them sitting at a corner table. He was groaning into his hat, but no one else in there even looked at him. I took another corner table, set down my scotch, lit my pipe, opened my copy of *Metamorphoses* and pretended to read. The other guys started giving me the eye then, including the one who was wailing into his hat. 'Gentlemen,' I said, from behind the cover of my book, 'it's a free country.' That had no effect, so I told the bartender to get them drinks, on me—there were only five of them in total. They left me in peace once they got their drinks.

It was quiet until a bunch of youngsters swept in and started shouting their orders all over the place. I raised my eyes from the line I'd been staring at for the past fifteen minutes or so and watched them. They used long words and called each other by nicknames that alluded to the classical world. Castor was present, and Pollux, and Patroclus and Achilles. College men, in town for the weekend. Three of them had a muttered dispute amongst themselves before heading over to where I sat. They drew out chairs, turned them around and sat on them. Usually it annoys me when people do that, but I wanted to know what they had to say. They asked me if I was S.J. Fox and I said, Yup. They named a few of my books and said they liked them. I said, Thanks. They called their friends over and announced my name. Looking round at the faces I could tell that some of them had no idea who I was, but they did an impressive job of pretending that wasn't the case. There's something to be said for good breeding. You get hypocrites out of it, but you get the odd respectful youngster, too. They called me sir, and boss, and wouldn't hear of me buying my own drinks. I put my book aside and answered their questions as well as I could. These boys all had names like Toby and Jed—their real names, that is. They didn't try to get me to call them by their Greek names. They reminded me of Daphne's set, kids who had never been poor and never would be, spouting cheerfully lopsided theories. Men of the world who didn't live in the world—not properly. Me, I'm a farmer's son. These boys reckoned the Europeans were about to get into a scrap over Czechoslovakia, and that there'd be war again, and we'd be in it again. They wanted to know what I thought about that. I reminded them that Germany had had its balls cut off—land taken, no army to speak of, no money—there wasn't going to be any war. I told them they weren't going to have to do what I did, that if they were looking for glory they'd better find another way. 'I hope you're right, Mr Fox,' Jed said, earnestly—or was it Toby? Blue sweatshirts and ears that stuck out. 'I hope you're right, but I don't think you are. Things are really boiling over—the Germans are saying all kinds of things, and France and England are running around trying to get promises—'

'Didn't you hear? We aren't promising anything. Roosevelt said we're staying neutral. What's Czechoslovakia got to do with us?'

Toby—or Jed—stared at me. 'What's Czechoslovakia got to do with us? Well, what's independence got to do with us? Liberty? The pursuit of happiness?'

All I could think of were a couple of lines someone else had recited to me a long time ago, in France. *To goodness and wisdom we only make promises; pain we obey.* That's Proust, y'know, the guy had told me. (Daphne should have said to me: 'You know what Proust says . . .' If she had, that little exchange of ours wouldn't have happened, or would have happened differently, maybe, would have ended without me having to shut the window in her face.) The boys went quiet, which means I'd said the lines aloud. They were all squinting at me, as if I was some figure in a fading photograph and each of them was vying to be the first to identify me. A pox on the young. I left without saying goodbye, just walked out.

I heard voices as I headed from my driveway to the front porch. Daphnc and a man. She was laughing. She sounded drunk. It was only three o'clock. I slowed my steps with a corner still to turn; hedges, luckily, so they couldn't see me. I heard the porch swing creak—the two of them were sitting on it. It was Jonas Pizarsky she was with, and they were talking about fairy tales, of all things. D had a pair of scissors, and a vaseful of water, and was arranging some flowers—whether she'd bought them, or he'd given them to her, I was sure the flower arranging was unnecessary—she always did it, stem by stem, even when presented with a bunch of flowers that already looked all right.

'Why have husbands got to keep themselves all locked up, that's what I want to know,' Daphne complained.

'Not all of them do,' Jonas told her. He wasn't drunk at all. I didn't like that—those two sat together, his voice measured and sober, and her saying just anything that occurred to her. He was going to remember the entire conversation and she would remember a quarter of it at the very most. Unfortunate.

'Oh, it's only the cold ones that do it, isn't it?'

'I don't know about cold, Daphne . . .'

'No, you don't know about cold. Because you're not cold, are you, J.P. ?'

He didn't answer. Too busy trying to think of some phrase that would make her see him as ardent, I'll bet.

'You're not Bluebeard? Or Reynardine?' I caught flashes of Daphne through the brambles; she was examining her arrangement of the flowers from a number of angles. She didn't ask his advice, and I was glad she didn't. She always asked my advice—not that I ever give a response she can make use of.

'Nor Fitcher, no.'

'Fitcher?'

Just what I was wondering. Pizarsky seemed to know his stuff, though. He'd told me himself that he'd been studying for a doctorate in anthropology until his father had demanded he help steer the family's jewellery business. A diamond mine in Africa and a gold mine in Nevada. Opal fields in Australia, and more. I don't like to think about how rich Pizarsky is. He doesn't seem to like thinking about it either. It's awkward that he has so much. What's left for him to want?

He told my wife a bizarre story. It started out almost too screwed up to even be a fairy tale. It was all about a magician called Fitcher who went around with a basket, begging for food. And any woman who pitied him and gave him food was compelled to jump into his basket and go home with him and be his wife.

'Yes,' Daphne said, laying down her scissors. 'I felt so sorry for him at first . . . all I wanted to do was make him happy . . .'

'Yes, well, Fitcher did this with three sisters in a row. He set each of them the don't-look-in-the-locked-room test—the first two sisters failed, of course. The only way for Fitcher's final wife, the third sister, to survive her danger was by becoming insane. If you think about it, it was inevitable. That woman went through a lot. She found her sisters all chopped up and sunk in blood, and she collected the parts and she joined them up. Only a very, very young child would think of a solution like that, and only an insane person would actually try it. It worked, though; they came back to life and she sent them home. On a clear afternoon in an empty house she covered herself in honey and rolled around in a barrel's worth of feathers, and a skeleton sat by in a chair the whole time; it was meant to take her place, and she didn't hesitate or falter because she'd gone nuts. She was scared right out of her mind. She had to be—to rescue herself. So she stopped working to make sense of things—we don't always realise it, but it's hard work we do almost every waking moment, building our thoughts and memories and actions around time, things that happened yesterday, and things that are happening right now, and what's coming tomorrow, layering all of that simultaneously and holding it in balance. She cut it out and just kept moving. She was nobody, she was nowhere, doing nothing, but doing it as hard and fast as she could. And once she was fully covered with honey and feathers she walked out into broad daylight and used the only words she hadn't forgotten, *I'm a bird, I'm Fitcher's bird.* If she'd ever been anyone other than Fitcher's bird, she didn't know a thing about it. What did she look like, all sticky with quills? What did her eyes say? Did she even understand the words she was saying? Never mind; her mouth said: *I'm a bird, I'm Fitcher's bird*. And nobody who heard her could doubt her. She met the bad magician; she met Fitcher himself, on her way home. *I'm a bird*, she told him. He didn't recognise her. I mean, she was gone. He looked into her eyes and there was no woman there. And he never caught her again.'

Daphne must have had a look on her face that made him stop talking. Neither of them said anything for quite a while.

'She went insane because of him,' Daphne said. 'I think that's happening to me.'

The swing creaked again. I looked out from behind the hedge; I had to see what they were doing. If they saw me, they saw me. But if I saw that he had his arms around her, or even just his hand on her arm, I was going to bust his head open. The conversation itself didn't matter. She was drunk. And he—I knew what he was doing with apparent idleness; using his halting, mysterious European accent to feed her a story that he knew she'd like because she could place herself in it, be the victim, be the heroine. I withdrew before either of them saw me.

'You don't have to go insane,' Pizarsky told Daphne. It doesn't have to go like that.'

'What shall I do, then? What shall I do?' She didn't sound as if she was especially interested in the answer to her question.

Her arms were bare and freckled, her eyes were closed, her head was resting against the back of the swing. Mine. I wanted to lift her up into my arms and carry her around with me, our bodies together, my neck her neck, her hands my hands. He wasn't touching her, he wasn't even sitting close to her, and I could only see the back of his head. But he was very still, hardly seemed to be breathing, and he was looking at her. That was bad.

'Daphne—what's going on?' he asked, eventually. 'What's wrong?'

'I wish I could tell you,' she said.

'You can. You can tell me anything.' He waited, but she didn't say anything. 'Maybe some other time. I think you should know, though, that there are other ways—apart from going crazy. Do you know the story of Mr Fox?'

'No.' Her voice was languid, reluctant. 'What happens in that one?'

'The usual—wooing, seduction, then—the discovery of a chopped-up predecessor. But the heroine, Lady Mary—'

'Lady Mary?' Daphne asks. I didn't need to look to know that she'd sat up.

Mary Foxe put a soft hand on my shoulder. 'Come away, Mr Fox,' she whispered. I shrugged her off. She was wearing what Daphne called her signature scent. I disapproved—and not just because the scent costs enough per ounce for me to momentarily consider asking the shopgirl to leave the price tag on so Daphne can realise how spoilt she is. Mary was Mary—she's been with me a long time, maybe even before I'd gone to France. She's handled a sickle at haymaking time, stacked and tromped the hay, helped me feed it to the cows and horses. She's stood dressed top to toe in mud, and she's braced herself against the barn beams when she's been too tired to stand. Mary Foxe shouldn't have anything to do with bottled fragrances.

'That farm stuff was before my time,' Mary said. 'Come away with me, Mr Fox.' There was a hard smile on her face. 'You said that Mrs Fox couldn't stop us, remember?'

Suddenly I was getting to be a little tired of Mary Foxe.

'Drop it,' I said to her. 'Just be quiet. In fact—you can't speak. You've just lost your voice, Mary. You're real hoarse today.' And I closed her voice up in my hand.

Mary's lips shaped words, a fast and furious stream of them, but none of them sounded. She clasped her throat, horrified. She'd been forgetting who was boss.

Undo this, she mimed, furiously.

In time, I mimed back.

But the damage was done. I'd addressed her too loudly; Daphne and Pizarsky had heard me, and they'd stopped talking. I couldn't stay where I was a second longer. I strode round the corner and stepped up onto the porch, car key dangling from my hand. 'Hi there, D. Afternoon, Pizarsky. Thanks for bringing her home. Had a nice time at—?'

'The Wainwrights',' they supplied, quickly. Oh, sure. The Wainwrights'.

Daphne got up and went into the house without kissing Pizarsky goodbye. It bugged me that she didn't kiss him goodbye, as if now even a simple kiss on the cheek could mean something between them. Pizarsky's leave-taking was good, quiet, neither hurried nor laboured—good in that I didn't really even have to say anything to him, or look his way. I thought that if our eyes met I'd have to take a swing at him.

Daphne went upstairs, but not into our room. She went into one of the spare bedrooms and put her flowers on the bedside table. I followed her in; the predominant smell was mothballs. We haven't had an overnight guest for a long time.

'Hi,' I said.

'Hi,' Daphne said. She fluffed the pillows, pushed all the blankets onto the floor and jumped onto the bed.

'Like the flowers?' She flung out an arm in their direction.

'They're okay,' I said.

'First prize for this afternoon's croquet. Pizarsky won them, but he doesn't care about flowers, so he let me have them.'

'Good of him.'

'I'm hot,' she said. 'Could you bring me some ice?'

'Just ice?'

'Just ice . . .'

'What are you going to do with it?'

'Look at it. Feel cool. God, St John. Does it matter what I do with the ice?'

'I'll get it in a second. What's going on? Why are you taking a nap in here? Don't you like your bed any more?'

'Oh—don't let's fight,' she said. My right hand was still closed up tight, to keep Mary quiet, and Daphne looked at that hand for a couple of seconds, then at my face. I guess she thought I was making a fist at her.

I wanted to ask her if she meant to spend the night here as well, but I didn't want her to say yes. It could be that she was in some kind of mood and just wanted a nap and my question might force her to adopt a stance. She does that, I've noticed; she lashes out when she thinks she's been given a cue.

'Is it okay if I host a luncheon for some under-privileged inner-city girls next Wednesday? Not too many; five or so.'

'Fine by me. Got your under-privileged inner-city girl bait? Want me to drive you down to the city so you can catch them?'

'Be serious. I want to join Bea Wainwright's Culture Club, and the luncheon is kind of an audition for me.'

'That's fine. Just don't let them into my study. I mean it—that's off-limits.'

'Of course.'

She stood up before I could go and get that ice she'd asked for. 'I'll get it myself, okay?' She went up on her tiptoes and kissed my forehead. Quite sadly, I thought.

On my study desk I found a brand-new notebook open on my desk, neatly placed in the centre. There was a list written on the first page. I looked at the list for a minute or two. Points in favor of 'D' and 'M'. It was almost my handwriting, so close that for a second it seemed to me that I'd made the list and forgotten about it. But I hadn't written it. These weren't even thoughts I recognised.

So Mary was writing things down now.

I looked up and she was laughing. Soundlessly, of course. She was even more appealing as a mute. Like an image my eye was chasing through one of those flick books—she wasn't moving, I was. I beckoned her.

'You wrote this,' I said. Mary came closer, gesturing helplessly towards her mouth.

'Just nod or shake your head,' I said. 'You wrote this, didn't you?'

She folded her arms.

'Did Daphne see this?'

No visible response. I closed the notebook and laid my fist on top of it. It was starting to ache, vaguely, but with a throbbing that promised to get stronger.

'This is childish, Mary. Don't do anything like this again.'

She curtseyed wickedly, and left me.

I tore the list out of the notebook and ripped it to shreds—I needed both hands for that. Even if Daphne had found the list and taken any notice of it, she must know that I couldn't write a thing like this in earnest and leave it somewhere she'd find it. But Daphne knew something, or thought she knew something. That tiny kiss on my forehead—why had she given me that? It stayed with me unbearably, like ashes at the start of Lent, the slap on the hand I got whenever I went to brush them away as a kid.

I must have been twenty-five years old when I realised Christ never came back from the dead. Some people would say it wasn't a big deal, it was just that I wised up. But I'm talking about something I'd always believed until then. I damn near knocked myself flat with these new thoughts. I mean, the resurrection could be true—it could be, I wasn't there so I can't say for sure. But it probably isn't true. So that means Christ was killed and that was the end for him. He'd gotten mixed up with some pretty intense people in his lifetime, though, and those people thought he was too important to let go. And they made themselves important with this idea that their friend couldn't be killed, told everyone all about it. And hundreds died because they believed Christ couldn't be killed, and thousands more suffered, I mean, the martyrs, think of all the martyrs, and—I was walking down a street in Salzburg, eating an apple when these thoughts came to me, and I just kept right on chewing and swallowing, chewing and swallowing, since it was something to do.

Love. I'm not capable of it, can't even approach it from the side, let alone head on. Nor am I alone in this—everyone is like this, the liars. Singing songs and painting pictures and telling each other stories about love and its mysteries and its marvellous properties, myths to keep morale up, maybe one day it'll materialise. But I can say it ten times a day, a hundred times, 'I love you,' to anyone and anything, to a woman, to a pair of pruning shears. I've said it without meaning it at all, taken love's name in vain and gone dismally unpunished. Love will never be real, or if it is, it has no power. No power. There's only covetousness, and if what we covet can't be won with gentle words—and often it can't—then there is force. Those boys at the bar downtown, coming round talking idly about more ideas to die for. Something terrible's coming, and everyone in the world is working to bring it on. They won't rest until they've brought it on. Mary, come back—distract me. No, stay away, you're the problem.

31 rules for lovers (circa 1186)[1]

From *the art of courtly love* by andreas cappelanus

1. **Marriage is no real excuse for not loving.**
2. He who is not jealous cannot love.
3. No one can be bound by a double love.
4. It is well known that love is always increasing or decreasing.
5. That which a lover takes against the will of his beloved has no relish.
6. Boys do not love until they arrive at the age of maturity.
7. When one lover dies, a widowhood of two years is required of the survivor.
8. **No one should be deprived of love without the very best of reasons.**
9. No one can love unless he is impelled by the persuasion of love.
10. Love is always a stranger in the home of avarice.
11. It is not proper to love any woman whom one would be ashamed to seek to marry.
12. A true lover does not desire to embrace in

love anyone except his beloved.

13. When made public love rarely endures.
14. The easy attainment of love makes it of little value; difficulty of attainment makes it prized.
15. Every lover regularly turns pale in the presence of his beloved.
16. When a lover suddenly catches sight of his beloved his heart palpitates.
17. A new love puts to flight an old one.
18. Good character alone makes any man worthy of love.
19. If love diminishes, it quickly fails and rarely revives.
20. **A man in love is always apprehensive.**
21. Real jealousy always increases the feeling of love.
22. Jealousy, and therefore love, are increased when one suspects his beloved.
23. He whom the thought of love vexes eats and sleeps very little.
24. Every act of a lover ends in the thought of his beloved.
25. A true lover considers nothing good except what he thinks will please his beloved.
26. Love can deny nothing to love.
27. A lover can never have enough of the solaces of his beloved.
28. A slight presumption causes a lover to suspect his beloved.
29. A man who is vexed by too much passion usually does not love.
30. A true lover is constantly and without intermission possessed by the thought of his beloved.

31. **Nothing forbids one woman being loved by two men or one man by two women.**
That nails it—I like this Cappelanus fellow! M.F.
Ha ha ha . . . indeed—S.J.F.
HMMMMM—D.F.

I stayed in bed almost all day Monday. To see if St John would notice, and if he did notice, to see what he would do about it. But he didn't notice, didn't even come up to ask me about dinner. Too busy with his book, I guess. It can't be easy killing people off the way he does, especially since each death has got to be meaningful. I heard him on the radio, once, before I even met him—a fan of his called in, ever so earnest, asking him why some character or other had died in such a meaningless way. St John's answer: 'I was going to say that the meaninglessness of her death has a meaning in itself, but the truth is, I missed that one. So thanks. I'm going to work harder.'

While he worked, he played a symphony I liked—he played it very loudly, but it was good that way, rising through the floorboards and welling up around me. I was lying on music, my arms and legs flopping down over a pillar of the stuff, my back the only straight line in me. If only my old dance teacher could have seen me; she'd have had a fit. I was always the girl who was 'just so'. It was the easiest thing in the world back then—if I felt as if taking too deep a breath would make me fall flat on my face that meant I was 'just so'.

There was housework to do, things to dust and

scrub and polish and move around and fret over, work that has never been visible to anyone else, and I took great pleasure in not doing any of it. I spent a few hours looking at a book of watercolors that just happened to be lying around, but they began to make me feel weepy. They were so faded, the landscapes, and they reminded me of some I'd started and put up in the glasshouse, half-finished, because painting them made me yawn so much, and I didn't suppose that anyone who came out there for a cocktail on a summer evening would care enough to ask if they were supposed to look like that. They've been there two summers and no one's asked yet.

When it got dark, Mary Foxe came and sat by me with a candle. I'd gone so dead in my senses and my brain that I'd been expecting her, and it was actually nice to have a change. She closed the door, so we'd have some privacy. I didn't protest. 'He won't be coming up,' Mary Foxe said. 'He's probably going to go to sleep in there tonight.'

'Again. I know.'

She was naked, and not a bit self-conscious about it. She didn't need to be. What I saw by candlelight made me sure that this was really going to happen—St John Fox had dreamed himself up a nice little companion who wasn't going to get old, and he was going to drop me and live with her. She looked younger than me, a lot younger than him—

'For God's sake, put some clothes on, will you,' I told her.

'I don't know where they've gone. I think I've annoyed him and he's trying to punish me. I'm sorry if I'm making you feel uncomfortable. Give me any old thing to wear and I'll put it on,' she said, in a very simple way. No guile, no false concern, just honesty. I couldn't really be mad at her when she spoke to me like that.

I got out of bed. 'Come on.' We went to my dressing room and I gave her a lilac shirtwaist to put on. I didn't tell her, but it was my favorite thing to wear. I'd worn it in Buenos Aires, on the first day of our honeymoon. There it was all over again, the first day, the first day, the first day, his hand in mine, all that woven into a dress. And there was no denying that Mary Foxe looked as cute as a button in my dress; its shade brought out interesting hues in her hair, or vice versa. I was glad we were the same dress size. It was something of a consolation to know that I'm nowhere near as fat as I sometimes think I am.

Mary Foxe sat in the chair at my dressing table and I stood beside the chair and she stared at me and I stared at her. It was just interesting to see what St John wanted in a woman. Her hair hung over her shoulder in a wispy plait, clumsily done. Someone should show her how to plait her hair. I wondered what would become of me. I didn't see him turning me out, not exactly—but I might be too proud to stay. He'd make me some sort of allowance, I suppose. I couldn't go back to my parents, though. Pops would forbid Maman from giving me a piece of her mind, and she wouldn't—not while he was there. But she'd give me that resigned look—*Messed up again, Daphne? Just what I expected.* The look I got when I stopped going to college, only ten times worse. I should fight this, make some kind of threat. Greta would fight like a hellcat. Twice now, some girl has tried to get Pizarsky to fall in love with her, and each time Greta's seen the girl off. She's not above fighting for her man. How do you threaten someone like Mary Foxe, though?

'I've never seen you this close up,' Mary Foxe said. 'I like looking at your face; it's a good face.'

I couldn't help laughing at her formality. I wanted to say I thought the same about her, but I couldn't make myself do it. Greta would have risen up in my mind like a ghoul, sneering. *That's right, pay her compliments while she replaces you.* I was always weak in the head—that must be it. I can't seem to care any more about what I'm supposed to do. This is not a typical scenario.

'What are you thinking about, Mrs Fox?' Mary Foxe asked. I laughed again.

'You're thinking of something funny?'

'He said you were British.'

'Mrs Fox,' she said. 'I think I'm more like you than not.'

'How can you know that?' Anger began to kick in. 'How can you know that?'

Mary Foxe looked up at me with big, thoughtful eyes. 'I'm glad there isn't a stapler around.'

Abruptly, I asked her if she knew whether I was pregnant. I'd cancelled my appointment with the doctor. It'd be a bad scene if I was pregnant and a bad scene if I wasn't.

'You don't look pregnant,' Mary Foxe said.

'Do you mean you don't know? If you don't, just say so.'

'I don't know. Of course I don't know. How could I know that? I'm not a doctor.'

'I thought you were . . . magical or something. Like a spirit.'

She opened her eyes very wide, wondering at

me. 'No, I don't think I am.'

'Okay. Not magical and not a doctor. Got it.'

She was really too amusing. Now that I'd asked if she was magical, I could see her wondering whether she might be magical, after all. What was this, me finding myself wanting to look out for this girl, thing, whatever she was?

'What do you want, Mary Foxe? My husband?'

'I believe in him,' she said, slowly. I wondered if she'd ever told him that, and if so, what he had to say about it. Someone you made up turns around and tells you they believe in you—what response could you possibly make? The scenario is just plain weird. And really kind of impertinent on her part, too. If it happened to me I think I'd be speechless for the rest of my life.

'I love him,' she added. That simple tone again; she thought this was something that was all right to say to me.

'That's nice. So do I.' We sized each other up again.

'Mrs Fox.' Mary put a hand on my arm, and we jumped away from each other in a hurry. The static, the awful static of her touch, it was exactly the way I imagined I'd feel if I ever brushed against an electric fence. My knees knocked together in a frenzy.

'That caused an unpleasant sensation and I won't do it again,' said the little comedian across the room.

'Good. Well, you were about to say something. Go on.'

'I wondered if you had eaten today.'

'No, I haven't. What's it to you?'

'I wondered—I wondered if we could go out to

dinner together. Someplace fancy. And if I could wear a nice hat.'

She wondered if we could go someplace fancy for dinner and whether she might wear a nice hat. One of mine, I suppose, since there weren't any other hats to hand. For all her shapeliness, this wasn't a woman I was dealing with. This wasn't the M I'd pictured when I'd looked over that list of things in her favor. She seemed a girl barely in her teens, mentally speaking. What if I worked on her a little, taught her a difficult attitude and sent her back to her master with it?

'I know a place,' I said. 'Let me just get dressed.'

She turned her back while I dressed. Then we tried all my hats on and I got caught up in the excitement of taking someone new—a brand-new person, almost—out to do something new. She got the giggles and so did I, so loudly that I thought St John was going to hear from all the way downstairs and come up to see what was going on. He didn't. She decided on a hat. Then changed her mind. And changed her mind and changed her mind. Very indecisive about hats, that Mary Foxe. Maybe she'd tire of St John and slope off somewhere. Maybe she'd vanish the moment I set foot in the restaurant and asked for a table for two. How foolish I'd look. But I was prepared to risk it. I wanted to see a smile on her face—some people make you want to see them smiling. And I like a project. I do like to have a project.

After about twenty minutes of hat changing, I'd insisted she stick with the black cloche hat she had on. She pinned on a brooch of mine and moved this way and that so it glinted at her in the mirror, eager magpie of a girl. We rang for a taxi, and I let her give our address—she recited it carefully, and looked so excited. She waited out on the porch, hopping, though she said she'd try to be patient, and I knocked at the door of St John's study.

'Daphne?' he called out. But not at first. He had begun to say 'Mary' and stopped himself. I went in, stayed near the door. He dropped his pen and stood up, strangely gallant. What for? It was only me.

'You're really something, you know that?' I told him. That wasn't what I'd meant to say, it just came out. It was the audacity of what he was doing, and the fact that I couldn't fathom how the hell he was doing it.

'Oh yes? Well, so are you,' he said, and looked admiring, turning his reply into a comment on the way I looked tonight. Our exchanges always seem to turn into whatever he wants them to. I don't think any woman can get the better of him. Keep things brief, Daphne, keep things brief, and you'll get out with your head still on your shoulders. This man is a deadly foe.

'I just wanted to say I'm going out to dinner at the Chop House.'

'Great. We haven't been there in a while, have we? Let me just finish my sentence, and—'

'Oh, no, you take as long as you need. I'm going with Greta.'

'Oh, then don't worry about *my* dinner, I don't need feeding at all. I get by on liquor and flattering notices in the newspapers,' he said, evenly. A dark man, my St John, tall and broad-shouldered and full of force he doesn't exert. I'm only just starting to see him clearly.

'Stop it. She asked me centuries ago.'

He inclined his head, to show that he had heard. He mumbled something. Against my better judgement, I asked him what he'd said.

'Just Greta?'

'What do you mean, "just Greta"?'

St John sat down again, scanning the page he'd just been working on. As he read he began to look baffled, as if someone else had snuck in and scrambled his sentences while he'd been talking to me. 'Wondered if she'd make Pizarsky tag along, that's all.' He attacked his page with short, exasperated scratches of his pen; crossing out. He didn't seem to like a single word he saw.

'Oh, J.P.—such a funny little man, isn't he?' I said. 'So short and squat. And I hardly know what he's talking about half the time.' St John didn't stop crossing things out, but his lips twitched; I think he was happy I'd said that. But I felt terribly guilty, because that isn't what I think about John Pizarsky at all. I honestly think he rescued me yesterday, and showed a sweet side I didn't know he had. And while it's true I'm not quite sure what he meant to tell me, it helped. It did help, and I'm grateful to him. I'd let J.P. down; I knew it in the pit of my stomach, but I told myself he'd never know that I'd talked about him like that. I'd make it up to him. I'd read that book he lent me six months ago, and I'd discuss it with him, and pretend it had changed my life.

That thing he'd told me about Lady Mary conquering Mr Fox just by telling him what she'd seen in his house . . . telling him right to his face in front of all the guests at that ghastly betrothal breakfast. And all Mr Fox could do was stand there denying it, his denials getting weaker and weaker as her story got more detailed. *I know what you're doing—I know what you are.* She had power after that, the knowing and the telling—power to walk away, or stay, save his life, order his death. I don't know what I'd have done in her place. It's easier to picture Greta in that kind of situation—Greta would've blackmailed him, for sure. Just for fun, and pocket change.

*   *   *

Mary caused quite a stir at dinner, and I was glad to be there. She was a little sad to have to take the hat off indoors, but she ate and drank and touched the knives and forks and spoons and her wine glass with such delight, you couldn't help but watch her. And she watched everyone, and told me what she thought of them. A group of four men moved tables so that they were in our line of vision, and whenever Mary looked over at them they toasted her. She got quite mischievous about it, and made them drop their cutlery at least ten times as they scrambled to lift their glasses. 'It's kind of like a Jack-in-the-box,' she said. She was blushing because of all the attention, her cheeks a gorgeous shade of pink, and I said, quoting something I'd read: 'Modesty is more effective than the most expensive rouge.' Then I realised I hadn't read it anywhere and I'd just made it up. 'Modesty is more effective than the most expensive rouge,' I said again.

'Hey, you should put that in your book,' Mary said, with a smile of approval. Two couples St John and I knew, the Comyns and the Nesbits, came over to say hello and get an eyeful. I introduced

Mary to them as 'a second cousin of St John's', which seemed to satisfy them, and they shook hands with her without any difficulty, though I was very worried that there would be. Mrs Nesbit is the yelling kind, and alarming her in any way is a sure-fire route to notoriety. The Nesbits and the Comyns were as nosy as they could be in a few brief minutes, and Mary told them she'd just come out of finishing school in Boston. She was a fluent liar, and really warm with it, really personal. If I hadn't seen her come to life before my very eyes I'd have believed her.

'You must come to dinner next week,' Mrs Nesbit said, before they left the restaurant. And Mary said she'd absolutely adore to. I began to foresee a disgustingly sociable future, then tried to see the three of us out for the evening; Mary, St John and I, and that jarred me out of my speculation.

'Mary . . . what was that about a book? What do you mean, my book?'

Mary poured us both more wine, fixed me with a suddenly keen gaze. 'Aren't you going to write one?'

I'd won a couple of prizes for essays and things at school, and a prize for a short story. But that was all so long ago. And it wasn't hard to shine at that sort of thing at my school; no one really studied hard because it was so unnecessary when you were going to marry well. Even so, maybe I would try. It could well go the way of the watercolor paintings, and the clay pottery, and the botany. But there would be many lonely hours ahead for me, and I thought it would be good to give them purpose.

'Did you put something in my wine, Mary? I'm just wondering how I'm keeping my temper. You just swan in, take my husband with one hand and offer me a hobby with the other . . .'

Mary's hand hovered over mine. 'We're going to be all right.' She flexed her fingers, closed her eyes ecstatically, and breathed in and out. It was embarrassing and I told her to stop making herself conspicuous.

'Sorry,' she said, not sounding sorry at all.

I had a lot of questions for her. Whether she and St John could read others' thoughts, what her first memory was, things like that. The first thing she remembered was a shilling with King George of England's head on it. It had been very well taken care of, polished and kept clean, and it shone in St John's dirty hand down where he crouched in the trench. He'd swapped something for it—she couldn't remember what he'd swapped, but she knew he'd wanted the shilling because it was bright. She told me about the first job St John took after the war. He'd been a bill collector, but he doesn't say much about those times. It was fascinating listening to her.

'He was one of the best,' Mary said, wolfing steak down as if she'd heard there was going to be a shortage. 'He hounded debtors door to door, plucking away the false names and new addresses they tried to hide behind. He developed a method. Firstly, he paid no visible attention to the poverty or misery of the people on his list. Secondly, once he caught up with them he'd only ever say one sentence, demanding what was owed. That was it, his method. He repeated that one sentence over and over without changing the formulation of it, until he was paid. You should have seen him, Mrs Fox. He was really kind of magnificent. Sometimes he'd get punched or interrupted or outshouted while he was saying his sentence. And, well, he'd just wait until the interruption was over. Then, rather than starting his sentence again, he just went on as if nothing had happened, picking up from the precise syllable where he had been forced to stop. It drove people nuts. His collection rate was outstanding. It doesn't take much to horrify people who are already frightened.'

She frowned. 'He was good at being a bill collector, but it wasn't good for him. For days at a time he hardly talked to anyone but me. And sometimes at the end of his work day he'd walk into walls and closed doors. He saw them up ahead but he just didn't stop walking.'

I asked her about the first story he wrote, and she told me about the crummy boarding house he was living in back then, just a bed, a desk, a chair, and a few easels, which he placed open books on, to look at. Art monographs and cookbooks, poetry, a guide to etiquette, a dictionary, a Bible. He'd get back from work and walk from easel to easel, picking up fleeting impressions. Mary turned the pages for him. *Gentility is neither in birth, manner, nor fashion—but in the MIND.* Next: *And what if excess of love// Bewildered them until they died?* And: *A woman is always consumed with jealousy over another woman's beauty, and she loses all pleasure in what she has . . .* After that: *Be careful that the cheese does not burn, and let it be equally melted.* Then he'd spend the night bent over his notebook, writing in zigzags, his pace irregular.

She was very reluctant to answer my other questions, about the war, and I thought it must be because of terrible things he'd done, or because he'd been a coward. But she said it wasn't that. 'If I answered the questions you're asking me,' she said, 'you'd wish I hadn't told you, because you wouldn't know what to say. I think he worries that people sneer at him for coming back safe and sound, or think that he must have been taken captive and put to work tending enemy vegetable patches. But just trust me. Mr Fox was decent in those times. He did what he could, and he was as decent and as brave as he could be.'

We changed the subject. Mary told me she had been doing some reading of her own. *Hedda Gabler*, and *The Three Musketeers*, so far. 'The women in these books are killers!' she said, her voice escalating with each word so that by the time she reached the last one the diners around us were looking around for the killers.

'Did you think they couldn't be?' I told her about one of my favorite villainesses, a flame-haired woman called Lydia Gwilt, who died changing her ways.

'Of course she did,' Mary said, frowning. 'This is worse than I thought. If you make the women wicked then killing them off becomes a moral imperative.'

My first thought was, *But they're not real,* and my second thought was, *Under absolutely no circumstances can you say that, you'll hurt her feelings*. So I devised a title for the book I was going to write—**Hedda Gabler and Other Monsters**, and she cheered up at the assurance that everyone would survive.

She wanted to experience things; she had a list. She planned to attend a big-band concert, and she planned to walk through a field of yellow rapeseed, and she planned to get an injection, and anything else I might recommend. She promised me she'd settle down soon, and I found myself telling her to take her time. Growing up I was glad to be the only girl, with big brothers who teased me and acted with unerring instinct to keep the heartbreakers away from me. But it might have been nice to have had a little sister, and to have helped her out from time to time, with advice, and chaperoning, etc.

Mary said she was going to sleep in St John's lighthouse, on Cloud Island. I told her I wouldn't hear of it, I wouldn't sleep for thinking of her all alone in that weird old place. But she'd already stolen the keys from him, and she said she thought it was nice out there. She said she liked to look at the sea, that it made her sing. 'The first time Charlotte Brontë saw the sea—she was about seventeen or eighteen, I think—she was utterly overcome . . .' she told me. She didn't seem to notice she'd slipped into a British accent, and I didn't point it out to her, I just listened. ' . . . after all those years on the moors. She'd imagined what the sea was like, over and over, of course, how could she not—but when she saw it, it was more than she imagined. Didn't someone write that nothing's greater than the imagination? I think that's nonsense, don't you?'

She said all this to me in the back of the taxi that was taking us home. She was sort of panting, then she was out and out sobbing, and to hell with the static, I held her and smoothed her hair and pushed the dimple in her cheek until she was able to smile. 'You're very kind,' she said. 'I'm sorry. It's just taken such a lot for me to get here.' I saw what she meant. All I could do to help was treat her as if she was ordinary.

Still—I had to know. I mean, it was a hell of a thing. 'How *did* you get—here, Mary?'

'We were fooling around with stories. We put ourselves in them,' she said flatly, as if she didn't even believe herself. Too much awe. Like someone explaining a house fire that burnt down their whole block: 'we were playing around with matches and gasoline.'

'What—where are these stories? Can I read them?'

She leaned forward and told the taxi driver to drop us off by the dock at Cloud Cove.

I told her that the last boat must have gone an hour ago. I told her to come back with me. I told her that St John would have to know what was going on sometime. That she was real now, that she ate steak and talked to the neighbors and was probably going to have everyone in town, men, women, children, trying to get next to her before the week was out.

'I'll swim over,' she said. 'I like having a secret from him. I'll be all right, honestly. Come and see me tomorrow, and you'll see I'm perfectly cosy out there.'

I looked back as the taxi drove away from the dock—she fiddled with her hair, seemed to be tying the lighthouse keys into a tight knot in her hair. That would be hard work to comb out in the morning. She peeled off my shirtwaist, my favourite lilac shirtwaist, discarded it, and dived into the water. The taxi driver saw her too. He raised his eyebrows, but not too high. He was a taxi driver. He'd seen a lot of things. 'Well, it *is* summer. And she's from out of town.' That's all he said.

* * *

St John came out of his study as soon as I opened the front door. Very quietly, he told me that Greta had phoned for me.

'Oh—what did she say?' I asked. Then I remembered that I was supposed to have been at dinner with her. And I shivered, a chill in my back that made me feel as if I was falling even though I stood quite still. He shivered, too. Much more noticeably, as if tugged by strings.

'She said she'd call back tomorrow.'

'Okay.' I switched a lamp on. It was frightening to be with him in the dark, seeing him shiver like that and listening to him speak so impassively. When I saw his expression I wanted to switch the lamp back off again. Anger. It was etched all over his face, the lines drawing up into a snarl.

'Why did you lie?'

I looked at him and didn't say anything. He took a step backwards, and I don't know how I didn't scream—he seemed to be readying himself to spring at me.

'Are you going to tell me who you were with?'

I don't think I could have managed a single word, even if I'd wanted to. I knew it looked bad. And it was going to look even worse if I told him who I'd really been with. It would look like mockery, throwing something he'd told me back in his face.

'I think I'm going to knock you down,' he said. 'If you just keep standing there like that I'm really just going to knock you down. Go—upstairs, to hell, get a room somewhere with your damn Pizarsky, just get out of here.'

That stunned me; I don't know why I laugh when I'm hurt. 'Oh, Pizarsky! Oh, you'd like that, wouldn't you? Then you could put another plus in Mary's column—doesn't run around with John Pizarsky.'

I turned towards the front door—but where, as a rational adult, did I mean to go? Did I mean to swim over to the island, as Mary had? Burst in on Greta and J.P., or the Wainwrights? I slid past him and went up to the spare room. I dragged a chest of drawers over to the door; it was just the right height for me to lodge a corner of it under the door handle, which turned ten minutes later, to no avail. Then he must have rammed a shoulder against the door—it shuddered and my heart hammered in my ears. He did that just once, without saying a word. Then he went away.

I sat up late, late, looking out over our garden. There was lightning, and rain battered the ground, and I thought of Mary Foxe, miles away, watching the storm through the lighthouse window. I thought of the things she knew about St John. I saw a shiny shilling and a dark-haired young man with eyes like stains on glass. Alone in a big city, walking into walls. Everyone hurts themselves in the city, then they just pick themselves up so as not to get in anyone else's way. And then he went home, to company devised for him alone, he went home to a girl who wasn't there. I envied Mary for being what she was, for being so close to him; I was so jealous it burned, and I knew I had to let it alone or I'd break something inside me.

The night changed me. I built a scene in my head, better than that line I'd come up with about modesty and rouge. I pictured a woman alone at her dressing table, getting ready to go onstage. She's exotic-looking—maybe dark-skinned, maybe an Indian—she's had hecklers before, guys saying really filthy things, and now she's really going at it with the makeup, just plastering it on, drama around the eyes, making herself look like a woman from another world so the audience will just sit there with their mouths open and let her sing her song and get out of there in peace. And while she's getting ready this woman is talking to someone sat behind a screen—I'm not sure who that someone is yet. Anyway, the woman at the dressing table—her heart's breaking. It breaks three times a week on account of people treating her so badly, and she knows that all you can do is laugh it off. She's saying: 'Let me tell you something, kid. Love is like a magic carpet with a mind of its own. You step on that carpet and it takes you places—marvellous places, odd places, terrifying places, places you'd never have been able to reach on foot. Yeah, love's a real adventure! But you go where the carpet goes; after you've stepped onto it you don't get to choose a goddamned thing. Well . . . there'd better be a market for magic carpets. 'Cause from tonight, mine's for sale.'

And that's how I plan to begin *Hedda Gabbler and Other Monsters*. I think I'll cut the part about the magic carpet being for sale, though. It might come off as tacky.

I moved the dresser away from the door at about four in the morning. I had to go to the bathroom. Then I went into our bedroom, mine and St John's. He wasn't there. I went downstairs and found him in his study, asleep at his desk, drooling a little on some newly written pages so that the ink ran. I pulled the pages out from under his arms and put them aside without looking at them. He woke up, but he didn't open his eyes. 'I can explain about dinner,' I said. 'In the morning. Just come out to Cloud Island with me, and I'll show you.' He made no answer, and I pinched him. He opened his eyes, then, and gave me a sulky look.

'How's the book going?'

He winced.

'Will you read me some? Please?'

'It's not ready.'

'Just a little.'

He read a couple of pages aloud, very quickly. Then he saw that I wanted to hear more and he slowed down. He writes beautifully but without hope. Odd that he could be responsible for a little dancing cinder like Mary. He reached a particularly stressful part of a chapter and I came to crisis and said, 'Oh, Lord,' before I could check myself. He looked up from the page. 'Bad things are going happen, D.'

'To the two of us?' I held out my hand to him. He took it and touched his lips to my wrist. Pins and needles, as if all my blood was rushing back into me.

'Yes, to the two of us. It's inevitable.'

'But good things are going to happen, too.' He opened his mouth, seemed to think better of it, closed his mouth. 'Were you going to say I sound like Mary?'

'Or Mary sounds like you . . .'

I came to him without substance, and six years later I'm still the same. Sometimes I say terrible things to him because I don't want him to know I'm sad, sometimes I fly off the handle to hide the fact that I don't know what I'm talking about. And other times—too often, maybe—I don't dare have an opinion in case it upsets anyone. I'm too stupid for him.

Have you ever heard a note in someone's voice that said 'This is the end'? I heard it in the next words he said to me, and I stopped listening. Have you ever wanted to try and cross an ending with some colossal revelation—'There's something I never told you. I'm a princess from the kingdom atop Mount Qaf', for example, 'my family live in eternal youth, and if you abide with me, you will, too. I kept this secret from you to see if you would cherish me for who I am.' Have you ever wished, wished, wished . . .

My head got so heavy, it sank down onto my chest. So say whatever it is you think you've got to say, St John. That you're not in love with me. That you need to be alone. Say it. I'm not going to like it, no, I won't like it at all. But I'll be all right.

I told him that I loved him. I've never, ever, said that to him before, because I just don't know how he'd take it. *I love you.* I mouthed the words because there didn't seem any point in interrupting him just then. I don't know if he saw. I hope he did, because I don't believe it's the sort of thing a woman can tell a man more than, say, three times in their life together. It's only really appropriate in the event of a life-threatening emergency, 'I love you.' It means a different thing to us than it means to them. God knows what it means to them. God knows what it means to us.

'. . . start again, D. Let's start all over again,' my husband said. He rested his hands on my shoulders for a moment, then took them away. 'Can we?'

Start again? Nice in theory, but what was he really trying to say? How far back would we have to fall? All that undoing . . .

Show you're game, Daphne.

'Sure,' I said. I held out my hand. 'Shake on it.'

We shook hands. He held on to my hand; his grip was tight, and our palms were sweaty. I looked up at him, he looked down at me, and I had absolutely no idea what was on his mind just then. I decided to wait. But after a few more speechless seconds I figured he must not know what to say next. Maybe he was scared of saying the wrong thing.

So I took the initiative. I broke the handshake and introduced myself. I said I was glad to meet him, and I asked him what his name was. I heard myself, all bubbles and sparkle. I'd had to drop my gaze to be able to pull off the playful act, though, and I felt him looking at me, still looking. I heard him stifle a yawn. Then he lifted my chin with his thumb, his lips grazed my cheek, my spine melted down my back, he murmured: 'Okay, but I was wondering if we couldn't go a little faster than that—'

I slid my hands up under his shirt, my fingers spread across the bareness of his chest, shaking as I felt the depth of the breaths he took. It felt nice, of course, but really I was just stalling him, trying to think of a way to give in without letting him think he could always get his own way. I needed some phrase that was simultaneously encouraging and disparaging.

'Well?' he said, and he was so close, smiling just a little, his lips not quite touching mine. I just couldn't find that phrase I wanted, so I gave his nose a good, hard, tweak—all the better for being sudden. He gave a pretty satisfying squawk after that, so I kissed him.

And, laughing a little, he kissed me back. He kissed me like ice cream, like a jazz waltz, the rough, gentle way the sea washed sand off my skin on the hottest day of the year. And the whole time there was that little laugh between us, sweet and silly.

* * *

We rode the ferry across to the lighthouse in the morning, having slept too late to walk across. Mary Foxe wasn't there. But she'd left us a note on the kitchen table, with the keys to the lighthouse on top of it.

Gone travelling! To Mexico via Mississippi. Met a beachcomber who said he'd take me as far as Virginia—not bad, huh? Don't know how long I'll be gone.

Mrs Fox—I'll send you a forwarding address when I know it, so you can send me pages of **Hedda Gabler and Other Monsters***—don't forget to write it. And don't talk yourself out of it—you can do it, and it's going to be really good. (Maybe I am slightly magical after all.)*

Mr Fox—don't worry. I'll come back to you. Maybe you'll be nicer to me once you've missed me a little. And hey, now you can do whatever you want. For a while.

I'm dying to know what it'll be like when I come home—the three of us(!) I almost wish I was there and back again already . . .

Take care of each other, okay?

M.F.

We'd found my shirtwaist by the dock, just where she'd left it, crumpled and ruined by the rain, so I could only hope she had some clothes on.

St John read the note over and over, his lips moving silently. He looked both stricken and relieved. I suspected that in the next few minutes he was going to start quizzing me pretty hard.

As for me, I'd noticed just how similar Mary's handwriting was to St John's and was thinking that perhaps a break from Mary Foxe wasn't such a bad idea after all.

some foxes

I

The little girl feared the fox cub, and the fox cub felt exactly the same way about her.

The woods went on for many miles, and a few foxes lived at the heart of it and didn't encounter people if they could help it. Yet the girl and the fox cub had been pointed out to each other—the girl's mother had used a picture book, and the fox cub's mother had brought him to peer in at a window once, when everyone in the girl's house was sound asleep—and each had been told: *That is your enemy.*

They grew up a bit. He learnt things, and so did she. They didn't unlearn their fear of each other.

The girl was pretty, though . . . and stubborn and strange.

And the young fox was curious and courageous and clever . . .

It was only natural that they would find each other.

The young girl was in love with mystery and secret knowledge. She learnt the names of demons, and summoned them. They never materialised. She didn't take offence. She wouldn't have bothered either, if she were them. The girl lived with her mother and her elder sister at the mouth of the woods—only a few steps away from town—less than ten steps, probably. Still, they didn't get many visitors. In the evenings the elder sister studied and studied, but our girl set up lanterns in her room and performed puppet shows with marionettes she had made herself. During his long illness the girl's father had shown her how to make puppets. Then he'd died. 'Come away from the window,' the elder sister would say, sharply, whenever she saw what the girl was doing. 'Don't draw attention to us. Who knows what's watching from the woods?'

But their mother intervened and told the elder girl to leave the younger be.

Our girl sang songs to accompany her performances, and the puppets cast shadows on the leaves and the grass outside her window. Our young fox observed all this from a distance; he stood stock-still, his narrow eyes just a faint shimmer amongst the shrubs. He heard the singing. The sound meant nothing to him, though it did not displease him. The fox knew about fox business. By now his mother had moved on somewhere and he didn't much miss her. His paws were swift, and he wouldn't let his eyes confuse his mind, so he was good at catching rabbits and squirrels. He slept late and woke early and travelled the whole wood wide, tasting the weather. He knew where the bees went to make their wild honey. He saw when cuckoos visited the nests and knew which birds were going to get a nasty shock come hatching time, and he waited for the spoils. The fox fought no one; he took things easy. When it was time to run away, he ran. But not this time.

What can it mean for a fox to approach a girl? Foxes are solitary. A fox that seeks out human company is planning evil. Or it has something the matter with it. Rabies, or something worse. The fox watched the girl at play, and he didn't understand what she was doing—it certainly wasn't fox business. Still, it interested him, and he gazed and gazed at her as she sat surrounded by all that greedy, dangerous fire that she kept in jars. He gazed and gazed though it served no purpose to do so, gazed without feeling satisfied and with the sensation of a deep scratch in his side (this was an awareness of time and its disappointments, the certainty that the girl would put out the lamps before he had looked his fill). And it was through observing the girl at play that our fox learnt to recognise beauty elsewhere in the wood. Whenever he became caught up in useless looking, he knew. Moonlight on the water brought rapture.

Think of a fox, dipping his paws in silver, muzzle dripping. He didn't want to drink the water, only to touch it while it looked like that. Another fox came by and laughed at him. But our fox didn't care.

As for the girl, she looked into the darkness of the woods, and she saw very little. Occasional motion, perhaps, but nothing definite. Our girl developed a distaste for fact. She stopped going to school. Her mother kept a shop in town, selling food, books, toys, linen, and anything else she could think of, and she did very well out of it. The girl joined her mother at the shop counter. She refused to sell people things she didn't think they needed, and argued with them until they saw her point. The elder sister grew more wan and studious, folding herself into her textbooks because she didn't like to live in the mouth of the woods, where things she couldn't see crept and shuddered all hours of the day and fell deathly still when she turned to look at them. The elder sister wanted to get away and go to a city, and be unknown and kick up her heels and have fun. All in time. She needed to get top marks first, and go away on a scholarship. 'What's to become of you?' the elder sister asked the younger, who shrugged and laughed and looked out of the window and dreamed.

Have you forgotten our fox?

The one who now had an eye for beauty, and an inclination to set it apart from other things . . .

The fox wished to thank the girl.

(The fox wished to know the girl.)

It took him a long time to make his mind up. He wasn't happy about it, but he didn't have a fever and he slept well and his appetite was fine, so he thought he must be well and that everything was all right, and that maybe just this once the things the elder foxes had said were wrong.

So the fox brought the girl berries. Plump, rust-red berries wrapped in the largest, greenest leaf he could find. He left the leaf out overnight first, so that it sparkled with dew. How to give them to her?

He watched and waited. The evening puppet shows had become less frequent; this was because the girl was becoming interested in young men and had begun dressing up to go out to dances with her sister. Their mother had previously refused to let the elder sister go alone. 'Young men are animals,' she said. So there were dances, and blushes, and letters written and exchanged, and sighs of longing and—the woods didn't seem quite as real to the girl any more. They were just some trees behind her house. A great number of trees, to be sure, but only trees. Men were quite interesting. They were new puzzles to work at, at least. And if she solved one of them she won a new life, and a new surname, and a companion who wouldn't tell her off for buying too many music scorebooks and new hats. These days the girl only tended to put on a puppet show when she'd fallen out with a suitor. Then a richly gowned female puppet berated a threadbare male puppet for half an hour at a time.

* * *

The fox didn't like the new tone that the puppet shows had taken. Something about it . . . anyway, here were the berries, and there was the girl and the lantern light. The time was right. He leapt up onto the windowsill with the leaf in his mouth, dropped it and retreated, farther than a stone's throw, but not so far that they were unable to see each other.

* * *

The young woman saw a streak of grey, saw a tail brush the windowpane, saw a green parcel fall. And her puppets fell from her hands with a clatter and lay on the ground with their knees bent as if they meant to spring up again on their own. The lantern flickered. The girl saw a fox a little way down the corridor of trees. The creature was watching her. She moved to the right and its gaze moved to the right. She moved to the left, far left, almost out of the window's frame, and the fox's head moved with her. It appeared to be smiling, but that was just a meaningless expression created by the look of its muzzle. There was an unfaltering clarity to the animal's gaze; thought without emotion. And yet. The fox was quivering. It had brought her something and it had stayed to see what she would do, and it was quivering. So the girl didn't draw the curtain, and she didn't turn away. She opened the window and slowly, very slowly, closed her hand around the bulky leaf. The fox did not approach—if anything, it drew further back. The girl opened the leaf. Berries, but they looked more like jewels. She tasted one, and it was delicious. She ate another and another, and she beckoned the fox. 'Come here, come here,' she said in a syrupy voice she used with very small children. The fox did not approach. The fox looked desperately from the girl's eyes to her berry-stained mouth. She didn't like the gift. She was angry. What was she saying, what was she saying . . .

'Won't you come closer? You're the one who sought me out, you know,' the girl said crossly, in her own voice.

The fox had had enough for one night, and fled.

Now the girl wished to thank the fox.

(The girl wished to know the fox.)

She wrapped herself in a shawl, took a lantern in her hand and slipped out of the house, thinking that she would follow the fox to its den and see how it lived. Our girl raised her lantern as she followed the paths between the trees. She ducked under the bigger branches, but the smaller ones raked her hair; she gasped at first, but then the pull became so frequent that it was caressing, a ceiling of hands. She stepped across shallow, pebbled brooks. Her skirt dragged in the water—the hem would be ruined, she thought, distantly. The fox was nowhere to be seen. The girl stopped beside a fallen log and swung her lantern around behind her, trying to remember the direction she had come from. She couldn't remember. She was lost, and she didn't know what to do. She sat down on the log and cried. Unfortunate girl—her tears were beautiful. From his hiding place, the fox watched her weep. All he could think was that she was doing something with her eyes; something that shone. He watched her until she fell asleep, and he kept watch over her while she slept.

This happened in winter. There was ice in the earth. When the sun was down, skin and clothing were of no use outside. You needed fur, or feathers, or you needed to be indoors. The girl caught a chill. A bad chill. Her breath cracked in her chest; she took a fever because her body needed the warmth. Her teeth chattered. She reminded the fox of leaves blown in the wind. When she woke up, she was weak, and, much to the delight of the fox, she lay on her log and wept again. Without knowing it she had walked a long, long way into the wood. Sunrise dazed the redwoods—birches wept, and so did the girl. Eventually she chose a direction and began to walk—the fox followed her, wondering where she was going. Home—her home, was the other way. Discreetly, he rattled some branches. She noticed him, and then he ran, too fast for her to catch him, but slow enough for her to keep up. The girl could hardly believe that she was following a fox again—it could be taking her anywhere. To her death in a deep pool; to a shallow pit crammed with tiny bones. Perhaps it didn't even mean for her to follow it, perhaps it was just bounding along enjoying its morning. The fox never looked back at her. A different fox?

She heard the search party before she saw them. The air rang with the sound of her name. The fox swerved and dashed past her, back to the heart of the wood. She put out a hand just in time and felt its warm fur against her palm.

There were no more puppet shows after that. Snow fell. The girl sank, and the girl shivered, and the girl raved, and the girl died. The cause of death was twofold—the extreme chill she'd taken alone in the night, and the berries, which were poisonous. The fox didn't know what was happening. He dared much, so he returned to watch the house. All the curtains were drawn. Steady lamplight escaped from a gap at the top of one pair of curtains, the pair in the girl's bedroom. He lost interest after a few nights of that view, and returned when he next remembered. There was no light that night. The whole house was dark. It was the same the next night, and the next. The fox was philosophical. From the moment he had recognised loveliness he had known it couldn't last. And he returned to fox business.

II

Now I will speak of another kind of fox. The other fox was a grey fox; this one is red. I am speaking now of a fox who had been hunted, a beast of the chase who was only alive because of luck and cowering and grim fighting—grim and miserable and low. This fox wasn't innocent—he had turned hutches into bloodbaths purely to divert himself. But he also knew wounds and weariness, had crawled into holes and lain like a rag wadded deep into the ground. He killed hens because they were there to be killed, and he understood that the hunters sought to do away with him for the same reason. The fox had started his life in a den heaving with cubs, but they had all been hunted down almost as soon as they were grown. A few times he had hidden alongside foxes who had been bred in captivity, but they never got away. Their wits were dull. The horizon made them run around in circles, confused.

This fox had no one. I've said that foxes are

solitary, but there's a difference between having no one because you've chosen it and having no one because everyone has been taken away. I'm not saying that I myself know what the difference is. But our fox knew.

One afternoon the fox jumped some fences and walked straight up to a farmhouse. He didn't want to be a fox any more. He didn't want to be anything. His head was down, so he didn't see the farm dogs, looking askance. They bristled and growled, but they didn't attack, not even when the farmer's wife came out and commanded it. The farm dogs knew a sick fox when they saw one. The farmer's wife went inside, but she left the door half open—she was coming back with something. The fox looked at the ground. He appeared to be smiling, but that was just a meaningless expression created by the look of his muzzle. The fox had no plan. Something might happen soon. Or it might not. Either way he was here, at the end of his nature.

A human form appeared near him—the dogs jumped at the sky and bayed in a way that wolves do sometimes when the full moon draws them. The fox didn't look. This person had been following him about for days. He couldn't remember when she had begun. He had been badly hurt and she was there, she was just there. She had sticky stuff that he had permitted her to smooth over his wounds. The wounds were just scars now; they'd healed fast. He had been too sore to move and she had dug up voles and snapped their necks and scraped at them and fed him. With her five fingers and her funny, flat palm she had placed food in his mouth. At night, when he was in too much pain to rest, she counted stars and whispered into the hollow of the tree he lay in, telling him how many she could see, until he fell asleep. There was no reason for her to do such things. He didn't know what this person wanted from him, and he hadn't come across anything like her before. So she probably didn't exist. The fox ignored her as best he could. Now she crouched down beside him and she touched him. She rubbed his neck. She spoke into one of his ears, and he understood. Whenever she spoke, he understood. Her voice had all sorts of sounds in it—the flow of water against rock, an acorn shaken in its shell, a bird asking for morning. Her voice wasn't loud, but he heard it throughout his body.

—Listen . . . that woman is looking for a gun.

A gun? Good . . . even if the fox had been able to reply, he wouldn't have.

—She's found the gun. Quickly: why did you come here?

The dogs became braver and crept close—she put out a hand and sent them away.

—It's true, then, fox? That you want to die?

He couldn't tell her the truth; he lacked the language.

She sighed.

—Very well. It is your right. Goodbye.

She stroked his back. She strolled away. The sound of the shotgun shattered the air and sent him after her, as hard and as fast as he could go. They both ran, but he overtook her. All things considered, two legs, etc., she wasn't a bad runner. 'Live,' she laughed, breathlessly. 'Live, live, live.' And when it was safe to stop, she collapsed against a stile in a fallow field and held her face between her hands and made noises that sounded like 'Hic, hic, hic.' He began to pay attention to her. Her eyes were set quite far apart. He had never been so close to one of his hunters, had never been this close to harm.

She told him that she had looked after him because of the white hairs on his forehead that grew into the shape of a star. Sometimes you see that someone is marked and you're helpless after that—you love. She wanted to tell him that, but she decided it was better not to. He hadn't known that there were such hairs on his forehead, or that such a thing could be of significance. She sat and he lay near her, and a little time passed, quiet and bright. Then they had to go, in case the farmer had been told of their trespass and decided to look for them.

They parted outside her hut. It was a ramshackle thing beside a stream. It had a heavily dented tin roof and its windows were coated with dust. All in all, it looked cross, and as if it had plenty of things to say to its inhabitant about having been left alone for so long.

'Come inside,' the woman said to the fox.

The fox demurred. Sadly, the woman watched him go his own way again.

Days went by. The woman made her peace with her hut. She gave it a thorough sweeping, built herself a new roof, washed the windows, plaited rugs. The woman picked herbs and grasses and boiled and bottled various concoctions. Sick people and their relatives sought her out in the forest; she took their money and they took her bottles away and were cured. 'Where have you been?' she was asked, again and again. 'Weeks we've been looking for you.'

And she answered. 'I fell in love.'

'Congratulations! Where is he?'

'I don't know. I don't know if I'll see him again.'

And her pupils grew vast as she spoke, as if her eyelids had been opened while she was still in the first stage of sleeping. Women like her are very serious once they have chosen. To everyone who saw her she said: 'If you see him, tell me. He wears a white star on his forehead.' She didn't tell anyone that he was a fox.

One of the village women went into labour, and our woman served as midwife. The days were full of screaming, and the nights were hoarse, and there were three of each until the baby was born. This happened in summer. When our woman came home, she jumped into the stream and washed; the blood and sweat whirled away and afterwards she sat outside until the sun dried her. She watched lizards and felt humming in her skin; tiny creatures bit her; they were alive and they wanted her to know. Her pulse slowed to its lowest ebb, and sped up again, flashed through her wrists, in her head. She was happy and unhappy. 'The fox has forgotten you,' she told herself. Yet all around her she saw white stars . . .

Because of a fox?

Because of him.

The woman went into her hut to find clothes to wear and found that she had been robbed. Bottles and picture frames were broken, her table and chairs were overturned, her papers had been rifled through, matches were scattered on the ground. The woman searched the hut for missing things. She wasn't aware of all her possessions, so really she was just looking for a gap. She found it on her bookshelf. The thief had taken a dictionary. Nothing else. She stood, looking at the gap, and thinking. Then thinking turned to wonder and she smiled into her hand.

Now think of a fox in his den, wrapped round a book. His front paws are resting on the pages, and his eyes are very close to the text. These shapes! They're useless. They frustrate him. The more he looks at them the more they mock him. He nudges the book into a sack and drags the sack along by its drawstring, through the forest. In the bushes by the village nursery, he listens to children saying their ABCs. He can see the blackboard. The teacher taps it with a ruler, going from letter to letter. His mind wanders . . . he bites his paw. Look and listen. His mind wanders again . . . he nips at his paw again, savagely this time. And again, and again, until his paw is bloody and he is learning.

First light finds the fox at his stolen book. No one else knows, no one sees what he's doing. But words are coming. The fox doesn't hunt any more—he doesn't hunt! He eats easy meat, forest rats. He stays near his den or he goes to the nursery school, he listens carefully, he connects pictures with words, he eavesdrops, he steals newspapers, he stumbles in his understanding and snarls and shreds the newspapers to pieces . . . but he will know this language, he must have this language.

Because of a woman?

Because of her.

The day came when the fox had words. Only a few, but enough to begin to talk to her. He went to the woman's hut. Her hair was grey, and there were lines on her face, but otherwise, she was the same. She had not been young when they'd met, and two years had tipped the balance. He wasn't young himself. The woman smiled and touched his forehead. So it was still there, this shape that she liked. Good.

—Come inside, the woman said, in that way that he heard from head to toe. One day he would ask her how she could do that.

The fox entered the hut.

The fox had brought the dictionary back. She'd long since bought a new one—just as well, since the stolen one was falling apart. He had also brought words. He had chewed them out of newspapers; long, patient work, and anxious work too, double-checking that each word meant what he thought it meant. If he had got it wrong, all wrong . . . if she laughed at him . . .

The woman settled in a chair and watched the fox sort through scraps of paper. She was holding her breath. She believed—she didn't know what she believed. It could not be. The fox looked lean and crazed. In her mind she ran through a list of concoctions that might do something for the beast . . .

Words began to spread at her feet.

Hello.

The fox looked up at her and panted. He curled his tail around his leg in an apprehensive 'L'.

The woman raised her hand and let it fall. 'Hello,' she said, aloud. She couldn't see clearly. All these tears. She brushed them away.

Can you help me.

He was very intent as she spoke. She answered three times, to be clear. 'I'll try. Tell me what you need.'

Quickly, remembering the afternoon at the farmhouse, she added: 'I can't help you die.'

The fox shuffled scraps of paper, chose two.

Not die.

He chose three more.

Please change me.

He thumped his paw on the last two words, his eyes on hers. Change me. Change me.

'Change you how?'

Not fox any more.

He'd had to tear the word 'fox' from the dictionary. It was tiny.

'No,' the woman said, slowly. 'No, I don't think I can do that. I haven't the skill.'

The fox lay down and closed his eyes. This lull, after all his striving, was enormous. It was like pain. The woman fell down beside him—her pity made her do it. The woman and the fox faced each other, nose to nose. Then he stood, nudged her aside, chose more words.

Stay with you.

I with you.

Please.

The fox applied himself to living as the woman lived. He ate at the table with her, and slept alongside her in her bed, and scrabbled around with soap in the stream. He read voraciously. He read more than she did. And as more words came to him, he told her of the hunt, of the horses and the hounds behind, and sometimes there were falcons, like a rain of beaks and claws. The woman listened, and as she listened, she realised that she was hearing him—that he was saying words instead of showing her. She made no remark, and treated it as normal. She asked him which would he rather be, if he could change—a horse, a bird, or a hound? None of those, he said. At night he suffered himself to be held, a thing that was unthinkable in the first days of their acquaintance, even when he had been very badly hurt. He had less and less trouble sleeping upright each night. Together they built a bigger hut, and a bigger bed. She saw that his claws had become thin and brittle—they were more like fingernails. Very long nails, it was true, but they weren't claws any more.

*   *   *

But what teeth he had. So:

The pleasure of biting. Or letting him. And afterwards the feel of a long wet tongue light against a hot wound. The different ways:

the hidden bite
the swollen bite
the point
the line of points
the coral and the jewel
the line of jewels
the broken cloud.

*   *   *

One medicine-making day, as they carried fresh water back to her hut in wooden buckets, he asked her: 'How old are we?'

And she answered: 'I have forgotten.'

She put down her bucket and tried to count

years on her fingers. He watched until she gave up, then put his arms about her—he stood a head higher than she did.

'What's so funny?' she asked him.

And he said: 'Nothing.'

III

I almost forgot to mention another fox I know of—a very wicked fox indeed. But you are tired of hearing about foxes now, so I won't go on.